Love Letters

Also By Julie Ma

Happy Families

Love Letters

JULIE MA

MLP

First published in 2024 by Mountain Leopard Press
An imprint of HEADLINE PUBLISHING GROUP

1

Cataloguing in Publication Data is available from the British Library

Paperback ISBN 978-1-80279-227-0

Printed and bound in Great Britain by Clays Ltd, Elcograf S.p.A.

MIX
Paper | Supporting
responsible forestry
FSC® C104740

Headline's policy is to use papers that are natural, renewable and recyclable
products and made from wood grown in well-managed forests and other controlled
sources. The logging and manufacturing processes are expected to conform to the
environmental regulations of the country of origin.

HEADLINE PUBLISHING GROUP
An Hachette UK Company
Carmelite House
50 Victoria Embankment
London EC4Y 0DZ

www.headline.co.uk
www.hachette.co.uk

Chapter One

'You can come and visit him any time you like.'

That's what Mr and Mrs Li told Asta. But whenever she took the detour on the way back from school and rang their doorbell, there was no answer. Then she'd lift the flap on the letterbox to see if the lead was on its hook by the front door. If it wasn't, she'd know to wend her miserable way home, feet dragging with disappointment. But if the lead was there and the blue mac and khaki parka that normally hung next to it were missing, she would creep around to the back of the house where she would see Steve stretched out on the cool tiles of the conservatory floor. His eyes would be closed, his shaggy white tummy rising and falling in the peace of an afternoon nap. Then she'd tap on the glass until he lifted his head. As soon as he saw who it was, he'd leap up and run to her, paws scratching track lines into the condensation his barking made on the window.

But today, as Asta bends down to lift the flap of the letterbox, she sees someone else looking back at her through glasses so thick she can hardly see the eyes.

She squeals and jumps backwards just as that someone flings open the door.

It is a small Chinese man in shirtsleeves and braces and wearing a flat cap indoors.

Asta doesn't know why she thinks of the man as Chinese. After all, so is Asta Fung, as her name and face testify.

It's like Chandler says in *Friends*. 'Of course, in China, they just call it food.'

Although they're not in China; they're a mere six thousand miles away in the small, boring and rubbish Welsh town of Cawsmenyn.

'*Ney*,' says the man, pointing at her with a wrinkly, stubby finger that he turns upside down to beckon her inside.

Once they get past the porch and through another door into the hallway, there is the sound of paws skidding across laminate and Steve is flinging himself against her legs. It's good to hear and feel the regular thump of his tail again. She kneels down so he can clean her face with his tongue like in the old days, only to jump back up when she spots a plump tabby of a cat saunter past and head into another room. She'd seen it curled up on one of the conservatory chairs loads of times and always thought it was a cushion. Well, it's come to something – Stephen Fung living in peace and harmony with a cat!

Asta follows the old man, bypassing Steve's dog bed that they'd handed over to give him comfort in his new home. It looks curiously unused. Once in the kitchen, the old man gestures at one of the chairs around the table so Asta sits down on it. He takes a seat himself and pours them both tea. It is proper Chinese tea like they serve whenever Asta gets taken to Chinatown and she always hates it and wants a Fanta instead. She takes a bitter sip and grimaces.

'*Ney*,' repeats the man.

You, thinks Asta, translating hopefully.

'. . . *nee gaw gau* . . .'

No, that's it, Asta is lost. No more Cantonese on her. She screws her eyes up and shakes her head to show she doesn't understand.

The old man adopts the policy of 1970s English holidaymakers on the Costa del Sol. It's not the different language that is the problem here. It is the lack of volume.

'. . . *NEE GAW GAU* . . .'

Steve whimpers, then disappears into the utility room, where the back door is opening and closing. He reappears moments later, followed by a woman whose face has both Mr Li's upturned nose and Mrs Li's high forehead. She is carrying a sack of Burns dried dog food. It is the best dog food but dog food all the same. Steve used to eat burgers and sausages off her plate when he was Asta's.

'Oh, hello,' the woman says, and noticing the way Steve is now sitting with his snout on Asta's knee, eyes rolled up to his former mistress so a crescent edge of white is visible, adds, 'you must be Asta. I'm Amy.'

The old man clears his throat and speaks to the new arrival. Asta recognises the lilting up and down of what he already said being repeated.

'He's saying, *This dog used to belong to you and he still misses you but also he has made himself happy in his new home and made new friends*,' says Amy. 'Basically, Tony Blair, that's the cat, my mum and dad and him. He's my grandfather, George.'

Asta turns and smiles at him gratefully. She is surprised by how much it means to her that Steve is happy rather than pining on a daily basis for her. Like she does for him.

'Can you tell him thanks for looking after my dog?' she asks.

'You just did.'

Asta looks puzzled.

'He understands English. It's just since his stroke he can't speak it.'

George nods eagerly and somewhat gummily.

'No teeth today?' says Amy.

The old man pats a pocket in his knitted waistcoat, where there is a crescent-shaped bulge, before speaking again. It's like when Asta used to visit her grandparents on her mum's side and a friendly auntie or cousin would helpfully translate. There had been none of that problem with the grandparents on her dad's side. Like her, they were proper BBC – British-born Chinese – English was their mutual first language.

George: (in Cantonese) 'So how's business in the
            takeaway now your parents have taken over?'

Amy: (in English) 'So how's business in the takeaway
            now your parents have taken over?'

Asta doesn't know where to look. At Amy who's
interpreting? Or at George? And if she is supposed to
look at him, where? Normally you look around the eyes
but she can hardly see them through the pebble-thick
lenses of his glasses. She decides to address her answers
to the top of Steve's head and his soft ears, one black,
one white.

Asta: 'Okay, I guess.'

She blanks out while George replies. What's the
point of picking out the odd word here and there? She's
never going to need the language of her forebears in the
real world; Mandarin is the preferred Chinese language.
And anyway, that's why Netflix has subtitles.

Amy: 'He's asking how you like living above the
            shop. He said to tell you' (rolls eyes) 'he was
            the one who bought it back in the 1950s and
            fitted it up as a takeaway.'

Asta: (shrugs) 'It's okay.' (sniffs)

How can she tell them what she really feels? She misses her old home. It was a flat above a takeaway too but in Traeth, forty winding miles down the road. It was called Sun House and it was right on the seafront, sandwiched between a bucket-and-spade-sticks-of-rock seaside shop and a newsagent. You could watch the sun set from behind the counter and when she used to walk out the door with Steve, they would be on the beach in a minute, in the sea in two. Where there was a long thin strip of garden at the back so when the man from the dogs' home came to check they could have young Steve, he said yes, as long as they secured the hole in the fence at the back. If he came to the crappy place they lived now, all he'd see is the service yard behind the shop that customers use as a car park, and potential squishing ground for a young pup. She misses her old school. It didn't have the greatest sixth form – another one of the reasons her parents said they had to move away – but it would have been *her* sixth form with teachers she knew and other familiar students. She misses the Syrian guy who ran the corner shop and who always wore long sleeves even on the hottest of summer days. She misses the wild swimmers who took a daily dip without fail whatever the weather, the women in jewel-coloured bathers while the solitary man might just as well have been wearing one, his skin puce with cold. She even misses the scruffy tramp who hung out at the bus stop and said pointed things at her about being a guest in this country in an accent that was more Perth than Pembroke. The Australian one.

It's gone quiet and she looks up to see both Amy and George looking at her, heads tilted to one side. George says something again.

'He's asking why don't you take the dog for a walk while you're here?' says Amy. She pauses as he carries on talking, then, 'Actually, why don't you make a regular thing of it? Before or after school? My parents are away at the moment on one of their mini-breaks so we've all been taking a share of the walks.'

Asta looks at George suspiciously. There's no way someone so old and wobbly could give Steve the quality of constitutional he needs.

'Not him,' says Amy, 'the rest of the family. We like doing it, don't get me wrong, but it would really help us out if you could do it sometimes as well?'

'Yes please,' says Asta, an unstoppable smile breaking out on her face. 'I'd love to!' And she dashes out to the porch, four paws and a shaggy tail skittering after her. A girl and her dog.

'Look how happy you made her,' says Amy. 'She's had a tough time these last few months. Moving house, changing school . . . everything else. I don't know why *Ah Mah* and *Ah Bah* didn't say she could walk the dog from the beginning.'

'I thought they did,' says George.

There is a ring at the doorbell.

'Short walk,' says Amy over her shoulder, as she goes to answer it.

Steve and Asta are standing winsomely on the doorstep. Amy feels like she should put fifty pence in the dog's head.

'I don't have poop bags,' says Asta. 'I don't suppose you've got any?'

Chapter Two

There is a note on the front door of the Yau Sum takeaway. Asta stops to read it as she bypasses the entrance to the shop to get into the kitchen at the back.

'What renovation work are we having done?' she asks as she waits for her mother, Mandy, to fry some chips for her. 'It must be massive if we have to close the shop. I live here and it's the first I've heard of it.'

'We told you ages ago,' says Tim, Asta's father. He's chopping onions with an enormous cleaver, cutting them into little squares before scooping them onto its shiny blade and depositing them into the Tupperware. 'Before we do the flat out, we're having the new stairs put in. You can't run a food business with sawdust all over the shop. It's only for a couple of days.'

'I don't know if there's any point now,' says Asta.

'I don't think Charlie would have wanted us to remember him by still having to get wet,' says Mandy.

It's one of the other things Asta hates about this stupid shop with its stupid incomprehensible Chinese name (Yau Sum) on the stupid junction in the middle of a stupid town (Cawsmenyn) - the only way you can get to the flat above the shop is by going outside to the side of the building and using the metal fire escape steps.

'It seems a bit pointless now though, doesn't it?' says Asta. 'Moving away so we could be closer to the big hospital in case Grandpa Charlie needed it.'

'Well, he did need it. It's just we hoped he hadn't needed it so soon,' says Mandy. 'And for such a short amount of time.'

'I wish we could move back to the Sun House,' says Asta.

Their old takeaway even had a better name than this awful place.

'Well, wishes don't wash dishes,' says Tim as he takes the chopping board over to the sink.

Asta goes over to get herself some gravy from the bain-marie, completely missing the significant stare Mandy is throwing across the kitchen at Tim.

'What was the best thing that happened in school today?' asks Mandy.

'I got to leave it at three-thirty,' says Asta, before remembering that today has been different. Then it's hard to stop the outpouring of excitement as she describes her reunion with Steve. 'And he still does the best poops. Nice and firm and easy to pick up,' she concludes.

'That was nice of Amy to say you could take Steve for walks,' says Mandy. 'Her parents suggested it right at the start but,' she looks over at Tim, 'some people said it would be much better for the two of you to have a clean break.'

'I still think that was a good idea,' says Tim, thumping the corner of the Tupperware to make sure it's closed properly.

Asta opens her mouth to say something. Mandy can spot the signs even if Tim can't. She deftly steps in to change the subject.

'So you met old George then? He knew your grandfather well when they were younger. And they got really close towards the end. I'm glad they got to be friends again.'

Asta still fancies an argument.

'How come I've never seen this George before, then, if they were so close?' says Asta. 'Why wasn't he at the funeral?'

'Well, I don't think you took a lot of interest in your grandfather's social diary all summer,' says Mandy. 'And he didn't come because he'd just had a stroke.'

'Oh,' says Asta, shame-faced.

'It's nice you've met George anyway,' says Mandy. 'I think your grandfather would have liked it. I suppose you are sort of related to him?'

'Not any more,' says Tim.

Asta scrunches up another piece of A4 and throws it in the bin. It should *not* be this hard. All she wants to work out is how her family – the Fungs of Traeth – are related to the Li family of Cawsmenyn. She found a template for a family tree online, managed to make a pretty good copy of it with all of her rulers, stencils and felt-tip pens, but kept getting stuck when it came to filling in the names. She wants to be able to do it on her own but eventually has to give up and run downstairs to ask her parents. She chews her lip as she watches Mandy and Tim disagree, contradict and talk over each other while they try to find the simplest way of explaining.

'So . . . it's like how Brody Jenner isn't related to Kim Kardashian any more after Caitlyn Jenner divorced Kris Jenner,' says Mandy.

'What?' says Tim.

'That doesn't help me,' says Asta.

'Let me have a go,' says Tim. 'It's probably better to say that George would be your step great-grandfather if he hadn't divorced your great-grandmother.'

'So somebody got divorced from somebody else and now we're not related any more?'

'No, not that,' says Tim and then a second later, 'Yes, that's exactly it. A bit lacking in detail, though.'

He turns around to scan Asta's failed attempts at a family tree.

'Here, I'll show you,' he says.

He takes his hands out of the sink and dries them inexpertly on his apron. Asta's glad she decided to use a Sharpie. The edges of the sheet of A4 dimple as his wrists, still damp with washing-up water, move down the page.

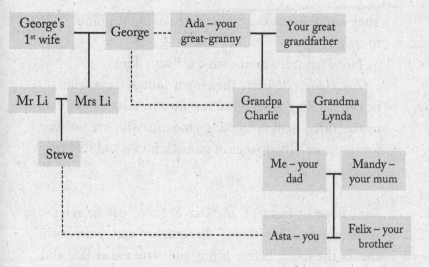

'What do the dotted lines mean?' Asta asks.

'That's an ex-relationship. The divorce I said about. George splitting from your great-grandmother? My granny? Your Grandpa Charlie's mum?'

Asta frowns down at the piece of paper.

'They're all the same person, not three different women,' says Tim.

'Yes, I get that,' says Asta. 'Why did you put a dotted line between me and Steve?'

'That's because it's an ex-relationship too. He's Mr and Mrs Li's dog now.'

Asta's face crumples.

'I thought you knew that,' says Tim.

'I did, but you don't have to say it out loud like that. It's like someone with a big mole on their face.

They know it but they don't like having it pointed out to them.'

'Not even from their own dad?' says Tim.

'*Especially* not from their own father,' says Mandy, before handing a Set Meal for Two to Asta. 'Take that to the three hungry-looking students who are waiting for it, please. Then you can go back home and I'll bring yours up to you.'

Asta flops in front of *The One Show* to eat her chips. After she finishes them, she quickly and pointlessly checks the room, before lifting the plate to her face and licking it clean of gravy. That used to be Steve's treat and she always felt like a proud parent as she watched the shiny underside of his tongue squeegeeing the meaty juices into his mouth. It was the look she used to see on her grandfather's face after he picked the cheek meat out of the fish's head to give to her.

'The best bits go to the best little 'uns,' he used to say.

That was when she was more of a baby. Once she got older, she wouldn't have been seen dead eating anything off a fish that wasn't coated in breadcrumbs.

Seen dead.

She goes to her room, gets into the bed still in her school uniform, pulls the duvet up over her head and closes her eyes.

'You should have this room,' said Charlie on the day they moved in.

Asta and Charlie had been sent upstairs to wait for the removal men. After Charlie had wheezed his way up the fire escape steps, he was pleased to flop into his wheelchair.

'We shoulda got the removal men to bring me up as well,' he'd joked, before he got Asta to push him all around the flat and inspect each room.

There was hardly any difference between pushing her grandfather and pushing the empty chair but as the wheels clicked over the metallic transition strip between each room, Charlie would sigh with fond recollection.

'You should have this room,' he said when they got to a small oblong at the front of the property. They could see the pole of the streetlamp blocking part of the window.

'Why?' said Asta, 'it's the smallest room. Felix should get this one, he's not even going to be living here properly when he goes to uni.'

"Cos this used to be my room when I lived here. I was only a bit older than you are now.'

'What? You lived here before?'

'You don't listen to anything any more, do yer?' he said. 'This is where I lived when I first moved to Wales from Liverpool.'

'I *was* listening. I thought you meant this town.'

'No, it was in this shop. Honestly, it was the making of me, moving down here. I'd fallen in with the wrong crowd back up there. If it wasn't for all this, I'd probably have been dead or in prison. Or both. I hated living here to begin with, it was so quiet and boring. Then I discovered the girls fancied someone who looked a bit different . . .'

'Oh yuck. Am I going to want to hear about this?'

'Anyways, this room was my room and it's the best 'cos the heat rises up from the kitchen downstairs to warm you up just right in the winter and 'cos it faces north, it's lovely and cool in the summer. And you won't need your nightlight 'cos that lamp post is out there.'

Asta fidgeted uncomfortably. Everyone in the family knew about the nightlight but she didn't like it being mentioned. Bit embarrassing still to be scared of the dark at sixteen.

'You've sold it to me,' she told her grandfather and when the removal men arrived, that's where she directed them to put her bed and wardrobe set.

Even with her eyes closed, Asta can tell someone else has come into the room. There's a familiar smell of chip fat and Nivea. She opens one eye just a millimetre to see the thin column of light from the hallway disappear as Mandy closes the door behind her. If it wasn't for the council's LED contribution, it would be completely dark in here.

'She was still in her day clothes,' she hears her mother say.

'Well, wake her up to go to bed then,' says Tim.

'Don't be dafter than usual.'

'I don't know why she's taking it so badly,' he says. 'He was my dad and even I'm over it now.'

'Of course you are,' says Mandy, and their voices drift down towards the kitchen until Asta can't hear them any more.

Chapter Three

If only Asta had known before.

A dog is a pretty good way to explore somewhere new. With Steve at her side, she feels there is good reason to slip down the paths and byways that spring off Cawsmenyn's main thoroughfares. Ambling along these single gravelled tracks with a green Mohican of grass running their entire length, she never actually sees anyone on them, although the evidence is there that other dogs visit. Steve isn't short of interesting smells to snuffle about in, clicking his teeth together at the intensity of the canine messages left behind. It is strange to think that only a few footsteps from the redbrick estates of new-builds, you could find yourself cutting down to a steep sided stream or a marshy field from which a lone horse glowered at you, daring you to come any closer. Sometimes there would be a fallen tree or the stump of one long ago chopped down and Asta would have a sit down while Steve tore around her, running around in figures of eight, before coming back to flop on the ground at her feet.

The route back to Mr and Mrs Li's bungalow leads them by the Yau Sum. Just as they pass the front door, it opens and out comes Asta's father, who looks back into the shop. The door is on a spring to make sure it closes itself after any customers who were born in a barn and he is holding it open for someone. Even though they've already gone past, Steve spins around and goes crazy, barking and stepping up onto his back legs. He lunges forwards, giving no thought to the throttling sensation around his neck.

'Hey! You! Tim! It's me! Me! I used to live with you!' Steve is barking. 'Pat me on the head! Scratch my ears!'

Tim jumps backwards. In the family vote to get a dog, he'd abstained.

'What are you up to?' he asks.

'Just walking a dog,' says Asta.

'Or is he walking you?'

Both Asta and Steve look appalled. It's the oldest, and unfunniest, thing you can say to anyone walking their dog, let alone your own daughter and your own ex-dog. It's the sort of thing you would say to a complete stranger to break the ice.

Tim stands aside as a middle-aged man, whose tummy presses urgently against the front of his boiler suit, appears from deep inside the shop.

'Back tomorrow, then?' says Tim, sounding much more Welsh than he usually does.

'Yes,' says the builder. 'We'll start the job properly tomorrow. Thanks for letting us drop some of the stuff off today.'

'No worries.'

'Means we can get straight to it tomorrow.'

'Very good,' says Tim.

Steve's not liking the level of repartee so decides to pipe up.

'You! Strange man! Do you want to be my friend? Me! ME!'

The builder drops to his knees and lavishes the scruffy loud hound with thigh scratches and chest rubs. Steve responds with ear licks and neck nuzzles. Tim pulls a face. The dog is on its walk, after all, where it is very likely to have been sniffing other dogs' bums and tasting dried splashes of their urine.

'Who's a good boy?' coos the builder. 'What's his name, then?'

'He was already called Stephen when we got him,' says Asta. 'But we decided to shorten it to Steve. He answers to both.'

'Stephen?' says the builder tentatively.

Steve's ears prick up.

'Steve,' he says more assertively.

Steve barks and then lunges up to plant his front paws on the man's chest and a wet tongue into the builder's left ear.

'Hey now . . . you need to at least buy me a drink before you do that.'

Asta muffles a snigger while Tim looks as if he is going to be sick.

'Well, Steve mate, it was good to meet you,' says the builder, 'and you too,' turning to Asta.

'I'll see you again though, won't I?' she asks.

The builder looks back at her blankly, as if trying to place her.

'Because you're putting the new stairs in for us?'

Recognition dawns on the builder's face. 'Oh, you live here too! I suppose it makes sense. I don't like to assume anything. Just because you're Chinese and you're walking past a Chinese takeaway doesn't mean you're anything to do with each other nowadays. Except you are. Typical.' He rubs his left temple, the one from which his mousy brown hair is receding just a little bit more. 'Yeah, I'll be back tomorrow. We'll meet again then, you handsome beast. Not you, Mr Fung, no offence.'

'None taken,' says Tim.

'Don't leave me!' Steve barks at the builder, who doesn't understand and disappears around the corner.

'Don't worry, Steve,' says Asta softly. 'I'm still here.'

He looks back up at her with worried eyes. She's left him behind before, she could easily do it again.

Not that Steve looks too bothered when she drops him off at the Li family bungalow.

The house is full of people she doesn't know when she creeps in through the back door. As soon as she unclips his lead, Steve has to weave in and out of several sets of legs to get to his water bowl. Everybody stops talking to listen to the sound of him lapping loudly. Asta understands why; it is one of the best sounds in the world.

'Ooooh,' says a small child, who is tottering about by where Steve is, her eyes stretched wide. She grabs two little fistfuls of fur and grunts with the exertion of pulling hard. Steve turns around and saturates the girl's face with his cool, freshly watered tongue. She giggles like mad, releasing Steve and dragging small palms down each cheek.

'Asta,' says Mrs Li. 'You here? We are having party. We not supposed to. Everybody come at the same time.'

She looks rosy and pleased to be unexpectedly surrounded by so many friends and family.

Asta goes to hang the lead up in the front porch and calls out, 'Thank you' and 'Bye!' like she always does before leaving through the front door. Instead of the accented echo she usually receives back, the human mash-up of Mr and Mrs Li – Amy – appears in the hallway.

'You're not going yet, are you?' she asks. 'Come in and have some super-sweet confectionary and bubble tea with us.'

Asta hesitates. She doesn't like to impose.

'We're on a mission to destroy the enamel in our teeth,' adds Amy.

That does it. Asta's brother, Felix, is in his first year at Bristol Uni studying dentistry. This has made him the apple of her parents' eye and created a Pavlovian response in Asta. If anyone mentions dental health, she feels the need to sink her teeth into an iced bun. Not an apple.

Back in the kitchen, small clusters of strangers stand or sit talking to one another. Asta gulps and is pleased when Mr Li hands her a glass of pistachio-green bubble tea and gestures for her to help herself from the cardboard bakery boxes laid out on the countertop.

A woman with big blue eyes and cropped chocolate-brown hair comes up. She is holding the adorable infant from before.

'We've been to Cardiff for the day so we stopped off in the Chinese bakery,' she says. 'Thought we'd drop some off here. We didn't know Amy and Elaine . . .' the woman looks over at a very tall woman with bobbed grey hair having an animated conversation with Mrs Li '. . . were going to be here too. Good job we got a big selection.'

Asta hesitates. There is so much choice.

'We like those,' says the woman, helpfully pointing at some egg tarts, twice the size and half the depth of an English egg custard and sitting in a paper case, not a foil tray. 'And these,' indicating some dazzlingly white puffy buns. 'They've got custard in them too. And these, sesame ones,' pointing at some perfectly round little balls of dough, golden brown and speckled with seeds. 'Why does everything deep-fried always taste so much better?'

'Have you ever had a deep-fried Mars bar?' Asta asks, finally deciding on a pineapple bun, its top transparently sticky with glaze.

'No, have you?'

'Yes, my grandfather did some for me and my brother when we were small. It was nice but Dad told him off because the next customer complained her chips tasted chocolatey. We only had them one more time after that. Dad deep-fried one last thing after the shop closed before they changed the oil but by the time we were up the next morning and he tried to give it to us for breakfast, it was all cold and congealed.'

Asta pulls a face at the memory. Strange how sometimes a horrible meal can linger as much as a nice one. It wasn't just the taste they didn't like. She remembers how disappointed her father looked when neither Felix nor she would finish it. Poor Dad. If it happened now, the two of them would stuff it all down anyway just to be polite but they didn't know any better back then. What made it worse was they'd gobbled up the ones Grandpa Charlie made and asked for more.

'Sorry to hear about your grandfather,' says a man who has Mr Li's thicket of unruly hair and Mrs Li's button nose. He takes the baby from the woman. 'I'm Roy. I suppose I'm Steve's brother now.'

'Oh shit,' says the woman. 'Where are my manners? I'm Lisa. I'm his wife and this horrible child here is Mattie.'

'Pleased to meet you,' says Asta.

'Likewise,' says Roy. 'I was surprised my parents agreed to adopt your dog. They're besotted with that cat of theirs but I think it's worked out. Ah Goong . . .'

Asta knows the expression but can't quite place it. She frowns and Lisa picks up on it.

'Don't worry, it took me ages to work out. He means George, over there.'

Everyone looks over at where George is sneaking the wrapper of his Werther's Original back into the bag. His cheek bulges luxuriously at fresh confectionary.

'It's the Cantonese,' Lisa continues. 'It's really specific on *how* you're related. So Ah Goong means George is his grandfather on his mother's side. And when you're talking about Roy's sister, Amy, you can't just say she's his sister, she's his younger sister. She's his *moy*. No, *muy*?'

Even though it is just one syllable, Lisa's tone changes each time, sometimes going up, sometimes going down. Wrong each time but not for want of trying.

'*Mui*,' says Amy accurately as she saunters over to join them. 'Are you talking about me?'

'Not really,' says Roy. 'I was about to say how much Ah Goong likes Asta's dog. They're practically inseparable.'

'Steve loves everybody,' says Asta, 'but he's always loved older people.'

It had led to a number of near misses, front paws threatening to sink into the chests and ribcages of the elderly of Pembrokeshire.

'Yeah,' says Amy, 'he arrived at just the right time really, back when Ah Goong could still take him out. Means they got a chance to get to know each other before his stroke. He sleeps on the ottoman at the end of his bed now, you know. It's like a symphony of snoring when I pop in for the early walk.'

'That's funny,' says Asta. 'He liked to sleep in my grandfather's room too. In that basket over there.'

Everybody turns to look at the unused, entirely kempt basket, at the other end of the room.

'I wonder if dogs understand it when somebody dies,' muses Asta, then chokes on the last bit of bun when she sees three sympathetic pairs of eyes looking at her. Four if you count the baby. She swallows hard before carrying on. 'Sometimes, it feels like my grandfather's just gone away for a few days, he'll come back and we'll have a good old laugh about how we thought he'd, you know . . . died.'

'Well,' says Amy. She offers Asta another cake from the plate of mixed pastries she's holding. Asta picks out something white and fluffy, like a small cloud. 'The best way to keep our loved ones alive is to keep talking about them.'

'I thought we weren't supposed to do that,' mutters Asta.

'Do what?' asks Lisa.

'Talk about them,' says Asta, so quietly that both Amy and Lisa have to lean in to catch what she's saying.

'Why not?' says Lisa.

'Because it makes us sad.'

Lisa leans forward to touch Asta's arm. Mattie takes the opportunity to join in.

'Yes, there is that,' says Amy. 'But it makes us happy as well, to remember him. The funny thing is,' she looks around the room, 'we all knew him.'

And it proves to be true. Even though they'd only moved here a few months ago, Charlie managed to make more of an impression on everyone than Asta, who'd spent most of her post-GCSE August staying with the cousins from her mother's side of the family (her *biu*, as she didn't know to call them) bemoaning the fact she'd been allowed to have her last day at her old school without even knowing it was her last. The move away from the old place (Sun House by name, Sun House by nature) had been a sudden one and sprung on her from nowhere. Her parents had been threatening the move for so long, nobody ever quite believed it would really happen. Until it did.

Asta smiles to hear these new stories about Charlie as if he is telling them to her himself. How he charmed the receptionists at the GP's surgery. The time they took him to the racetrack at Ffos Las and he'd picked a rank outsider who romped home. When Lisa was told off for parking in the disabled spot, only for Charlie to be helped out of the shop in his wheelchair, shouting loudly in his still-thick Liverpool accent to the 'interfering old bat to mind her own business'.

Best of all were the memories George has about Charlie as a young man. When George took Charlie to buy his first suit at Davies & Valentine, the gentlemen's outfitters. The time the two of them tried to go fishing in a coracle. How Charlie borrowed George's glasses so nobody would punch him in the face and made the mistake of looking through, not over them, and promptly walked into a lamp post. Amy and Ray relay these tales to everyone else. George's face moves expressively out of synch with what they're all hearing, a bit like watching the sign language interpreter in the corner of the screen. You can't exactly link what's being said with what's being translated but you can tell from their face and the way they move their hands when it's meant to be happy, sad, serious or funny.

'I suppose you knew him longer than any of us,' Asta tells George.

'Yes, but there was a long gap in the middle,' he replies.

'Yes, but there was a long gap in the middle,' Amy translates.

George raises his cup of tea and gives a toast that transcends the language barrier.

'*Charl-ay!*' he shouts.

'Charlie!' everyone echoes.

Chapter Four

Asta reaches for her phone and shoots out of bed immediately.

It is 08:40, the exact time she should be standing at the bus stop underneath the market clock, waiting to climb on board the school bus. Or the time she should be crossing the bridge over the railway line on the long walk to school, part of the human crocodile that wends its way through the industrial estate that divides Cawsmenyn from its high school. If a drone was filming this daily odyssey of adolescent souls, it would see clusters of schoolchildren bumping and joshing their way to classes. Very occasionally, it would pick out an isolated dot walking alone. Asta would be one of those dots.

She opens the bedroom door, dashes straight to the bathroom and completes her morning ablutions in an angry rush. It's just as the electric buzz of her toothbrush stops that she realises she can't hear her parents' pneumatic symphony of sleep through the thin walls of the flat.

Oh yeah, they've gone to see Felix in Bristol. And to look for a new sofa. And to get some more paint. She remembers it now. Her father creeping in to say they were leaving and she should remember to get up in time for school. Her groaning and pulling the duvet over her head. The front door banging shut and feet clattering down the fire escape steps. She wants to blame her parents for not calling her from the car to double-check, but why would they? On any other day, Asta gets herself efficiently to school while her parents sleep on after their late-night finishing time downstairs.

As she hurries from bathroom to bedroom to kitchen to living room, getting ready for school, she becomes faintly aware of a change in the atmosphere. There is a different smell all through the flat. Everything seems fresher, more outdoorsy than usual. The light is shining differently, casting unexpected shadows everywhere. There is more dust in the air, motes lifted up into sunbeams and dancing as if no one is looking. Except Asta is looking and amazed that her father's new-found obsession with cleaning has allowed them to be here in the first place. It's only as she hurries to the front door to slip on her shoes and unhook her coat from the rack that she sees why.

The floor that leads to the front door has disappeared. There is a vast expanse of empty space where the hall rug used to live and at the other end, the key is still in the lock. She could maybe attempt an Attenborough jump, a gazelle's leap across the void to perch on the tiny ledge there, but she's just as likely to do a mountain goat tumble into the abyss of downstairs.

She is a prisoner in her own home.

Oh damn, no school, bad luck.

It is, of course, the builder and the new stairs being installed. Grandpa Charlie always said she could sleep through an earthquake. It looks like she pretty much has. She tiptoes to the edge of the precipice and peeps over. There is nothing to be seen down below, just an expanse of white dust sheet like a grubby layer of snow shrouding the chessboard tiled floor. Someone must have left the shop door open because she can hear Zoe Ball introducing the next record and revving engines ticking over at the nearby junction.

That someone must be coming because a reedy, whistled version of *Perfect* is getting louder and louder. Asta steps back quickly, slips on something, and the next thing she's bumped her arse onto the floor and her lower legs are dangling over the edge of the hole in the ground.

'It's raining bits of paper,' she hears someone say.

'And human legs,' says another voice.

Asta scrambles backwards on her elbows until her feet are back on solid floorboard before getting up.

'Are you all right up there?'

Asta tucks her hair behind each ear so she can still see as she peeps over the edge.

'Fine, thanks,' she calls down to the two upturned faces, one she recognises as yesterday's builder, the other a younger, smoother-faced version of him. 'But I think I'm trapped upstairs.'

'You again?' says the older builder. 'I hope no dogs are going to come hurtling down towards us.' He pulls an agonised face and crosses his arms above his head like people do in films when they think a heavy weight is about to fall on them.

'Steve doesn't live here.'

'Aren't you supposed to be in school?'

Asta nods.

'I'm sure your mum and dad told me there wasn't going to be anyone in so we didn't have to worry about there being no stairs for most of the day. You've put a bit of a crimp in that, young . . .'

He pauses, waiting for Asta to supply her name so she does.

'Well, Asda, my name's Vince and this is my boy, Josh.'

Asta rolls her eyes. She is used to this.

'I'm *not* named after a supermarket, it's Asta!' she snarls. She isn't being unpleasant, merely accurate. And you can't say Asta properly without having to spit out the bit in the middle. 'It's short for Augusta.'

The younger builder turns away quickly, stifling a laugh.

'And *that's* why I shortened it to Asta.'

'It's different. I'll give it that,' says Vince. 'And it better have a tick against it on the school register.' He claps his hands together. 'All right, let's get on. Josh, fetch the ladder so we can get this young lady to school.'

'I might as well stay off now,' says Asta, 'I've missed the first lesson already.'

'No need to miss any more,' says Vince, 'We're going down to Screwfix now anyway so we'll give you a lift in the van.'

It was her mum who suggested Asta not be offended when Mrs Li said there was no need for Asta to call and walk Steve every single day of the week.

'I'm sure they like you but there's like and like, isn't there?' she'd said cryptically.

What was that supposed to mean? Asta couldn't afford to put a foot wrong in case Mr and Mrs Li decided they didn't need help walking Steve at all any more.

What if they *minded* her going to their house all the time?

They minded *her* going to their house all the time?

They minded her *going to their house* all the time?

They minded her going to their house *all the time*?

It must be this last one, mustn't it? Everyone deserves a bit of privacy and not to be woken from an armchair nap by a strange teenager tapping at the window.

Anyway, it means she gets home from school at the proper time today. Even though she was late, the school day didn't feel any shorter or more bearable. She doesn't know what her problem is, it's not as if she left a weeping squad of besties behind in her old school. There are friends and there are *Friends*, aren't there? Most of them have seen each other for five days a week, forty-two weeks a year for the last eleven years but now that spell of proximity has been broken, there is nothing to hold them together. As for the new school, it isn't as if anyone is particularly horrible to her. It's just nobody is particularly nice either.

She tries to get into the flat around the side as usual, only to find the fire escape steps have disappeared. The only sign they've ever been there are the two pale strips high up on each side of the entrance where the metal rails used to be attached. She looks up at what is now literally a door to nowhere. Her parents aren't back yet either – no sign of the car – although the builders' van is still there which is a relief as she only has the key to the flat's now unreachable ex-front door with her.

'Hello,' says Vince, turning to greet her as she walks into the shop. 'How was school?'

She shrugs vaguely. He responds with some sympathetic head bobbing before adding, 'Like that, is it?'

Asta knits her brows together. It is her default facial expression which she thinks makes her look thoughtful and serious. Everyone else in the family claims it makes her look scowling and furious. How come she's only known the builder five minutes and he understands her in a way her parents can't? All Mandy ever says is, 'Don't worry, things will get better, it takes time to settle in,' while Tim is all, 'I don't know what you've got to complain about,' or, 'It can't be as bad as all that.'

'School's school,' she says. 'You go there to study. It's not a popularity contest.'

Vince gives a low whistle which Asta chooses to ignore as she walks through the flap in the counter, which is already flipped up, and turns into the vestibule. She gasps. Instead of a small dark room filled with the whiff of coats and broken umbrellas, light is pouring in from upstairs. There are three steps that lead to a small landing before a ninety-degree turn and a wooden stair-case that takes you all the way up to the flat. There is a pleasing smell of glue, varnish and sawdust. She dashes back out again.

'It looks amazing!' she says to Vince. He pulls his face into an 'aw shucks' expression. 'Can I go up them?'

'Yup, they're ready to use. Help yourself.'

Asta leaps up the first few steps before turning and springing up the rest, two at a time. She has to stop at the top though. A length of ribbon is tied across from the new handrail to the new bannister. Josh appears from the kitchen and presents Asta with a pair of scissors.

'For the official opening,' he says.

Asta takes the scissors, snips at the ribbon and says, 'I declare these stairs open.'

Then she runs to the toilet because she is bursting.

Asta's changed out of her school uniform into joggers and a T-shirt and is standing by the fridge eating yoghurt. She wonders if Charlie ever did the same thing when he lived here. Not the yoghurt part – he was lactose intolerant – but did he just slop about the flat on his own like this? Lie on his tummy on the floor kicking his heels up as he read a magazine? Carefully squeeze a spot in the bathroom mirror and dab at it with TCP until it stopped bleeding? Lean out of his bedroom window and watch the starlings swoop and swirl around those cedar trees on the other side of town?

She rinses the yoghurt pot out and places it carefully down on the draining board to dry, considers putting the licked-clean spoon back into the cutlery drawer before doing the right thing and placing it in the dishwasher. Then she sits back down at the kitchen table and looks at what Vince and Josh gave her when they finished up for the day.

'Don't oversleep tomorrow,' Vince said. 'We're painting the stairs and we want to get an early start 'cos it'll need drying time.'

'As your mum and dad aren't back yet, can we leave these with you?'

This was Josh, who was holding a bundle of something Asta recognised as the bits of paper she'd slipped on this morning, the ones that went confettiing down through the gap in the floor. Or ceiling, from where Vince and Josh were standing.

'We found them when we took the floorboards up. Looks like someone who lived here before you left them behind by mistake. Pity.'

'Why's it a pity?' asked Asta.

'You'll see,' said Josh.

'Have you looked at them already?' said Asta. 'They're not even yours.'

'They're not yours either.'

'They're more mine than they are yours.'

'Finders keepers,' says Josh.

'Losers weepers,' says Asta, snatching them off him.

'Well,' says Vince. 'That escalated quickly. We'll go home now and that exchange between the two of you will not make it in any ways awkward the next time we all meet again.'

'Sorry,' Asta calls out after the two of them, as their rigger boots traipse down the stairs. She thinks she hears footsteps stutter in recognition but nobody says anything back.

Asta spreads out the pieces of paper until they cover the kitchen table. The writing on them all is from the same old-fashioned hand, every single letter joined to the next by threads of black ink. All her year had learned cursive in primary school but as soon as they got to big school, they'd each developed their own writing style – lifting their pen off the paper after they wrote an x or an r, swirling a super-loopy d or a y above or below the line, BLOCK PRINTING EVERYTHING IN TINY CAPITALS, dotting the letter i with a heart, circle or smiley face. This handwriting was not like that. It was proper writing like Charles Dickens or Thomas Hardy's. There were even splotches of ink that meant a fountain pen was used, occasional crossings-out too, all the evidence of being written in a rush. It's hard to read so she fetches her glasses from her school bag and things swim into focus.

The builder must have just stacked everything into a pile after they fluttered to the ground floor. There's no logical order to them and it feels like watching episode four of a show before episode two and then moving onto episode five. She should get them into the right order before reading them; so she begins laying them out on the kitchen table, placing each piece of correspondence – some of which stretch to several pages, some just a few words on a postcard – into its own pile. She checks the dates, the postmarks, to try and get them into chronological order so she can read them properly but her eyes can't help skimming a few lines every now and again.

Lots of them seem quite mundane, describing the weather or the minutiae of a stranger's boring everyday but occasionally, she'll come across a sentence or a paragraph that makes her gasp. She thinks of Mr Feather, her English teacher's face when he reads out Shakespeare's 'Sonnet 18'.

Shall I compare thee to a summer's day?
Thou art more lovely and more temperate.

Isn't it curious? How did the letters end up here and how long have they been here? Why is there only one side of the correspondence? If the couple had lived happily ever after, wouldn't she be seeing letters from both sides of the story? And they wouldn't be hidden away under years of stamping, dancing, tiptoeing feet. They'd be treasured, something special to show the grandchildren. *How I Met Your Grandmother*.

She is sitting there, chin in hands, impressed by the Indian ink curlicues, neat and straight, across unlined paper, when there is the sound of a car turning into the service yard. Her parents are back.

Asta doesn't know why but she instinctively scoops everything up off the kitchen table. She dashes into her room and opens up the middle drawer. It's the one that attracts the least attention; they always go for the top or bottom first when they come a-snooping. She drops the letters next to the unused vape, the leaflet from Talk to Frank. She re-adjusts a T-shirt on top of everything when two words leap out at her from one of the letters.

Dearest Charlie

She bends forward for a closer look, just as her parents reach what used to be the hallway but, Asta supposes, is now the landing. She can hear her mother's voice.

'They've done a really good job on these stairs, haven't they?'

'It's all right,' her father replies.

Asta drops the T-shirt, smooths some knickers and socks over everything and shoves the drawer shut. She saunters out onto the landing.

'How was Felix?' she asks.

Chapter Five

Asta waits until she hears the Tudum of Netflix coming from the living room.

Then she hops off the bed, fetches the letters out of the drawer, and settles down onto the floor where there will be enough space to spread them all out. She'd had to fake a lavish yawn, a Y-shaped stretch to the ceiling, to get out of *The End of the F*cking World* with her parents.

'I don't know how you can be more tired than me when I've driven to Bristol and back and visited every furniture and paint shop in the South West,' Tim had said.

'We don't often get a chance to do stuff together in the evenings,' said Mandy. 'Perhaps a bit of nap and we'll wait for you before we start?'

'No, you go ahead. I'm really, really tired,' Asta lied. 'Going to call it a night.'

She makes sure her back is pressed firmly against the door before she places the letters out carefully in front of her once again. Getting like with like, matching up the several sheets that make up one letter, is like matching the suits in a game of patience. She doesn't know the last time the letters were laid out like this, it was on this exact same floor although it was covered in Marley tiles back then, not speckled carpet. Once it's done, she scans them again and she sees that lots of the letters are addressed to a 'Dearest Charlie' but also some have been written for a 'Darling', a 'Sweetheart', a 'My Love'. Even so, Asta is certain they were all written from the same person to one other person.

She switches between looking over these vintage examples of human interaction in the twentieth century with the most current example of the same in the early twenty-first. She taps things into her phone she sees mentioned in the letters – Winston Churchill's funeral, Goldie the Eagle escapes, Sydney Silverman and his bill to abolish the death penalty – and she can get an idea of what the world must have been like when they were written. The earliest letter she can find is dated 1964, the latest 1965. She gets up and treads carefully over to the windowsill where she left that family tree, the one that connected her family with the Li family. Yes, it works out right, and looking through what the letters actually say, she can't be wrong. Dearest Charlie is Grandpa Charlie and the woman writing to him is not Grandma Lynda.

Asta loves Grandma Lynda with the pure affection of a small child because she died when Asta was nine. She remembers how sad Grandpa Charlie was, how she often sat with him to try and cheer him up with stories and drawings and games and how it usually worked. Not always, though. Once or twice, the sadness was too much and instead of her cheering him up, he ended up making her feel sad. She'd cried with the unashamed bawling children are still allowed before they learn to hide their feelings. She often wishes she could still get away with that.

Asta squints at the final page of a few of the letters and it takes a while to decipher the name of the person who wrote them. It's the 'x' at the end of the name that throws her off to begin with until she sees the number of them expand exponentially. They are not part of the name; they are kisses and name of the writer is revealed.

Elax

Ela xx

Ela xxx

It goes against the grain of her generation not to skim through the letters, see what she can find with a super-ficial scan. But if she wants to know Ela's surname, she will have to do this properly.

She starts reading.

11 Seaview Cottages
Porthgynffon
South Glamorgan
3rd June 1964

Darling Charlie,

I'm sitting on the bench in Auntie Gaynor's back garden. Everyone else has already gone to bed. It's nearly dark, but not quite and I have left the kitchen light on so I can see properly to write this to you. It's a warm night, not chilly enough for a cardigan even, and if I look out west, towards Cawsmenyn, the sky is striped with lilac clouds and fading orange sunlight. It looks like it will be a shepherd's delight in the morning so you'd better watch out for Hafod and his gang. They will be ravenous after a good day's sheep shearing!

Although we are very close to the beach and in spite of its name, you can no longer view the sea from any of the cottages in the street. Not since they built over the recreation ground with a block of flats. Auntie Gaynor says the people who live there can 'see the sea lovely from where they are' and she hopes 'they choke on it'. Still, even though you can't see it, you know it's there. The air is briny and by midday, if you lick your

wrist, you can taste the salt. Even now, I can hear
the waves gently lap lap lapping, in and out. The sea
must be in a good mood today. Other days she roars
and I can hear her beating herself up the beach, over
the promenade and onto the main road, leaving layers
of sand and pebbles behind when she goes back out
again. I remember Sali telling me about it before, how
when there is a storm and a mess, someone eventually
comes along to clear it up.

How is Sali? Well, she's getting better but Auntie
Gaynor says she will keep Sali with her now and
she is not to set foot in Cawsmenyn ever again.
Apparently, she was allowed to run wild when she
was living with us. My mam's ears must have been
on fire back home. Did you see any smoke coming
from our house? What Auntie Gaynor doesn't seem
to remember is that she shifted Sali down to live
with Mam and me because she couldn't keep up
with her here in the first place!

The colour's not back in Sali's face. When I think
of those two peachy pink flushes she had on each
of those little round cheeks and the rest of her like
a jug of cream from the dairy. Now she looks so
ashen and her face as if it's caved in on itself. That's
because of the not eating, of course. She says she's

got no appetite but the doctor says there should be no physical reason for that now.

Yes, we've had to tell the doctor here what happened too but nobody else knows. As far as everyone else thinks, she had a funny turn at the top of the stairs. Was that tumble down them part of the plan? Or was she hoping the half bottle of gin and hot bath would do the trick? I suppose we'll never know but the trick has most certainly been done now.

Of course, we all wondered who it was and Sali told me just this morning it could only have been Miguel Garcia. She cried when she said, because she loves him and wanted me to find out from you if he's been asking after her but I think it's best if you don't tell me either way. That way I won't have to pretend not to know or worry about letting anything slip. As for Miguel, I know he is your friend and he looks like butter wouldn't melt in his mouth but I will be giving him a flea in his ear next time I see him.

I know you both had your wily ways with the girls in the old days. Still, as I tell the others, 'Charlie's with Ela Hennessy now so you'd better all keep your mitts off!' It looks like Miguel is still available though, more's the pity.

Don't say anything to Miguel. I couldn't get it out of Sali what she said to him and what exactly happened. Please don't let anyone else see this letter. Perhaps you should burn it after reading or hide it somewhere very safe. Please don't just throw it in the bin where anyone can find it.

I think Sali will need me for a little longer yet and I know it's annoying when we were supposed to have the whole summer together. Still, it's only June and ages until term starts again. I have lots of reading to do for my final year and I am trying to do as much of it as I can now here in Porthgynffon so my time when I get home will be free to spend with you. The added benefit is that if I read them out loud, they send Sali off to sleep pretty quick. Better than a pill, she says, the cheeky thing!

It's getting very dark so I am going to finish writing for now and hope to catch the first post in the morning.

Ela x

Chapter Six

'Asta Fung's got more chins than the Chinese phonebook.'

Asta remembers this joke from Year Eight as she taps Ela Hennessy into the BT website.

She was still puppyish in fat back then and even now she isn't sure if that joke is racist or not.

'What do you think, Grandpa Charlie?' she'd asked.

'Don't think so,' had come the reply. 'Not compared to what it was like when I was your age. And it literally is not the same kettle of fish when you compare it with what me mam had to put up with.'

'Not literally, surely,' she'd said, picturing a fish's head poking out of the spout, scaly tails flipping about so you couldn't close the lid properly. Of course, she should have asked Charlie about what happened to his mother, who was also her great-grandmother, but instead she chose to call him out on using the word 'literally' incorrectly. She flushes with embarrassment, pressing a hand against her hot cheek, before turning back to the screen.

The phonebook website has spoken.

We're sorry we couldn't find any results for Ela Hennessy.

Please could you try the following:
Double check your spelling.

She does – double n and double s. All correct. Still nothing.

Try using an initial.

Good thinking. She scrolls back up and deletes the -la from Ela. Still still nothing.

Try widening your search.

She clicks into the box for 'county' and adds 'shire', then the small magnifying glass to the right of it.

Success! There are three households listed under the name of E. Hennessy in the whole of the county. Three who choose not to be ex-directory anyway. Asta thinks about how many households still actually have the landline that would make them eligible to be in the phone book in the first place. Probably just the really old folk, which works out well, not like her first Google search for Ela Hennessy. All of them had been young, filtered and fake. She hopes *her* Ela Hennessy is as committed to the spaghetti of cables that linked the phone to the outside world as Grandpa Charlie was. He wouldn't even let them have a cordless handset.

Someone is coming upstairs and straightaway Asta knows it's her mother. That was something else she used to miss from the Sun House after they moved here – the external staircase – being able to tell who's coming up by the sound of their feet alone. The regular light Cortez tread of her mother. Her father's DM-ed baby elephant stampede. Her brother's irregular beat as he sprang up two steps at a time, then one, then two again. Another thing she misses is having a desk in her own bedroom. There's no room for it in Grandpa Charlie's old bedroom. Instead, she has to do everything at the big table in the living room, sharing it with everyone else and this demands a certain level of wiliness. She quickly opens up a new tab to hide what she's doing before realising the sudden appearance of the white Google homepage is about as useful as closing your eyes and hoping you won't be seen. She quickly taps something into the address bar to bring something up but oh no, not Write4U. Not now. Quick, change it!

Too late . . .

'Should you be doing that again?' asks Mandy, sticking her head in to check on her only daughter, the baby of the family. 'What about your schoolwork?'

'I've done it all,' says Asta and it was true. Unlike her classmates, who had each other to distract them from their studies, she had no one.

'Well, all right then,' said Mandy, completely convinced, entirely unquestioning. 'I've just come upstairs to put some eyedrops in. It's smoky down there tonight. We'll have to get the engineer in to check the extraction system.'

Asta doesn't pay attention to this last bit. The way she sees it she's never going to have to worry about the day-to-day management of a Chinese takeaway, not when she is already proprietor and sole employee of her own online calligraphy and lettering store. Today – *occasionally* selling inspirational messages, lines from a poem or quotes from a film she's carefully etched onto 260gsm card. Tomorrow – *consistently* selling inspirational messages, lines from a poem or quotes from a film she's carefully etched onto 260 gsm card.

Write4U is Asta's online shop. It's not like the others that sell mass-produced wall art, fed into a computer and churned out by a printer. Oh no, Asta's products are all handwritten by her personally. She lavishes care and attention on every item she produces, on each single stroke of her pen. She knows the thick and thin, rise and fall of each letter. Like all good calligraphers, she draws them into existence. Her own handwriting is basic but her lettering work is, even if she says so herself, rather brilliant.

She needs to work on her marketing plan. Even though she has got a full fifteen five-star reviews, a third of them are from contributors called Mandy, Tim, Charlie and Felix. There's even one from a Steve Collie-Cross. They were the early ones of course when that was the shape of her family. Things have changed since then but it does mean she's fully earned every good review afterwards. It's turned from hobby into a profitable side hustle, although she regrets letting her nagging parents know that.

'You do know your main hustle is being in school, don't you?'

That was Mandy, the good cop. Tim was the bad cop.

'I don't know why you bother,' he said. 'It's not like we don't give you pocket money. We didn't move forty miles up the road so you could mess about with a fountain pen for the rest of your life.'

'I don't use a fountain pen,' said Asta. 'That's the old-fashioned way of doing it. What I do is modern calligraphy with modern pens.'

'I don't care if you pluck some feathers off a chicken's arse to make a quill,' said Tim. 'We haven't gone through all this upheaval so you can fail your A levels.'

'Not that you will fail them,' added Mandy, daggers practically flying across the room from her eyes into Tim's.

Asta waits five minutes after Mandy's feet have pitter-pattered down the stairs again before going back to finding her E. Hennessy. She could just call them and ask them if they remember Charlie but what if they don't?

In the old days, they probably wrote to each other in the post like people WhatsApp each other now. Nobody remembers the ins and outs of everyone they've clicked the send button for. What if it's the same thing with these letters? Perhaps this Ela was in the habit of falling in love everywhere she went and there are small deposits of letters like these under floorboards all over the country.

Or she went on to marry someone else and live so happily ever after with him, this relationship with Grandpa Charlie means nothing to her. *Charlie who?* she might ask.

What if none of these women are the right one? Because Grandpa Charlie had a hidden split personality in his younger days? He wrote the love letters to himself. He was both Charlie *and* Ela which could mean a curious congenital time bomb for her and Felix.

Do you have any first- or second-degree relatives with a history of mental health issues?

Asta shakes her head like Steve after a hot summer's day in the long grass. She thinks about things far too much. Still, she can't deny the possibilities for catastrophe are endless. The possibility of success much less likely. She blows hot and cold on herself, torn between thinking the letters are the work of the truly lovelorn, a heartless serial romancer of people's grandfathers or the manifestation of a troubled mind.

She'll just enter the first E. Hennessy's numbers into her phone to see how it feels. She doesn't have to press the green dialling button after that. But she does. It rings and rings for such a long time, Asta is convinced it's going to go to voicemail but then . . .

'Hello?'

The voice of someone who had to take the plums out of their mouth before answering the phone.

'Good evening,' Asta replies. 'Could I possibly please speak to E. Hennessy?'

'Yes, you're speaking to Edward Hennessy now. What is it you want?'

'I don't suppose your wife is called Ela, by any chance?'

'Just one moment. Darling, is your name Ela?'

In the background, Asta can hear someone say, 'No, it's Carol,' before Edward comes back on and says 'No, she's called Carol.'

This is so weird. Asta is literally speechless while simultaneously appreciating her own correct usage of the word literally.

'Is there anything else?' asks Edward Hennessy.

'I don't suppose there is anyone there called Ela Hennessy by any chance?'

'Mum? Granny?' she hears Edward saying. 'Either of you called Ela?'

Asta can hear someone say Delyth while someone else chimes in with Lydia.

'Did you catch any of that?' says Edward.

'Yes,' says Asta, before adding weakly, 'is anyone called Ela in your family?'

'No, it doesn't look like it, does it?'

'Sorry,' whispers Asta, 'I think I've got a wrong number.'

'It rather looks like you have.'

*

She who fails to plan, plans to fail.

How could Asta have forgotten this? It was her first proper Write4U commission that she got paid for in cash, not hugs and kisses, a lift into town or a pat on the head. That last one was from Felix. It takes a few days to work up the courage but by the time she's ready to call the two other candidates for E. Hennessy, she has prepared the arse out of it. She has flowcharts. She has different scripts as to what to say. She even has a prop.

The phone rings out for so long Asta nearly hangs up and then the answer machine kicks in. Ah yes, answer machine. Asta riffles through her revision cards for the right one. In the meantime, a robotic voice informs her, 'There is nobody to take your call at the moment. Please leave a message after the tone.'

Beep.

Asta clears her throat and reads the script.

'Hello. I'm looking for E. Hennessy. I'm very sorry to interrupt you and take up your valuable time. You don't know me but I think I have found a purse and the bank card in it says E. Hennessy. I looked it up in the phone book and found your number so I was just wondering if this could maybe, possibly, be you. There seems to be something which I think may be of great sentimental value to the actual owner so even if it's not yours, do you think it might be possible for you to confirm it isn't, so I can tick you off the list and eliminate you from my investigation?'

Asta's voice is getting wispier and more faded as conviction in her plan ebbs away. She's spun the story about the purse to get anyone who is screening their calls to answer and she's being super-verbose in order to give elderly hips and legs time to walk to the phone.

'I'm sorry to have missed you on this occasion. I will call you back again . . .'

'Hello. Hello. Are you still there?'

The voice is breathless from having to run to answer. It also sounds quite young but not all people get that roughened tree-bark effect to their voice as they get older. Look at Tom Jones. Or rather, listen to him.

'Are you E. Hennessy?' Asta asks.

'Hello. Yeah, it's me, I'm E. Hennessy. You found my purse, right?'

'You've actually lost your purse?!'

This was not supposed to happen. Asta opens up the prop purse, an old one of Mandy's, and finds a greying Boots receipt in there. Vicks decongestant, it says. £2.99.

'Yeah, and you've found it. It's mine. Is my money still in there? Mastercard? Visa?'

Asta flips through the revision cards. She's definitely failed to plan for this.

'It might be,' says Asta eventually. 'What does your purse look like?'

'What does *your* purse look like?'

'It's dark blue with a pale blue lining,' says Asta.

'Yeah, that's it. That's mine. I'll meet you outside Caffè Nero. Today. You bring it to me.'

'It's not dark blue with a blue lining!'

'I made a mistake, right. I'm colour-blind so I can never get the colours right when I'm talking. You should be feeling sorry for me for being colour blind. And for losing my purse.'

'There is no way it can be your purse. I know it isn't.'

'How do you know that, then?'

'It just can't, right? I'll bet you haven't even lost one. You're a big liar.'

'Takes one to know one,' says the other voice, before rounding the call off with a choice selection of obscenities arranged to give vivid and maximum offence.

Asta feels like giving up, crawling into bed and pulling the duvet over her head again, but she figures she should get back on the horse immediately. After all, there's only one more number to call. Then she can give up, knowing she gave it a good go. She brings up the last E. Hennessy and dials again. It's voice mail this time and the speaker clears her throat before enunciating in classic Welsh old lady tones.

'Hello. If you would like to leave a message for Eleanor Hennessy, please do so after the beep. Thank you.'

Asta opens her mouth to leave a message, decides against it and instead presses the red button. Then she gets up and does a little dance around the sofa before coming back to the screen to make a note of where Eleanor Hennessy lives.

11 Seaview Cottages
Porthgynffon
South Glamorgan
8th June 1964

Darling C,

While I was cooking breakfast this morning, there was a sound on the stairs and next thing, Sali came into the kitchen still in her nightie. At last! My policy of frying a full breakfast every day has paid off. She used to love extra dripping on her fried bread and was a fiend for an egg with the yolk cooked until it's rubbery. We've been trying to waft the smell of it up to her room every day and it's finally paid off. I think she might be turning a corner and once she's taken it, I can come home.

Now I do have a bone to pick with you about your not taking Doris out for me. Never mind your confession to it in your last letter, Mam said she's been languishing in that shed for weeks, longing for someone to give her some TLC. I know you think I'm silly for thinking Doris cares whether she gets taken out or not and she is only a bicycle and not a pony or a dog. Still, everything has a purpose in life. A flower craves to be sniffed, a pen wants you use up its ink and a bicycle wishes someone would ride it.

Doris won't mind that you're a bit wobbly on her. I know that you didn't learn to ride a bike like everyone else does because your daddy died when you were small. I can't quite believe you only learnt to pedal after Miguel shoved you onto his bike at the top of the grassy bank and let go. It's like chucking someone into the river and hoping he'll swim. Typical of him.

The trick is balance. Remember that time I took you out for a frontie on the handlebars, how we moved and tilted and found the perfect equilibrium — the two of us together? That's how it should feel when you're with my Doris.

Even if Sali doesn't feel she can cope here on her own with Auntie Gaynor, I am going to try to get home for a day at least so I can make sure Mam's coping. And to see you of course!

Missing you lots, wish you were here,

Ela x

Chapter Seven

They are reading *Sense and Sensibility* for A-level English and some of the class got together at the weekend to watch the film version. Asta wasn't invited, of course. It's not personal, she tells herself, and she wouldn't have gone anyway.

But still, it would have been nice to have been asked.

Mr Feather isn't in the classroom when the lesson starts so they all spread out across the middle two rows. He can make them move further forward when he comes in if he wants to.

'Was the film any good?' asks Sophie. She didn't go because she went to Cardiff with her boyfriend who is called Lambert after Lambert and Butler cigarettes. He is quite small for a seventeen-year-old. 'But perfectly formed,' Sophie unnecessarily likes to inform the others on a regular basis.

'The best part is when Professor Snape comes on,' says Callum, the only boy doing English A-level and who manspreads himself accordingly. 'And you're supposed to believe he's not too old to marry Rose from *Titanic*.'

'Colonel Brandon?' says Asta, confused.

'Yeah, that's right, Alan Rickman,' says Paige, who is sitting next to her, mobile phone gripped firmly under the desk, thumbs ablur.

Asta doesn't know Alan Rickman is in the film. She was momentarily flummoxed by how Hogwarts had turned up in rural Devonshire in the eighteenth century. She looks around. Nobody seems to have noticed her mistake so she resolves to shut up and keep it that way.

'Dirty old man,' says Callum but the rest of the class of girls disagree. They find Alan Rickman's brooding moodiness infinitely superior to the floppy-haired prettiness of Hugh Grant's Edward Ferrars. Asta decides doubly to shut up.

'Well, I think it's wrong,' says Callum, flicking through his Penguin Classic. 'Where does it say how big the gap between them is? At least twenty years!'

'And what's so bad about that?' says Mr Feather as he comes in, closing the door behind him.

'Colonel Brandon's a dirty old man, Sir,' says Callum.

'He's thirty-five, Callum', says Mr Feather. 'Even though I have yet to reach that milestone myself, I can assure you, it's not "old".'

'Still dirty, though,' says Callum. 'How old is Marianne, anyway?'

'She's sixteen,' says Asta, but nobody notices because she's drowned out by Sophie's louder voice.

'Same age as us, isn't she?'

'Well done, Sophie,' says Mr Feather. 'And what do all of you think of the romantic match between Marianne and Colonel Brandon?'

Voices overlap, small insults exchanged, opposing views held up and shot down. Good-humoured teenage debate. Asta doesn't join in. Instead, she looks down at her bag where her mobile phone is. She wonders why Eleanor Hennessy is never in when she calls. Perhaps she should stop withholding her number when she calls her? Or even leave an actual message to ask her to call back? What would Ela say if she got through to Asta's voicemail?

Hello, I don't want to talk to you. Your grandfather broke my heart nearly sixty years ago and I've never forgiven him. Yes, we were very much in love before. Do you want to make something of it? Do you?

'What about it, Asta?' says Mr Feather. 'Asta? Are you listening?'

He's looking at her expectantly.

'Well, it all depends on how you choose to interpret it, doesn't it?'

She makes this vaguest of assertions with absolute conviction. She's not spent years intermittently daydreaming in class for no reason.

A small smile spreads across Mr Feather's face.

'I was just asking, Asta, if you wouldn't mind popping next door and asking Mrs Pritchard if she could give me back my stunningly well-annotated copy of *Sense and Sensibility*?'

Asta scrapes her chair backwards, gets up and heads next door. It's only as she closes the classroom door behind her that she realises she should have said something. Like, 'Yes, Sir,' or, 'Not at all, of course I wouldn't mind.' Several different kinds of embarrassed mortification flit through her mind as she waits for Mrs Pritchard to finish rummaging in the book store. Finally, Mr Feather's copy is found. It's so ancient and well-loved, it still has an orange spine and a cover glistening with layers of Fablon.

When she steps back into the classroom, everyone turns. She feels the heat of many pairs of eyes trained upon her.

'What?' she asks nervously, looking down at herself. It's like that stress dream where you suddenly find you're in school standing in front of everyone else in just your underwear. She knows that when other people have this dream, they're naked, but even in this tiny way, she has to fall short of the norm.

The whole class bursts into laughter. It's awful and she's tempted to turn around and run out of the room, out of the school, out of the town, out of everything. But instead, she goes forward to put the book into Mr Feather's outstretched hand.

'I'm sorry about that, Asta,' said Mr Feather. 'Callum was doing his rather good impersonation of the headmaster and I think everyone was worried it was him at the door instead of you. The class was not laughing at you, they were . . .'

Asta braces herself for the inevitable 'laughing *with* you' which never makes sense. It never makes her feel better about it either.

'. . . releasing tension during a moment of stress.' He tilts his head in that kindly yet patronising way Asta is used to. 'Although I realise it probably didn't feel like that from where you were standing. It really was nothing to do with you. They would have laughed even if Greta Thunberg had come into the room.'

'*Especially* if Thunderbergs had come in,' says Callum.

There is another wave of laughter. Not because it's funny but just like the first time, it relieves the tension. As Asta sits back down, Paige leans over and whispers, 'Sorry.' Asta pulls that half-smile she's used to doing but is surprised to find that this time, she means it.

18 Rupert Street
London
SE1 8AW
22nd January 1964

Dear Mr Charlie Fung,

Thank you for your letter dated 16th January.

I'm afraid I was dumbfounded as to why you were writing to me in this way and was completely unaware of the circumstances you describe. I was also utterly mystified as to how you have my London address.

Fortunately, the second post was able to solve the mystery for me when a letter from my cousin Sali arrived. She has explained that it was she who gave my address to you although I am at a loss as to why she did so.

Regarding the matter for which you are sending your apology, yes, it is true I am regularly at the bus stop opposite the library. I don't recall the incident you recount. Although I have a hazy recollection of your friend Miguel Garcia making some pointed comments in my direction, I didn't think he was talking to me so wasn't paying sufficient attention to hear what he said. Following receipt of your letter though, I am now fully aware that he was calling me a 'goody two-shoes', 'teacher's pet' who 'always has her nose stuck in a book' and thinks 'she's a cut above the likes of us'.

So thank you for informing me about something concerning which I could have lived on in blissful ignorance.

The fact of the matter is that I largely agree with Miguel's opinion of me although I would seek to phrase it slightly differently. I do work hard and keep out of mischief (goody two-shoes) and this inevitably will have made me a favoured pupil in school (teacher's pet). I very much enjoy reading which explains why I often have my 'nose stuck in a book'. However, I do not think I am a cut above anyone else and the fact that I am studying for a university degree in London is hardly different from Miguel's plumbing apprenticeship or your work with your parents in the Yau Sum shop.

In spite of all this, I do appreciate your kindness in writing. It takes guts to stand up and apologise for not, as you say, 'shutting Miguel's big fat mouth right there and then'.

Please don't give this incident or its aftermath a second thought.

I know I certainly won't.

Yours sincerely,

Ela Hennessy (Miss)

Chapter Eight

The builders are coming back to put fitted wardrobes into her parents' bedroom this morning. It explains why Asta woke from a dream where she was being crushed to death by marshmallows only to find Mandy and Tim had piled most of the clothes they owned on top of her while she slept. As she rolled over to try to get comfortable, she felt the soft slap of Mandy's enormous rubber plant on her forehead. It had been shoved up against the bed. She should be grateful, she thought, there's no chance of over-sleeping with so much stuff crowding her personal space.

And here she is, up nice and early because she has to get out of the flat before Vince and Josh get here. The two of them have been back and forth intermittently over the last few weeks working on different parts of the shop and the flat and Asta has a 100 per cent success rate in avoiding them. As Vince had predicted, it would be utter mortification to have to speak to either of them after that incident when the letters were handed over.

But Josh is the only other person who's read them or she thinks so, judging by what he said.

We found them when we took the floorboards up. Looks like someone who lived here before you left them behind by mistake. Pity.

But on the other hand, don't builders find all kinds of personal stuff when they're going about their work anyway? Earrings that have fallen between gaps in the floor, biscuit tins filled with cash hidden in wall cavities, treasure maps used as carpet underlay. Josh isn't even related to Charlie like she is. He won't remember having seen the letters, he probably forgot about them five minutes after he handed them over. Otherwise perhaps he could help with the search for Ela? She thinks about it for a bit. Asking someone else for help instead of doing it on her own?

No chance.

She still doesn't fancy bumping into Josh, though, so to fill the extra time before school, she's taking the long way round. She'll go past the Li family bungalow and nip around the back so she can get an early morning glimpse of Steve. That will keep her going until 3.45 and their next scheduled walk.

All the curtains are still drawn at the front of the house. She realises she's never been around here this early before and certainly not when a morning walk hasn't been pre-arranged. Didn't they say Steve slept in the old man's bedroom? Would he close his bedroom door properly at night meaning Steve *couldn't* be in the conservatory? It's a concern and it occurs to her to go straight to school to avoid any prospect of disappointment. But she's here now so she creeps around the side of the bungalow on the tippiest of tiptoes looking for all the world like the sneakiest of sneaky cartoon burglars. As she turns the corner past the vegetable garden and onto the lawn at the back of the house, her heart leaps into her throat. A small ninja has his back to her and is throwing some tai chi stances.

She's just chastising herself when a shaggy mess of black, tan and white hurtles toward her. She drops down onto her knees so Steve can prop a paw on each of her shoulders and press a hot furry cheek against hers. Steve doesn't judge her for doing a racism; the ninja is George in black Marks and Spencer pyjamas and he is clearly attempting a neat little mountain pose, just like they do during the yoga that comprises non-competitive PE. Which is her favourite sort of PE.

'*Ay yah!*' says George.

He spots her just as he is turning into a Warrior pose, although it's hardly worthy of the name. More like a Pacifist, a very wobbly one that Asta has to rush forward to catch. She doesn't get there in time but it doesn't matter because George readjusts a leg, shuffles a foot and rights himself.

'Hello,' says Asta. 'Sorry, I was just passing.'

'Hello,' says George.

'Oh, are you feeling better? Do you speak good English now?'

Asta winces. She's done another racism. Out loud this time too.

George doesn't seem to notice though. He shakes his head before replying with something incomprehensible in Cantonese which he thoughtfully accompanies with actions – pointing towards the kitchen, pointing towards Steve, doing a walking motion with his middle and index fingers and sipping an imaginary cup of tea. He rounds it off by shrugging his shoulders and gesturing towards the back door with both hands.

Asta can see the kitchen clock from here. It says 7.40.

'Are you sure?' she asks George, who nods so she follows him inside, Steve barging forward to lead the way.

A large tablet is propped on the kitchen worktop next to the sink and George stops to give Carol Kirkwood an admiring look before putting the kettle on. Then he gets some Weetabix out of the cupboard and a pint of milk out of the fridge. He puts them on the table, looking at Asta significantly and smiling down at Steve before disappearing out of the room. Asta doesn't like cereal in the mornings. Or at any time of the day or night but George doesn't know that. As a guest, she should act accordingly so she hunts around in the cupboards and drawers for a suitable bowl and spoon before coming across *that* drawer – the one that's filled with a lifetime of household tat. She shouldn't really but she hesitates before closing it to get an eyeful of the contents. Loose batteries. A ball of string in multi-colour shades and textures because it's made up of shorter pieces of string tied together. Odd chopsticks, odd as in single, not odd as in weird.

By the time she has found a suitable bowl, tipped a solitary wheaty biscuit in and covered it with semi-skimmed, George has returned, fully dressed in his daytime outfit of shirt and trousers, braces and belt. Asta quickly takes a spoonful of mushed-up cereal and brings herself to take a bite when George shouts at her to stop. Well, he shouts at her and she does stop at any rate. George peers into the bowl, frowns and holds up two fingers.

How rude, thinks Asta, as George points just one finger into the bowl and cocks an eyebrow. She nods. George sighs, takes the bowl over to the worktop where he fetches another Weetabix out of the packet, adds it on top. He pours more milk on and starts bashing everything around with the spoon, reducing it to mush. He turns and heads back towards Asta. She gulps and feels a little bit of bile rise in her throat only for it to drop back down again when George plops the bowl onto the far end of the kitchen table opposite her. A delighted Steve hops onto the nearest chair, shoves his snout into the bowl and starts lapping.

Steve never got breakfast when he was Asta's. He didn't get to sit at the kitchen table either. She can't wait to tell her father, who used to accuse Steve of being the world's most spoilt dog, just because they let him sit on the sofa to watch *Countryfile* on Sunday nights.

George shuffles back to the worktop and pours hot water into a bowl containing a brick of ramen noodles. After a poke with a pair of chopsticks, he goes to fetch two fat croissants that Asta hadn't noticed warming up on the toaster. He brings over a butter dish and a jar of jam, its label blurred from being repeatedly wiped clean of sticky spills. Finally, the noodles are ready and divided into two small bowls and two small glasses of Tropicana appear. George places a tea strainer before he pours his glass to catch the bits, which he tips into the food waste bin under the sink.

Asta isn't sure what to make of this curious international hybrid of breakfast and lunch at this time of day but she knows she likes it.

'My dad says you knew my grandfather when he was my age?'

George nods, while slurping a curly noodle into his mouth.

'What was he like?'

George smiles, then frowns, then pulls a nonchalant face.

What does that mean?

'Was he happy when he lived here?'

George nods.

'And you got married to his mum, my granny? We're sort of related to each other?'

George nods twice.

'Did you know my Grandma Lynda?'

Nod and a smile.

'Before he met her, was my grandfather,' Asta tries to think of how best to say it, 'a bit of a player?'

George frowns.

'Did he have lots of girlfriends?'

George bursts out laughing. He opens his mouth to speak, checks himself when he realises he doesn't have access to the right language, hesitates but ploughs on in Cantonese anyway. His one concession to this is to speak extremely slowly as if addressing an imbecile, which isn't helping. Asta nods along for a bit uncomprehendingly before she has her brainwave. She fetches her bag from under the table and digs around for her mobile. It's at times like this she wishes she kept it in its purpose-built phone-sized pocket instead of chucking it in with everything else and hoping for the best.

After what seems like ages of rummaging, she gives up and starts removing the top layer of crap out of her bag and laying it out on the table until, at last, it's her phone. She finds the translation app quickly, flips it on and puts the phone on the table between herself and George.

'Carry on talking,' says Asta. 'Tell me about Grandpa Charlie.'

George says something carefully and slowly.

I'm listening the app says.

George looks at the screen. He knows he didn't say he was listening. Asta frowns and presses the small microphone icon again and nods encouragingly at George. He repeats himself and although the app claims it's still listening, it clearly doesn't fancy doing any translating.

'It can't hear you properly,' Asta says.

She picks the phone up and thrusts it toward George. He leans in and says something into it slowly and clearly.

What do you want to know? appears on the screen.

'What was Grandpa Charlie like when he was a young man?' she says.

George speaks. Sentences flash up, words appearing and disappearing as the context of what George is saying eliminates certain expressions and replaces them with more suitable ones.

To begin with, we liked each other not very much. He was a boy with no father, naughty too, his mother letter said. I wanted a help in my kitchen. My wife was dead. I was lonely.

Asta has to stop George then because the app has stopped translating. She presses the microphone icon again.

I'm listening.

George begins again. It's a bit stop–start but they are getting somewhere.

Work hard very good company all day together like wi-fi and otter. Singing Alouette on whiskers? Triangle shape forge striped monster all along the disestablishmentarianism.

Asta waves a hand to stop George. She frowns as she reads the screen. Either George is messing her about and talking nonsense or the app isn't working. She holds the screen out to George.

'Is that what you were saying?'

Even though the screen is small, George turns his head from side to side as he reads, moving his lips as he reads the English 'translation'. He shakes his head.

'Try again,' says Asta. So he does.

Gold whiskers do not work. Cow sheep explodes. Hmmmm?

Modern technology isn't everything it's made out to be after all. Asta gives it one last go and whispers one of the few Cantonese words she does know, taking care to turn away from George as she says it.

Lumberjack.

Well, at least the last two letters are the same as last two letters in the word she actually said.

All of a sudden, Gary, the local newsreader, appears on the tablet's screen and tells them it's 8.25.

'We'll have to see if we can get it to work another time,' says Asta, sweeping everything back into her bag. 'I have to get to school now.'

George has picked something up and is examining it closely. It has Japanese text on it, which is probably what caught George's eye, because it's her soft-tip Tombow Fudenosuke, one of her best calligraphy pens. He takes the top off, examines the tip of the brush and taps it against his thumbnail where it leaves a jet black dab. George looks delighted and does some experimental writing of a Chinese character on the back of a nearby envelope. As he writes, Asta notices the lines he summons up onto the paper vary in thickness and thinness just like her strokes do when she's practising her own calligraphy. Normally she hates it when anyone else uses one of her good pens because they never respect it. They just write as they always do, whether that's a careful script or a messy scrawl, and rely on the pen to work its magic and beautify their handwriting. Which it always does but is a bit like applying a Chanel lipstick to a grubby face. Better, but a bit of a waste.

But George isn't doing that. She can see he's guiding the pen, making the strokes thinner or thicker just by varying the pressure onto the paper. He finishes what he's writing and hands it to Asta.

'Fung,' he says, pointing at her. He offers her the piece of paper. She takes it.

'Thank you,' she says before hoisting her bag over her shoulder.

She stops to ruffle Steve's ears as she runs out the back door and it's only when she leaves the housing estate and joins the main road towards school that she realises George still has her pen.

18 Rupert Street
London
SE1 8AW
1st February 1964

Dear Charlie,

What a sight for sore eyes your letter was when I
saw it on the hall table when I got in this evening! I
knew it was from you even before I saw the postmark.
Your handwriting is so much neater than the average
boy. That's a compliment!

I picked it up and ran straight upstairs to my
room, secretly pleased it has been on the hall table
all day so the others can see that I do, in fact,
receive letters because I do, in fact, have people to
write to me. Clemmie, who has the attic room, has
at least three letters every single day. She went to a
boarding school so there are lots of chums in almost
every town in the land to write to her, not to mention the letters with Swiss stamps from her friend in
the finishing school. I asked her if she would have
preferred to go to finishing school instead and she
said, 'Not bloody likely.'

Anyway, nice as Clemmie is, you don't want to
hear about her.

Of course, I don't mind you telling me about it all.
A problem shared is a problem halved, as they say.
(Who are 'they'? I never know!)

It might be a good idea to look on the bright side
of your mother's expansion plans to open up another
takeaway shop nearby. You must see it how she sees it.
Having made such a success of things with Yau Sum,
she doesn't want all of you to rest on your laurels.

' It strikes me as a very good idea if your moving
there can avoid a repeat of what happened when you
went to see the empty shop in Dyffryn. While I can
just about forgive a seven-year-old for saying, 'Look!
A Chinese man!', the father should be shushing his
child, not joining in and saying, 'I've never seen one of
them before.' I understand your mother rushing off in
embarrassment but good on you for smiling and waving back at them.

I don't think tiny one-street Llyn would be a good
choice, never mind what that estate agent said but
Traeth is a lovely town. We used to go there for day
trips every weekend when I was small. I think I know
the shop you mean on the seafront. It used to sell
sweeties and we always went there for candyfloss and
sticks of rock. That would be my choice but, of course,
I haven't seen all the candidate locations as you have

done. Reading between the lines, though, I think that's the one you like best. Am I right?

Next week, I am coming home for a reading week. Mam also wants me to help with the spring cleaning, especially as one of her lodgers, Miss Grealy, has left to get married. A travelling salesman is coming to take the room for a few weeks as he has some business in the area. Harri has stayed with us before and can turn on the charm like any salesman. Mam likes him. I find him a bit much myself.

I hope we are able to speak in person next week. I love our letters — what would Clemmie say if she knew my correspondent was Cawsmenyn's answer to Paul McCartney complete with mop top and accent! — but it will be very nice to meet properly now we've got to know each other a bit better.

I'm glad we agreed to be pen pals and you are quite right, the thoughts of a Welsh girl in England and an Englishman with a Chinese face living in Wales definitely count as very educational cultural exchanges.

Yours sincerely,

Ela

Chapter Nine

Well, it's definitely been a day of doing things for the first time and the day isn't even anywhere near over yet.

Asta groans as she looks through the long thin window in the door into the classroom. There are already a dozen other students standing around or sitting on desks with their feet on the chairs. She doesn't know any of them, only recognises them from the corridors and the playground. She realises with horror there is only one Year Eleven and above doing detention and that's her. She wonders if detention is going to be like prison and whether it's a good idea to ask each other what they did.

Although, it soon becomes quite apparent that most of them are doing time for the same offence as her. Mrs Yates, the headmaster's pit bull of a PA, comes in with a high-sided metal tray that has six mobile phones laid out on it. Their screens light up with the movement of her weaving in and out of desks and chairs to get to the front and Asta spots her screensaver of Steve eating a Mr Whippy on the beach. When Mrs Yates gets to the front, she glares at Asta. Asta glares back.

It was the beginning of afternoon break and Asta had figured mid-afternoon on a weekday was one of the few times of the day or night she hadn't yet tried to call Eleanor Hennessy. She must be the most in-demand pensioner in the county as she was never in and never answered her own phone. She hadn't moved away or gone on holiday because, in spite of the number of silent voicemail messages Asta had inadvertently left while dithering over whether to speak or not, the box never filled up. This must mean she was deleting them. Which means she *must* be there, just not answering the phone. Asta had tried all the little tricks she knew people told their friends and family to do to ensure a ringing landline got picked up: call until voicemail picks up and then hang up and phone again immediately; three rings and hang up; call on the dot of the hour. Nothing had worked so far and Asta was beginning to think she'd have to go to Plan B which was to take the forty-five-minute bus journey to Eleanor's village, find out where she lived, and call in on Eleanor whether she liked it or not.

Asta *really* wanted to call Eleanor today so she took the risk of sneaking into the bin store. It was the only place to get any privacy because it was out of bounds. Once there, she crept inside and began scrolling through her recent numbers. She pressed the phone so tightly against her head, she could feel the back of her earring.

Ring ring

It stinks in here.

Ring ring

Wouldn't it be amazing if she answered!

Ring ring

And I could talk to her about Charlie without having to use that stupid translation app.

Ring ring

Unless that village she lives in means she can only speak Welsh?

Ring ring

Like she does on her outgoing message, you stupid idiot!

Ring ring

'Hello?'

That's funny, her voicemail sounds a bit different today. Did she record a new message?

'Hello? Is anyone there? If this is one of those scam calls targeting the elderly, I can tell you now that you're wasting your time . . .'

'Hello,' said Asta breathlessly, having overcome her shock at finally making contact with the real, live human Eleanor Hennessy. 'You don't know me but . . .'

'What are you doing here? Students are not allowed in this part of the school and certainly not to use their mobile phones.'

Asta looked up to see Mrs Yates holding two big bags of shredding.

'Hello?' said a tinny faraway voice that was only twenty-two miles up the road.

Mrs Yates dropped the bags, took the phone out of Asta's hand and terminated the call. Asta screamed, first a general noise of frustration, and then words that will later come back to haunt her. Words like 'jumped up' and 'not even a teacher' and 'will respect authority when authority's earned it'. She was a little bitch; there was no other way to describe it. She hated it when people wrote her parents off for 'just' running a takeaway. She'd done a snobbery and she knew it. What she didn't know was Lance Corporal Geraldine Yates used to be in the army and was commended for her service in Northern Ireland. Perhaps that's why she never took any shit from anyone.

Anyway, the end result is detention. An hour of, well, Asta doesn't know what but she hopes it's not like when Bart has to do lines on the blackboard at the start of *The Simpsons*.

Everyone is just settling down into their seats when the member of staff who is actually taking detention bounces in on the balls of his feet. It's Mr Feather, one of Asta's actual teachers, and not some random she's never going to have to see again. Typical.

He goes to the front of the classroom and does a visible double-take when he sees Asta before looking down quickly at the rap sheet. Mrs Yates whispers in his ear and hands him the tray of phones before leaving.

Mr Feather reads out a list of names which includes Asta.

'Right, all of you can spend the next hour writing me an essay on "Twenty-four hours without a mobile phone". I do not want to see three pages of the word "misery" and its many synonyms.'

'What's that mean, Sir?' asks a Year Eight sitting next to Asta.

'Look it up on your phone,' says Mr Feather. 'Oh you can't, can you? Well, there's a dictionary over there on the shelf.'

'What's "snim"?' the boy asks Asta out of the left-hand side corner of his mouth.

Asta tells him out of the right-hand side corner of her mouth.

'I like my detentions like I like my haircuts,' says Mr Feather, appearing between the two of them. He drops the dictionary heavily onto the boy's desk. 'In silence.'

It doesn't take long for Asta to warm to her subject. More walking with Steve. Reading a fun book for herself, not for her A levels. Practising her calligraphy, learning new fonts and variations.

When I have my pens, pencils and paper, my guidelines etched out and I start to draw the letters (yes, DRAW the letters!), I know it's all down to me. I don't have to rely on anyone else and nobody can let me down. Calligraphy is my mindfulness. It lets me concentrate on making one thing beautiful and, for a bit, the rest of the world disappears.

Asta leans back in her chair. She knows she enjoys her calligraphy but has never been forced to think about why before now. It's good to see it written down in front of her and the thought of letting Mr Feather see a small part of her when he reads the essay, even if he is only her English teacher and not, like, her uncle or something, feels good.

When detention ends an hour later, they all queue up to hand in their work and collect their phones.

'I hope we won't be meeting here like this ever again,' says Mr Feather to Asta.

'Thanks, Sir,' she says, as he hands her iPhone back to her.

She speeds out of the room. Is Steve wondering where she is? Then she smacks her hand against her forehead. Whoops! She did it again. She'd just left without replying properly to Mr Feather.

'I hope and fully intend never to get detention ever again either, Sir,' she should have said.

She runs back into the classroom; just in time to see Mr Feather tearing all of the detention essays into pieces and throwing them into the bin.

Chapter Ten

Steve is chewing away on a huge knucklebone that Asta can smell before she sees it. When he spots her, he thumps his tail against the patio and gives it a farewell lick before getting up and following her into the house.

Mrs Li is sitting at the kitchen table with her best friend Elaine and they are both reading. Judging by the familiar logo on the front of Mrs Li's book, it's something to do with *Jurassic Park*. She can't see what Elaine's reading because it's on a Kindle. The amazing thing is that until Asta arrived, they were just sitting together doing something that didn't really need the other person there. Asta is usually leaving the house by the time Elaine arrives and she doesn't know her except to say hello because they normally cross over. Is this really what Elaine calls around to do? Couldn't she just as easily read her book at home on her own? Like Asta does.

Mrs Li picks up her mug, sees it's empty and puts it back down again. Without saying anything, Elaine gets up and fills the kettle, rattles about with the hot beverage apparatus all laid out on the worktop.

'I'm sorry I'm late,' Asta says. 'It's too boring to explain why.'

It's actually too embarrassing.

'Steve no mind,' says Mrs Li. 'Dogs got lots of leisure time.'

She pronounces leisure *lee-zhur* which is a classic sign that she's been watching too many episodes of *The Real Wives of Atlanta County Hills* or whatever.

In the porch, Steve holds his chin up nicely so Asta can clip him on.

'You are a good boy,' she tells him. 'You're the best.'

Steve dips his head modestly before tugging Asta through the house and out of the back door. Mrs Li and Elaine call out goodbye as they pass.

Asta decides to walk Steve through town today. It's not something she does very often, in case she bumps into someone she knows from school. Detention has put everything back by an hour though and the sleepy town centre shops are already using that last hour between five and six to wind down. What Asta doesn't realise is the flexi-office workers have been finishing since four o'clock and what do their dogs demand as soon as they get home? Walkies and a lovely street pee.

Steve doesn't know what's hit him. Every other person he passes has a dog, an actual dog, not just the trace they leave behind for him on trees and lampposts. Lots of them have very bulgy eyes and flat little faces. Almost all of them are littler than him. He stops to sniff the bum of a tiny Pomeranian and presents his so it can sniff him back, but it is too small to reach. Steve doesn't like it when the Pom jumps up and press its paws into his bum cheeks to get closer to the action. He spins away and the Pom takes offence, yapping its Cesar breath into his face. He barks back and the Pom turns tail and scampers back to its owner.

'Don't go,' Steve barks after them. 'I didn't mean it. Come back. Be friends!'

'Too late, mate,' says Asta. 'You blew your chances there.'

Steve feels Asta pulling him closer as they pass an enormous dog with piercing blue eyes. Blue eyes on a dog, Steve's never seen that before and he wants a closer look but Asta has inserted herself in between the two dogs. Unfair!

'Look at how tall he's holding his tail, Steve. That dog does not want to be your friend.'

And true enough, when Steve and Asta cross with the husky and its owner, the husky growls and there is a brief skitter of paws as it lunges towards them. Steve wonders why it's kept on such a short lead compared to the long floppy one Asta usually lets him run about on. Then he notices she's wrapped most of their lead tightly around her fist, her fingertips clenched and turning red against the strapping.

When they get to the patch of grass by the bus station, there is a golden retriever already there, nose down, sucking up all the sniffs, but when the aroma of Steve wafts over, it looks up, mouth parted in a goofy grin. Its tail thumps against its owner's legs with the rhythmic beat of a marching bass drum. The retriever does the play bow so it's only polite for Steve to do the same back. Then, like in a Jane Austen novel, they begin to dance, except neither Jane Bennet nor Mr Bingley were on a lead. Both dogs twist and turn until they're well and truly snarled up. The owners do much laughing, untangling and separating of leads before the two dogs are allowed to sit and pant at each other for a bit.

This is a good walk, thinks Steve, which, of course, are famous last words.

Even after closing time, café culture is still on, even in Cawsmenyn. There are people outside the local branch of a chain of coffee bars hunched over a fag and a hot chocolate. Amongst them is a guide dog, sitting quietly under the table while its owner is chatting away to a woman sitting further along. The guide dog is wearing a harness and its hi-vis jacket. Asta knows not to let Steve interfere with it when it's working so they give the entire area a wide berth. She's pleased about how sociable Steve has been with all these dogs today. He's not had much practice at it, not after those times he went to puppy class and got frozen out by all the cocka-, cava- and jack-a-poos. Like ex-owner, like dog.

They have got half way up the street when Asta hears something.

Steve can hear it too, the sound of a lead dragging along the ground. Has the old young owner dropped it again? She does that sometimes when she needs to tie her shoelace or is fumbling with her phone, trying to take yet another selfie with him. Strange, he can still feel the tension of his neck's connection to her hand. He turns to see a strange dog in a yellow jacket trailing a harness behind him. He's hurtling towards them, teeth bared and using the kind of language he's never heard before, even in the dogs' home. Steve must protect the old young owner; his grandfather was an English mastiff after all.

Asta holds limply onto one end of the lead while its other end is a mess of fangs and growls and fur. Strange, Asta always thought Steve was a lover not a fighter but it looks like he takes advice from Mr Miyagi. Fighting is for defence only and Steve can defend himself when needed. If it wasn't for that strange keening noise he's making, he'd be pretty good.

Hmm, it doesn't appear to be Steve making that noise but Asta herself.

Two dogs can only fight for so long before they have to break like boxers do. Human boxers, not the breed of dog. When it eventually happens, Asta yanks Steve quickly away. The guide dog attempts a regrip but Asta is already bending over Steve, cradling his head, shielding him. She doesn't care if she gets bitten instead but luckily she doesn't. Even delinquent guide dogs know what's off limits. She looks up to see the owner running towards them and she can't help thinking he's doing that extremely well for someone who's blind. Her hand is getting wet from blood dripping off Steve's face and then she feels his body jolt. He whines and tries to struggle free because the other dog has sunk its teeth into Steve's rump and is not letting go.

The blind man with miraculously good eyesight has reached them and is tugging away at the guide dog's collar, but his dog doesn't care. It shakes its head and Steve swings from side to side. Asta reaches forward to try to part the dog's jaws.

'Don't do that,' shouts the owner, 'he could go for you.'

'Rather me than my dog,' says Asta.

The blind man gives a heavy sigh, takes a step back and kicks his own dog sharply between the back legs. It howls with pain and lets go of Steve, who gets dragged clear by Asta. There is a raw red outline of the dog's bitemark in the blood-clumped fur on Steve's bum.

'What sort of guide dog have you got?' Asta asks the blind man furiously as he picks up his dog's harness.

'Guide dog?' says the man. 'What makes you think he's a guide dog?'

'Because of his outfit,' says Asta. 'And you're wearing dark glasses on a cloudy day?'

'That's his jacket. My proper glasses are broken,' says the man. 'This pair is the only other prescription set I have.'

He leads his dog away without so much as an apology. Steve and Asta exchange a look before beginning the long limp back to the bungalow.

By the time they reach Steve's back door, Asta has had to pick him up and carry him. He's not a heavy dog but he's no lap dog either. He was walking so slowly. He's been doing some shivery trembles too so by the time they get to the back door of the bungalow, Asta has to shout for help.

Very soon, Mrs Li and Elaine are crowding around her and Steve in the utility room. Asta's trying hard not to cry even though she must have started hallucinating, because she thinks she can see her English teacher, Mr Feather, eating a bit of cheesecake in the kitchen. It's all that fucking detention's fault. If she'd been able to walk Steve at the usual time, none of this would have happened.

'*Ay yah*, Steve,' says Mrs Li. 'What happening?'

She takes him out of Asta's arms and goes into the kitchen where she lays him down in the rarely used dog basket.

'That's not a good sign. He never stays in that thing normally when he can go on the furniture instead,' says Elaine. 'And you, Asta dear, you look like you've been through the wringer too.'

'What's a wringer?' Asta asks.

'It's not important,' says Elaine. 'Perhaps you should go and wash your hands.'

Asta looks down to see Steve's blood and judging by the puncture mark on her thumb, her own too. This must have been when she was trying to open the other dog's lock tight jaws off of Steve's arse. Still, she doesn't move, but just rubs her bloody hand up and down the tops of her tights.

Mrs Li is already running the hot water tap into a bowl, tipping salt into it too and fetching a cloth to clean the patient's wounds. Meanwhile Steve's eyelids are getting heavy.

'I think that dog needs to go to the vet,' says Asta's hallucination.

Asta is about to repeat this, because Mrs Li and Elaine won't be able to hear the product of her delirious imagination, when Elaine speaks.

'Who's going to take him? I didn't bring the car.'

'I can do it,' says the hallucination, adding, 'don't worry, Asta, these things often look worse than they are but it's just as well to be certain.'

'It's really you,' says Asta, as Mr Feather reaches across the kitchen table for his car keys. 'What are you doing here?'

'Explanations later, dog emergencies first,' he says, before picking up the dog basket, complete with Steve still in it. Steve lifts his head and gives Mr Feather's wrist a weak lick. 'Mum, you phone ahead and tell the vet we're coming.'

Elaine fishes around on her person for her mobile phone while Mrs Li opens the back door. She settles Steve onto the back seat of Mr Feather's car.

'Can I come too?' asks Asta.

'I promise I'll get him to the vet and call you as soon as we know anything,' Mr Feather shouts through the passenger side window. 'In the meantime, no news is good news, remember that.'

That's a no, then.

As the car drives off, Mrs Li steers Asta back inside where Elaine already has a big mug of hot sweet tea ready for her.

11 Seaview Cottages
Porthgynffon
South Glamorgan
3rd August 1964

Dearest Bravest Charlie,

Are you all right? Mam told me. She said about you dragging Harri off of her. She said she didn't know what would have happened if you hadn't turned up. He'd already held her hand against the bakestone. It wasn't as hot as it could be because she'd already finished making the Welsh cakes. Still, it was hot enough for her to have to put some butter on it afterwards, not that I've ever found it works. I hope the steak she gave you to put on your eye did a better job. It made me laugh, a little bit, when Mam said it was the steak she'd bought in for Harri in the first place. I think your black eye was more deserving than his tummy.

You said you were glad I wasn't there but I can tell you now it would never have happened if I had been. I've been telling Mam for years she should really only have lady lodgers but she keeps making an exception for Harri. He can be charming when he's not drunk or he's not missed his sales target. Then he loses his temper but he's never raised a hand to any of us before, just come home looking worse for wear after fisticuffs in town.

Mam said Harri said some horrible things about you and me being together, kept some especially nasty names back just for you. I know I don't care what he thinks but the fact he thinks them, that anyone thinks filthy things like that, it makes me so angry I could spit nails. Mam said we should shake it off, like water off a duck's back. 'Sticks and stones will break your bones but names will never hurt you,' she said, which is quite ironic from someone who couldn't hold the phone properly because of her bandaged-up hand.

The important thing is we never have to see that Harri ever again so all's well that ends well.

I will be home just as soon as Auntie Gaynor comes back from her stay in Southwold. Sali sends her love. As, of course, do I!

Ela xx

Chapter Eleven

Asta decides that Elaine, Mrs Li's best friend, is really lovely.

After the hot sweet tea, which makes Asta feel much better, Elaine takes it on herself to call Asta's parents and explain what is happening.

'And your mother confirmed you are completely up-to-date with your tetanus injections so there is no need to go to A and E,' says Elaine kindly. 'That's a big relief. We'll just keep an eye on your hand, look out for any signs of infection.'

She also sits down with Asta and listens patiently, without interrupting, to her account of what happened. When her phone makes a pinging sound, she shows Asta the text from Mr Feather.

> Bit of a Q and vet nurse says we are not emergency.
> Steve seems OK, prob just shock. Might need stitches?
> More later Xx

'Can I stay here until Steve gets back?' Asta asks.

Mrs Li is putting the first-aid kit away after cleaning and dressing where the 'guide' dog's teeth have been. She turns and, with a look, relays the message to Elaine to deliver far better than she could herself.

'Of course,' says Elaine. 'We wouldn't expect anything less.'

'Can I ask you something?' Asta says. 'What was Mr Feather doing here?'

'Oh Max,' says Elaine. 'He's always hanging around here with his big sister.'

'That be me,' says Mrs Li. 'He my baby brother.'

The two women laugh at Asta's astonished face. It's clearly a reaction they're well used to.

'And I'm Max's . . . Mr Feather's mother,' says Elaine.

'Are you Mrs Li's mother too?' asks Asta, failing to hide a bamboozled look on her face. 'Are you old enough?'

'No, of course not,' says Elaine, laughing and looking over at Mrs Li. 'To both of those questions.'

'So that means Mrs Li's father is Mr Feather's father as well? Is that right?'

Bang on cue, George shuffles into the kitchen wearing pool slides that show off his very thick toenails. In the top pocket of his shirt, next to a shiny Parker ballpoint, is Asta's Tombow Fudenosuke pen from this morning.

'So if you,' Asta says, addressing George who is now digging around in *that* kitchen drawer, 'used to be my Grandpa Charlie's stepfather, that means . . . well I don't really know what it means except I'm somehow related to my own English teacher.'

'Don't worry, it's all water under the bridge,' says Elaine. 'If it makes you feel better, you probably were related to all of us once upon a time but not any more.'

George comes and joins the rest of them at the kitchen table. He's holding some paper, a felt-tip pen and a plastic bottle half full of the blackest substance Asta has ever seen. Liquified black holes probably.

Mrs Li rolls her eyes and exchanges a few words with her father. He looks quite devastated as he blurts out something that sounds like *'ah gau zai!'* but at another indecipherable word from his daughter, rallies around and sits himself down next to Asta. He spreads outs the paper and takes the top off the pen to reveal not a fibre tip but a tiny fine brush. Unlike a watercolour paint brush from The Works that has nylon hairs splaying out into a wedge, this pen looks like it came off some unfortunate creature's pelt and tapers finely to a delicate point. He reaches for one of the saucers already on the table, only to have it snatched away by Mrs Li who replaces it with a small chipped egg cup.

Asta watches as he tips from the plastic bottle into his improvised ink well before dipping the brush into it. He wipes it gently against the rim of the egg cup before beginning to make strokes on the paper. She has no idea what he's writing, of course, but it is beautiful to watch, especially from such a wrinkly set of sausage fingers and the unusual grip, a bit like the way a hairdresser holds the scissors. She hopes she will still be able to wield her pens as well when she's his age. Asta recognises it as soon as it's finished and she rummages in her pocket for the piece of paper he gave her this morning.

'Fung?' she says and George nods.

Set side by side, her surname in Chinese written once using traditional calligraphy tools and once using the modern equivalent, Asta tilts her head, wondering whether convenience trumps tradition. She can't decide unless . . .

'Can I have a go?'

George nods and hands her the brush, moving her hand to get her to hold it properly, flicking its shaft upwards so she holds it vertically like a Chinese calligrapher, not a Western one. It doesn't come easily and there are many botches and misplaced strokes. Eventually, she comes up with a half-decent pictogram of her own name and then she swaps places with George, showing him how to write his name in a basic English script with all the downward strokes nice and fat and the upward strokes delicately thin.

'You're a natural at this,' she tells him and he smiles, points at her and does a thumbs-up.

The two of them are so engrossed in what they're doing that they don't even notice the back door opening, voices in the utility room and Steve striding into the kitchen, resplendent in his Elizabethan collar of canine warfare. He goes and sits in between George and Asta, tail thumping, hopeful of sympathy.

'*Ah Steve!*' shouts George.

'Steve!' squeals Asta.

'Old new owner!' barks Steve and then, 'Young old owner!'

'You've got stitches in your face,' says Asta.

'And on his bum,' says Mr Feather. 'Nothing serious, the vet said. He might have a scar on the one on his face and a bald patch on his bum. They will make him look well hard.'

He's carrying the old dog basket which he puts back in its place in the corner of the kitchen. Everyone holds their breath as they watch Steve get in and turn around and around on the spot.

'He can't be feeling himself if he's willing to sleep in there,' says Elaine.

Mrs Li is watching with her hand over her mouth, brow furrowed with concern.

But at the last minute, Steve hops out and disappears into the hallway. They hear one of the bedroom doors creak open and the hoppity-skip sound a dog makes jumping into bed.

'You see, he's all right,' says Elaine. 'All's well that ends well.'

Chapter Twelve

Half-term, so at least Asta doesn't have to see her new brother/cousin/uncle/whatever for a week. Well, not in school, at least. Mr Feather has started to spend an awful lot of time at his big sister's house, quite often when Asta happens to be there to take Steve for his walk.

'You should call me Max when we see each other here like this,' he said.

'I won't. If you don't mind, Sir,' she replied.

Mr Feather shrugged and carried on eating his fried egg sandwich.

'I shan't be seeing you tomorrow, Steve,' she tells him after he's followed her to the front door. 'I know there's no school, but I've got something on.'

Steve doesn't like this nugget of information one bit and turns to go back into the kitchen. He normally waits until she's gone out of the door.

'Be like that, then,' says Asta, as he flashes the bald patch on his bum where the fur refuses to grow back, the only sign that *The Incident of the Guide Dog Who Wasn't* ever happened. That and the small round black scar on his left cheek that looks like a beauty spot.

It has been a busy week for Asta. She spent yesterday morning writing out thirty place cards for someone's wedding at £2.50 a pop. In the afternoon, she started work on the Philip Larkin a customer wants to frame and give as a present. The customer only wants the very end of the poem but Asta had to read it in full to get a feel for it, to see how she should lay it out. She had a bit of a sniffle when she remembered that new absence the day after Grandpa Charlie died. She approves of those last few lines, about being kind when you still have the time. She wishes she'd been more kind.

She finishes it off this morning as soon as she gets home and soon, all the busy thoughts about irrelevant things disappear as she makes her guidelines on the paper. Her pencil is so soft it barely leaves a mark, the wheels of her rolling ruler glide gently down the page. She narrows her eyes as she considers the start point halfway along the line, that solitary comma, the lonely full stop. She thinks of where best to place them, how they will fit together in a sea of white. Then she begins, breaking down each word into its individual letters, each letter into its individual strokes, each stroke into its upward or downward movement. It clears her mind of all else and only the muscle memory remains. All those hours of writing practice and drills, like a musician playing scales and arpeggios, means she rarely makes mistakes. She can't afford to; any false move from her pen and she will have to start again. No room for any Tipp-Ex or correction labels here.

Asta notices a lemony smell as she works, doesn't know where it's coming from. Still, the whiff of citrus gives her a boost and as soon as everything's done, she packs it all up to catch the post.

The three-storey Post Office building takes up a good portion of Cawsmenyn High Street. Its yellow sandstone façade, with dozens of mullioned windows and separate entrance and exit at each end, demonstrate the importance of Her Majesty's General Post Office as a hub at the very heart of the community when it opened at the end of the nineteenth century. By the beginning of the twenty-first century, it's a far cry from its glory days of First Day Covers, Postal Orders and Urgent Telegrams. There is a buddleia growing from a second-floor window and bombs of pigeon shit have detonated on the pavement outside.

Its glory days are over because the business of the Post Office has been relegated to a concession at the back of a mini-market across the road. That's where Asta stands now shivering in the queue between some chicken drumsticks and a special offer on mature Cheddar. The queue is enormously long as usual and has snaked out of the designated post office area into the chiller aisle.

There are only two clerks manning the counters. One of them is busy with someone sending a suitcase load of identical small brown parcels to every fathomable corner of the United Kingdom. The other is preoccupied with helping someone fill in their passport form which includes having to take their photograph. Everybody in the queue has to move to make room so the prospective international jetsetter can stand against the bit of bare white wall that makes an acceptable background for the modern passport.

'And . . . *don't* smile,' says the clerk as she presses the shutter.

When Asta steps backward, she nearly bumps into a boy reaching to get something from the top shelf.

'Sorry,' she says, looking up only to see Josh with a crooked armful of shopping and a chocolate milkshake in each hand.

He looks almost as embarrassed as she feels and mutters a greeting as he puts one of the milkshakes back.

'You have two milkshakes if you like,' says Asta.

Josh hesitates, goes to get the milkshake, decides against it, changes his mind again and finally chooses a banana-flavoured one instead.

'Fruit is good for you,' he says apologetically.

Asta is mystified as to why the builder's son wants to discuss nutrition with her.

The man behind Asta in the queue coughs loudly but it's not a cough, it's a passive-aggressive message to get her to budge up, which she does wordlessly.

Josh looks nonplussed and disappears to the checkout.

Asta eventually reaches the front of the queue where there is a quick weight and dimensions check to get both of her parcels on their way. Cashier number two looks relieved to have such a straightforward transaction.

When Asta leaves, Josh is still outside. He's talking to a Jack Russell who's not really interested, its eyes staring into the shop, impatient for the return of its owner. But when Josh puts his hand out and reaches for that magic spot near the base of its stumpy tail, it slouches down onto the ground, one of its back legs kicking involuntarily. It turns around and presents Josh with its head, which it slides under his downturned palm. Josh takes the hint and begins smoothing from between its ears down to its studded leather collar.

Asta hopes Josh is so preoccupied he doesn't see her and he doesn't. For a bit. She hears him saying goodbye to the dog and the next thing she knows he's walking down the narrow pavement with her.

'Funny bumping into you here,' says Josh. 'I thought I might have seen you at your place while we've been working on it.'

'Yes,' says Asta.

'But you must be pretty busy with school stuff, I guess.'

'Sort of.'

'Your mum and dad said they moved you down here to do your A levels?'

Asta wants to say that Oscar Wilde was wrong. There *is* something worse thing than not being talked about and that is to have your parents talk about you with the builder's son, but instead she just says, 'Yes.'

'I was hoping to see you. To ask if you got a chance to read those letters we found under the floorboards.'

Asta stops walking suddenly and the woman behind her pushing a shopping trolley has to swerve around. She gives Asta and Josh a dirty backwards glance.

'Not really,' she says eventually, as she starts walking again.

'You should. I didn't get a chance to read them all but they were . . . they reminded me of when the English teacher used to read sonnets out in class. Beautiful. And real as well, not that we don't know the sonnets aren't real.'

'You did English A-level?' asks Asta.

Josh nods.

'In Cawsmenyn High?'

Josh nods again.

Perhaps Asta could have got away with a poncy quote from Oscar Wilde after all.

She jumps as someone honks their horn very nearby and they turn to see Vince pull up alongside them in his van. He leans out.

'You were supposed to wait for me outside. Did they have the vegan pastie? And the kefir?'

Josh nods.

'Oh hello there, young Asta,' says Vince. 'Skiving off school again?'

'It's half-term,' she says indignantly.

'Oh right, you forget about that kind of thing when your youngest leaves school.'

He leans out and digs his knuckles affectionately into Josh's heavy fringe. Behind them, someone else is honking their horn.

'All right, all right, keep your pants on,' Vince shouts. 'Right, youngling, get in.'

'It was nice bumping into you,' says Josh, as he hurries around to the passenger side. 'See you again soon maybe?'

'Um, yeah,' says Asta, because it would be rude to say, 'Not if I see you first.'

Chapter Thirteen

Asta is the only person to get off the bus at Mynydd Iawn Uchaf and as soon as she gets off, she wants to get back on again.

But it's too late. The bus's doors have folded shut and all she can see are its tail lights as it disappears into a dip in the road and rises up again a few metres later. Asta scratches her head, looks around her. A road in the sort of village you drive through to get to somewhere more interesting. She'd checked it out on Google Maps, tried to get a glimpse of it on Street View, but Mr Google and his photography vehicle haven't visited in years and certainly never turned off the main road onto any of the B roads. She knows there was a load of scaffolding just over there but it seems to have disappeared now.

'If this is the bus stop,' she mutters to herself, 'then I need to take the next turning right down there.'

There are semi-detached houses on each side of the road. Where the scaffolding used to be all down one side of the road, there are now completed new-build homes, their block-paved drives empty of vehicles, blinds pulled down or louvres shut, a red box flashing on the front of the house to prove the alarm is on. The other side of the road has the old houses, their fronts pebble-dashed, but with years of different colours and paints covering up the original roughcast. Here there are net curtains, china ornaments in the window and the backs of photo frames facing onto the street. When the houses run out, so does the pavement. There is only a grassy verge and an unmarked single-track road that turns right.

'Is it this one?' she asks herself.

She loiters on the side of the road, poking about on her phone. There isn't enough signal to download anything so she's pleased she emailed the directions to herself. The problem is that when it says 'turn right onto Penwaig Coch', how is she supposed to know it's Penwaig Coch when there is not a street name to be seen anywhere?

She decides to turn right anyway and follow the track. There is nobody to ask and no other vehicle passes her to reassure her she is not about to walk off the edge of the Earth and fall down into the space where monsters be. It starts to rain, persistent drizzle speckling everything all around her. She pulls up her hoodie and tightens the strings around her head. Then it stops raining. She leaves the hoodie where it is. After about five minutes of walking in stop–start showers, she begins seeing discarded farm equipment on the side of the road, big metal claws and undefinable bits of metal tubing, an enormous tyre big enough to stuff her dead body into before rolling her downhill into a shallow grave. She gulps but keeps going. Eventually, the track opens up into a big yard, undeniably a farmyard with barns, bales of hay and a blue merle sheepdog who looks surprised to see her. It barks but doesn't move from where it's standing next to several discarded oil drums.

This can't be where Eleanor lives. There was no indication she lived on a farm. Asta must have taken a wrong turn. She sighs as she realises she has to retrace her slightly scary footsteps. Soon enough, she's back on the main road. That track she went down can't be the road she was supposed to take. It was just the entrance to a farm. She knows she's supposed to turn right somewhere so she re-joins the main road and walks along until she reaches the next turning.

It all feels much better because there is regular traffic on this road. Still no pavement though so she is careful to walk on the right-hand side and all the vehicles coming the other way give her a wide berth. She smiles hopefully at each one, hoping to catch a smile back like the game she used to play with Felix during long car journeys. They had to stop playing when Felix hit puberty and decided swapping smiles and waves with other drivers was soppy. He took to flicking the v sign or flipping the birdy instead. Nobody smiled back after that. Nobody is willing to smile back at her today.

After fifteen minutes of trudging along with nothing to do but notice the mud starting to creep up around the edge of her trainers, she realises she should have reached Eleanor's house by now. She must have walked a mile and there has literally been nothing other than hedges, thick tree trunks, big fields and sheep. If everything had gone as she'd imagined it, by this time she should be sharing a lovely cup of tea and a biscuit with Eleanor, who would have told Asta everything she knew about young Grandpa Charlie and how the course of true love never did run smooth.

Should she keep going? Or should she cut her losses and turn back? What if it is down this way and she misses it by just a minute? Should she stay the course or go back the way she came? The sight of a badger up ahead, completely intact and seemingly uninjured but clearly very dead, decides it for her. She's not willing to walk past its furry corpse so back she goes again the way she came except this time, she crosses the road so she can see oncoming traffic, as per the Highway Code. When she reaches the other side, she nearly steps on a dead mouse.

So this is the countryside, Anita Rani?

She starts traipsing her way back to the junction.

She reaches the main road and heads for the bus stop. She doesn't like to give up but sometimes you've just got to know when you're beat. She'll take the next bus home and have a think about another plan of action. A letter that Eleanor will have to sign for maybe? That would make more sense, seeing how letters were how the whole thing got started in the first place.

But annoyingly, as she passes the single-track path down to the farm she visited before, her phone catches one bar of signal from somewhere.

It pings to life and says, 'Turn left. You have reached your destination.'

She checks her watch, wonders if she should perhaps knock at the farmhouse door to see if they can help. She pivots. Bus stop or farm? Bus stop or farm?

Farm.

Almost immediately, a black four-by-four pulls up and a man with the sort of thick black beard sported only by pirates or police mug shots asks her if she wants a lift.

'We're definitely going in the same direction, aren't we, so might as well. There's only one way down here. It's the dead end.'

Asta looks at him suspiciously. She has seen *The Silence of the Lambs*, after all.

'No, thank you,' she says primly.

It doesn't occur to her until she reaches the farmyard and sees the Land Rover parked up that the bearded man is the farmer and now she's going to have to knock on his door and ask him about Eleanor. When he answers, he brings with him a smiley red-faced woman.

'We meet again,' he says. 'I've brought a chaperone with me this time.'

'I'm looking for where the Hennessys live,' says Asta. 'I don't know if you know if it's around here?' She turns to look back up the farm track she's just walked down.

'Oh yes, Eleanor,' says the woman, looking sad. 'The residential cottages are over there. You go through this farm and through the next farm and you can't miss them. Three cottages, it's the middle one you want. Not sure if anyone's there right now but yes, another five minutes' walk in that direction.'

Asta remembers to thank them instead of just marching off. She kicks herself for the time she wasted by not stopping to ask at the farmhouse when she was here the first time but still, who would have guessed you need to go through two farms to get to somebody's house? Not her.

The other farm has a dairy herd in the next field and the cows come up to the fence and watch Asta as she crunches along the gritted path. She eyes one of them nervously as it licks its nose with an offally long tongue. Another cow behind it moos in quite an angry way making Asta jump. She backs away from that side of the path to get away from the herd but it means she isn't looking where she's going and the next thing, she's face down on the ground. She gets up and examines the damage. Small stones stuck in the heels of her hands which she brushes off to reveal Morse code dots and dashes of blood. She blows a painful raspberry to get the grit out of her mouth and all down her front is a coating of dried mud. If there hadn't already been tears in her jeans when she bought them, there definitely would be now. She thinks she can feel a trickle of blood down her left knee and when she presses against it, the denim turns a slightly deeper shade of blue. She keeps walking and very soon, is relieved to see the three cottages up ahead. There is a car parked outside the middle one. She walks gingerly up to the front door, rattles the letterbox and holds her breath.

Chapter Fourteen

'Hello, I'm looking for Mrs Hennessy.'

The woman who answers the door looks Asta up and down.

'What happened to you?' she asks.

Well, *she* can't be Eleanor Hennessy. She's too young for one thing. Also, she has an Australian accent.

'It's nothing, I just slipped and fell outside. I'd really like to see if I can speak to Mrs Hennessy if she's around. Please.'

'You'd better come in.'

Asta follows the woman through a short corridor into a cosy-looking parlour with a lumpy armchair next to a coal fire that's really a gas fire. Stretched along the entire length of one wall is a Welsh dresser, only half of it filled with the usual full matching set of dishes, plates and tureens. The rest are stacked up on a small wooden table. She catches a glimpse of herself in the large shield-shaped rimless mirror above the fire. Her lower lip is rather fatter than it usually is. She bites at it gently and winces.

'I'm sorry I can't offer you any tea or coffee,' says the woman. 'I'm all a bit at odds and ends. You know how it is.' She looks again at Asta, seems to notice how young she is and adds, 'Well, maybe you don't. Now why did you want to speak with my mother?'

Years of parental manipulation have honed Asta's skills in hamming it up to get her way so she gives this woman a highly edited, rather subjective account, of what's happened. Anything to get to meet Eleanor Hennessy.

'And I know it didn't last but they were each other's first love so it would be good to know what happened, how it turned out.'

'That's a beautiful story,' says the woman. 'I really hope you find the lady who wrote the letters to your grandfather. If she's still around.'

'But she's your mother, isn't she?' says Asta. 'I know you won't recognise any of the stuff I just told you but she'll remember it though? So do you think I could get to speak with Mrs Hennessy herself?'

She gets up and looks back towards the parlour, the hallway and the staircase that leads upstairs.

'Is she having a nap?' Asta asks. She knows how much the olders rate their naps.

'Sweetheart,' says the woman, looking very serious. 'I don't even know your name?'

Asta tells her.

'Well, Asta, my name's Georgina Dupont and my maiden name was Hennessy.'

Asta's got a real bad feeling about this.

'And my mum, her maiden name was, well, I won't tell you in case you are part of an elaborate scam to divide me from this magnificent inheritance you see before you.'

'Inheritance?' Asta sits down again.

'Mum passed away three months ago. To the day.'

Asta gasps.

'So did Grandpa Charlie.'

Georgina seems to have lost the ability to speak. She gets up and starts banging about in various kitchen cupboards and drawers until Asta hands her a tissue from the pocket packet in her bag. She has to use one herself too.

'And in any case, Mum and Dad,' Georgina continues, 'they were childhood sweethearts. They used to play together as children. There was nobody else ever for either of them. So, you see, she can't be the one who wrote those letters.'

'Couldn't they have been on a break?' asks Asta.

Georgina laughs and shakes her head.

'They didn't go on breaks in those days.'

'But nobody really knows what your mum and dad did before they had you. It's not something anybody's parents ever talk about in that way.'

'Perhaps. But there is one thing you can't get around. Hennessy was Mum's married name and your Hennessy, she wasn't married to anyone else when she wrote those letters. You said it was her first love.'

Asta has to admit defeat.

'But there's nobody else that fits the bill,' she says.

'It's been a long time. This other Eleanor Hennessy you're looking for? She might not even be with us any more.'

'Don't say that,' says Asta. 'She has to be, I'm just not looking hard enough for her.'

Georgina smiles at Asta.

'Tell me, what was your grandfather like?' she asks.

Asta loves talking about Grandpa Charlie, bringing him alive, introducing him to someone new. And now she gets to meet this other Eleanor Hennessy too, through the eyes of her youngest daughter.

'I think they would have got on if they'd met,' says Georgina.

'I think so too,' says Asta.

A clunking sound comes from the parlour and Asta is thrilled to hear the sound of a cuckoo clock. She rushes out just in time to see the cuckoo retreating back into its hole in the wall.

'I used to love waiting for the cuckoo to come out too,' says Georgina. 'I can't believe it still works. You have to wind it up, you know, and nobody did for ages before I got here last month. I'm definitely taking it back to Auckland with me.'

'Auckland? I thought you were Australian.'

Georgina laughs.

'And I thought we were getting on so well too!'

*

When Asta leaves the wrong Hennessy house, she has two Perky Nana chocolate bars in her bag that she didn't have before and twenty minutes to get back onto the main road before the bus arrives. Plenty of time.

As she reaches the end of the farm track, a little procession of traffic is passing on the main road – a tractor is keeping a couple of cars, a bus and a van dawdling behind it and there is a steady stream of vehicles coming the other way so none of them can overtake. Asta had to negotiate the 30 mph sign when she took the wrong turning earlier on, so she knows that half the traffic is speeding through Mynydd Iawn Uchaf, while the other half would like to if it wasn't for the tractor.

It's only when she gets to the bus stop and there is nobody else there waiting for the last bus back into town that a cold feeling comes over her. She checks the time. It seems like only just now the cuckoo declared it was five o'clock but according to her phone, it was forty minutes ago and the bus leaves at half past five. Georgina's clock may have sprung to life after it was wound up again but it clearly can't keep up with the pace of modern life.

Shit, what is she going to do?

In the old days, she knew she could, and did, rely on Felix to fetch her out of a hole but now he's in Bristol, it's an awfully long way to come.

'Hello?'

'Sunshine Cabs, all your transport needs, can I help you?'

'Yes, I was wondering how much it costs to go from Mynydd Iawn Uchaf to Cawsmenyn?'

The sound of a taxi operator sucking air in through their teeth.

'That's about twenty miles, is it? Oh, fifty quid or thereabouts?'

Well, thirty painstakingly etched place cards will cover that.

'Can I book it then please? How long before it gets here?'

'Bit busy at the moment, half-term, you see.' Tapping sounds, air being sucked through teeth again. 'We can be there in about an hour.'

Asta looks up at the velvet navy curtain that is slowly draping itself over the hills from east to west.

'No thanks, I can't wait that long.' Not here, not stuck in a creepy bus stop in the middle of nowhere. Not in the dark. 'I'll have to sort something else out.'

'Please yourself,' and the line goes dead.

Who else is there? Her parents? But it's past opening time and they would have to close up to drive out here. Disruption. Lost profits. She wouldn't hear the end of it from Tim while Mandy would want to know exactly what she was doing out here. That's something she's not prepared to share, not until she's found the real Ela, at least.

Asta is truly stuck. She scrolls through her phone looking for someone to save her. It's at times like this she wishes she had actual *Friends* from school. Although it wouldn't be that much use as most of them aren't old enough to drive and of the ones who are, only Paige has managed to pass even her theory.

Does it have to be another one of the students from school though? Could she depend on the kindness of strangers? Or perhaps long-lost family is more important than friends?

Hi I know this may seem a bit inappropriate but I was wondering if you are free to do me a little bit of a favour?

Asta keeps the torch on at the back of her phone and its beam falls on a bit of trodden-in chewing gum on the kerb. Is it in the shape of a duck? Or a rabbit? She's using it to distract herself from how it's getting darker without getting actually dark yet. It's only a matter of time though and soon, she'll be stuck here without even a streetlight to keep her company, just the remaining 84 per cent of battery life left on her phone to keep the blackness at bay.

She jumps every time a car passes but none slow down or pull up. Perhaps she should run out into the road, flag every car down to make sure she doesn't get missed. She decides instead to lean out of the bus stop, plaster a hopeful look onto her face for each set of headlights that whizz past. She could swear they speed up as soon as they spot her.

The lights have started to come on in the windows of the houses across the road. Asta has to turn on her mobile's torch app and she dabs repeatedly at the screen to keep it illuminated as well. Eventually, a vehicle slows and stops, its window slides downwards.

'Hiya.'

'Sorry,' says Asta.

'It's no problem. It's nice to be wanted.'

Asta fidgets nervously.

'Well, hop in then.'

Asta gets in, buckles up her seat belt while he does a one-handed three-point turn.

'Thanks for this,' she says. 'I didn't know who else to call.'

'*Dim problemo*,' says Josh, sounding super-casual.

Asta turns towards Josh to see if he means it but it's too dark and she can only really see the side of his head. He is sporting a stubby workman's pencil behind one ear and it's holding his floppy fringe back revealing a rather pleasing profile. There's his high-vis work jacket too, like someone's run a highlighter pen over his torso.

'I was surprised to hear from you on Messenger,' says Josh. 'I've never been able to find you on Facebook before. Or any of the socials.'

That's because she deactivated all of her accounts as soon as she realised she was as unpopular in the virtual world as in the real one. It seemed the best way and also wise to hang onto them, just in case, which meant they were available to reactivate to summon help when needed. Like just now.

'I missed the last bus home,' she says. 'I wasn't supposed to be taking the last bus. I should have got the one before.'

'Oh yeah? What were you doing all the way out here anyway? Visiting someone? Couldn't he have given you a lift home?'

'Well, not really, no,' Asta says, while thinking about how Josh has done a sexism by assuming she was visiting someone male. 'I was trying to find somebody, but I got it wrong. They weren't who I was looking for.'

'Is it something to do with those letters?' asks Josh. 'What made you think Charlie lives out here? Or is it Ela you were looking for?'

'Ela,' says Asta. 'But it wasn't the right one. I know who the Charlie is, though. He's my Grandpa Charlie.'

'Wow! What did he say when you showed them to him?' asks Josh.

'I couldn't. He died last year.'

'Sorry.'

'I so wanted to find the Ela and I was certain this Eleanor Hennessy was going to be the right one . . .'

And because the car is nice and warm and they're sitting side by side and don't have to face each other or put up with any of that awkward eye contact, Asta finds herself telling Josh about everything that's happened and how she has now reached a pretty comprehensive dead end.

'Don't say that,' says Josh. 'We can find her.'

'We?'

'Yes. The fact you're sitting here is evidence you can't do it on your own.'

'That's what you think,' says Asta under her breath.

'Not thinking about anything much, really,' Josh replies. 'Just driving along in the van. Mindful driving, I guess.'

'Oh,' says Asta. 'Good.'

She looks out of the window and watches the empty fields, the intermittent lights of smallholdings flashing past in the distance. They don't know each other anywhere near well enough for the silence between them to be comfortable.

If in doubt, change the subject.

'Your dad seems nice,' says Asta.

'Yours too,' says Josh.

'Really?' says Asta.

'Yeah. Comes in every few hours with two mugs of tea. Full-fat milk, not skimmed. Has sweeteners ready for my dad. Otherwise leaves us alone to get on with the job. Offers to make us lunch. Tells us what he wants and sticks to it. Keeps on top of all the sawdust and mess for us. We told him he didn't have to.'

'You're doing him a favour there. He's always loved his Henry Hoover just that little bit too much, but ever since . . .'

'Ever since what?' says Josh.

Asta wants to tell him about how her father's been different ever since they had to say goodbye to Grandpa

Charlie. He has an extra layer of sadness she wishes she could peel off and throw in the bin for him. She hears her mother whispering suggestions, trying to get him to talk to her about it and all he does is say he's fine while cleaning, dusting and polishing until his hands are red raw. Felix moving away hasn't helped. She can't tell Josh any of this though because that would mean bringing up Grandpa Charlie and the whole point of this was to change the subject.

'I like your dad and Steve likes him too. Steve is a very good judge of character.'

'Who's Steve? Is he your boyfriend?' That super-casual tone of voice again.

'No, he's my dog, sort of. The other thing is your dad understands how I feel about school.'

'Yeah, well, he had a hard time when he was in school. He didn't find out he was dyslexic until after he left. After they'd all given him such a hard time.'

'The olden days, eh?' says Asta.

They reach the outskirts of town and have to overtake a man on his bike. Josh takes his eyes off the road ahead just for a moment and as he looks quickly over his left shoulder and back again, they pass under a bright LED lamp post.

'Shit, what happened to your face?' he asks.

'Charming,' says Asta but she pulls the sun visor down to see her lip now looking very swollen indeed. 'Oh that, I fell on it.' She flips the mirror back up. 'Don't worry, it looks much worse than it is.'

'Are you really allowed out on your own?' Josh asks.

'Oi,' says Asta, directing a slap at Josh's arm. It's surprisingly firm. 'I'm the Lone Ranger. I'm Jack Reacher. I'm Jane Eyre.'

'More like Robert De Niro in *Taxi Driver*,' says Josh.

'I've never seen it,' says Asta.

'You should. We could watch it together,' says Josh. After a little think he adds, 'Or perhaps, maybe not. I definitely think two heads are better than one, though, on this searching for the Ela who wrote the letters.'

Asta's silence is heavy with sulk. Josh dashes in to fill it.

'You know you wouldn't be able to find the Charlie in those letters now. It's pretty likely that you won't be able to find the Ela either, but you could find her family. Her family would probably like to see the letters, wouldn't they?'

'I don't know,' says Asta, giving Josh a sideways glance. 'I almost wish I'd never seen them.'

Josh's eyes are locked into looking ahead.

'Really?'

'What's the point, though? I've gone on this wild goose chase today that's come to nothing. I'm nowhere nearer to finding my grandfather's ex, who you say is probably dead anyway. I can't tell my dad about it in case he gets even more upset about his dad. I can't tell my mum because she tells Dad everything.'

'Seems like a pity to give up so easily,' says Josh, hands gripping the steering wheel tightly.

'ARE YOU CALLING ME A QUITTER?' says Asta, then winces inwardly. Too much.

'No, I'm not calling you one,' says Josh. 'I suppose they're your letters. It's your decision. It's the wrong decision but it's your decision.'

'The whole thing has been a complete waste of my time,' says Asta. 'I'm just going to enjoy the letters for what they are. Sweet and all in the past.'

'If that's what you want,' says Josh.

18 Rupert Street
London
SE1 8AW
27th January 1964

Dear Charlie,

Thank you for your letter. It was very kind of you
to write to me again. In retrospect, I accept that the
tone of my previous letter was somewhat 'prickly' but
I think it a bit much for you to expect anything else
under the circumstances.

I have known Miguel Garcia since we were both in
primary school. He used to run up to the girls and
either kiss or pinch us, then run away. It made us
squeal with disgust. He was an extremely handsome
boy and, objectively speaking, he is an extremely
handsome young man. It does not mean he can
keep kissing and pinching all the girls and running
away though even if the squeals are no longer ones
of disgust.

Still, I accept he is your friend and I do admire
your loyalty towards him.

It was such a nice surprise to find your letter
waiting for me when I got home after a full day of
lectures although much as I enjoyed being updated

on everything I'm missing while I'm away, there really is no need for you to write again. By your own account, you are incredibly busy working with your mother and stepfather in their shop so you needn't be wasting your valuable time on the likes of me.

Yours sincerely,

Ela Hennessy

*

Unknown number: Hiya, how you getting on?

Asta: OK ... Um, how are you please?

Unknown number: I'm fine thanks for asking. You?

Asta: Meant to say who are you please?

Unknown number: It's me! Josh! Didn't you save my number? I'm hurt. ☹

Asta: I have now. Am good thanks. Why you asking? Did you get me mixed up with someone who's not well?

Josh: No, it's you I wanted.
Josh: Any updates on Finding Ela?

Asta: Not really

Josh: My offer is still there ... if you want any help with it.

Asta: not necessary, thanks all the same ... nice to hear from you though.

Josh: you don't mind me messaging then?

Asta: course not!

Asta doesn't add that apart from people she's related to, nobody ever does message her.

Chapter Fifteen

The sixth form entrance at Cawsmenyn High isn't working. Apparently, over half-term, someone with a grudge against the school – approximately 23 per cent of the local population aged between eleven and eighteen – came along and put superglue in the lock, so the school's crème de la crème is being allowed to enter through the visitors' main entrance.

Asta's never been in this way before and she stops to take it all in. As soon as you arrive, you are confronted with the reception desk where Mrs Yates usually sits, guarding the only entrance to the headmaster's office. Much to his regret, he can only come in or leave his office by walking through reception which always prompts her to ask where he's going. He'd never be able to conduct an affair, not that he wants to. What's worse is he can't ever nip out for a sneaky Toffee Crisp or packet of Smoky Bacon from the corner shop.

The rest of the reception is a tribute to celebrating pupils past and present which, for a comprehensive school not quite in the back of the Welsh beyond, has done rather well for itself. Rugby players for the Welsh National Team. A singer at the Eurovision Song Contest. A scientist based at CERN. There is also a list of Head Boys and Girls past and present and Asta notices one of them is now an MP. More interesting is the name of the Head Boy before the current one. He is called Joshua Palazzo. Her Josh! Well, not her Josh, she corrects herself.

As she hurries along the short unfamiliar corridor into the main school building, past the cleaner's cupboard and open door of the staff room, she hears a voice she's reluctantly got to know all too well. She can't help turning her head to see Mr Feather, in his young fogey knitted waistcoat, handing a cup of tea to a little old lady.

Stop doing an ageism, Asta tells herself, she is just a woman in a twinset and pearls, her hair in a silvery grey updo. Doesn't this amount to much the same thing? It is unusual to see anyone really old in school, though; the teachers try to retire by the time they're sixty and most of them succeed. She wonders who it is and then remembers the vast age gap between Mr Feather and his sister – Mrs Li – and how his father – George – is easily old enough to be his grandfather. She decides the mystery woman is probably his girlfriend.

Mrs and Mrs Li have gone on one of their mini-breaks again. To the Lake District this time. When this happens, they arrange for their back-up care team to kick in for George and for the first time ever, Asta's been picked for a team! She feels the honour deeply and determines to merit her inclusion.

'I can look after myself,' George presents to Asta on a sheet of paper when she is sitting with him at the kitchen table after school. Elaine has asked her to stay on after dropping Steve off so she can go to her yoga class.

Instead of being all straight and stick-like, as his writing in English used to be, it's in hasty faux-calligraphy, all scratchy where he used a biro that's on its last legs.

'You missed that downstroke there, it should be a thick one,' says Asta, pointing at the emaciated 'y'. 'What happened to the Tombow I gave you?'

George brings it out from his shirt pocket. It is completely squished from middle to tip and there are canine teeth marks all down it.

'Steve!' says Asta. 'Bad doggo!'

He's not even in the room. He's in the lounge watching the local news with Tony Blair.

'I know you can look after yourself,' says Asta. 'It's me that needs looking after.'

George laughs and shakes his head. Asta nods and while her head is bobbing up and down, she has another one of her brainwaves. She hopes this one works out better than the last one did.

'Have you heard of the yes/no game?' she asks him.

George shakes his head.

'It doesn't matter,' says Asta. 'Because this is the exact opposite of the yes/no game. In that one, you ask each other questions and the person answering is not allowed to say yes or no. So you end up asking questions to try and get the other person to say yes or no so you can win. But I am going to ask you questions and you will only be able to answer with yes or no. How does that sound?'

Asta could kick herself. Her very first question is one that can't be answered yes or no.

'Can you do that?' she asks.

George nods.

'Very good.'

George points at the piece of paper and wields his pen.

'And you want to write the answers sometimes if you can?'

George nods. Then writes 'yes' on the paper.

'All right, here we go,' says Asta.

George nods.

'Did you used to know my Grandpa Charlie when he was about my age?'

George nods.

'So he was quite young when you first met him?'

George nods again.

'And quite old when we moved here last year? You knew him at both ends of his life. Do you think he'd changed a lot?'

George shrugs.

'When I asked before about him being popular with lots of girls, you laughed.'

George nods.

'Why did you do that?'

He stares blankly at Asta before writing on the paper, 'Yes? No?' and crossing it out.

Asta purses her lips, tries to think of how to pose the question to get a yes/no answer.

'Do you think he had any girlfriends when he lived in Liverpool?'

George is adding degrees of enthusiasm to his head movements to add some colour to this very one-sided conversation. He shakes vigorously.

'So, he really only started dating down here?' Asta doesn't wait for a reply before ploughing on. 'And it was mainly local Welsh girls?'

Two nods.

'But my Grandma Lynda wasn't Welsh. She was Chinese? From England too?'

One nod.

'Was Grandma Lynda his first serious girlfriend?'

George nods.

'So you don't remember if he had any serious girlfriends before that? With anyone local?'

George knits his brow, thinks for a while, then shakes his head again.

'So there was nobody called Ela? Ela Hennessy?'

A pause before George shakes his head slowly, uncertainly.

'Were you close? If he had a girlfriend he liked more than the others, would he have told you?'

George leans forward, writes something on the paper. Asta leans forward excitedly.

It's a rather good drawing of the happy turd emoji.

Asta shrugs, she has no idea what *that's* supposed to mean but she gets her answer when George stands up and leaves the room. She hears the cloakroom door open and shut. When he comes out again, he goes into the lounge and the music for *Emmerdale* comes on. Steve doesn't like the soaps. He hops off the sofa and appears in the kitchen doorway staring at her.

'What?' she snaps.

*

Asta: Did you used to be Head Boy?

Josh: Yes.

Asta: Why didn't you say anything about it?

Josh: It never came up.

Asta: I suppose not.
Asta: Did you ever lose all hope?

Josh: Wow, keep it light, Asta!

Asta: Not *all* hope.
I just finished talking to the one person who remembers Ela ...
but he's refusing to talk back to me

Josh: Who is it? Where are you?

Asta: It's too complicated to tell you. I think I've
reached a dead end.
I really am a quitter after all.

Josh: Does it count as quitting if it's an impossible task?

Asta: ???

Josh: if we can't find Ela perhaps she just can't be
found ...
We've done everything we can haven't we?

Asta: *We?*

Josh: Maybe it's time to Let It Go, Asta.
Like you said, we got to enjoy the letters for what they
were.
Sweet and all in the past.

By the time Elaine gets back, Asta's had her spot of online Zen coaching from Josh and is sitting calmly on the bench in the hallway, reading. Steve is splayed out at her feet, spooning with Tony Blair.

'How was he?' Elaine asks.

'Fine,' says Asta. 'He can probably look after himself for a few hours, you know.'

'Well, better safe than sorry,' says Elaine. 'It's like looking after someone else's children. When it's your own, you let them run around naked with only a hammer and a box of matches to play with. When it's someone else's, you find yourself being much more careful.'

Asta follows Elaine into the kitchen to fetch her bag but is persuaded to stay when she is offered hot chocolate and one of the doughnuts Elaine picked up on the way back.

'I burnt a lot of calories doing yoga,' Elaine says with a wink.

As she watches Elaine moving about the kitchen in all of her tight yoga pants and top, Asta hopes she looks half as trim when she gets that old. It's hard to believe she is an old woman really.

'You'll never guess who I saw when I was getting these,' says Elaine, offering the bag of doughnuts to Asta.

'Lady Gaga?' says Asta, taking a sip from her mug. 'Beyoncé?'

She isn't really sure if she's supposed to make a guess or if Elaine is asking a completely different sort of question to which the correct answer is presumably no.

'Wrong,' says Elaine. 'I saw that phoney guide dog who bit Steve. And you'll never guess where I saw him and his owner?'

Asta doesn't think she is supposed to reply so she doesn't.

'Talking to the security guard in Tesco, trying to get her to say yes to that vicious brute being allowed into the store as some sort of emotional support dog. He's put a bow tie around its neck as well as making it wear that silly high-visibility jacket. Makes him look cute, I suppose, like butter wouldn't melt in his mouth.'

'What did you just say?' asks Asta.

Elaine peels a bit of her doughnut off and gives it to Steve.

'I said about that dog wearing a bow tie and a high-visibility jacket. He did carry it off, I suppose; not many humans could.'

'No,' says Asta. 'After that.'

Elaine mutters to herself while she rewinds what she said.

'Something about trying to make his dog look all innocent, like butter wouldn't melt in his mouth?'

She lets Steve lick the sugar off her fingers.

'Don't you worry, boy, I made sure to tell the Customer Service Desk so they knew what was going on and to put the kibosh on it. They messaged the security guard right away and I saw her send the man away with a flea in his ear. No better than he deserves. He didn't even say sorry to you that time, did he?'

It's another rhetorical question because Elaine is already out of her seat, going over to wash her hands.

It's just as well. Asta has stopped listening. She gathers all her things up into her bag and says hasty goodbyes to everyone. She needs to get home quickly. There's something she has to double-check.

Chapter Sixteen

'Did you have your tea yet?'

It's what Tim asks Asta as soon as she gets home.

It's a question Asta knows must have been asked a few thousand times over the years here in this Chinese take-away in a Cantonese language she can't speak but reads about online. *Did you eat your rice yet?* Only, when all the ghost residents of the past were asking, it was just another greeting. Her dad means it literally. In any case, Asta likes it, that the two phrases are so similar, that it unites how she feels on the inside and how she looks on the outside.

'Yes, I had it with George and Steve.'

'Are you still hungry?' Tim asks.

'A bit.'

'I'll bring you something up when we're done with this order.'

When she gets up to her room, Asta rushes straight to where she keeps Ela's letters. No longer a pile of folded and unfolded bits of paper, curled at the edges, showing the strain of lying unexamined for over forty years; they have been flattened out, unsmoothed and arranged in as close to chronological order as they can be. They're kept in a battered box file she's pinched from her brother the student dentist. It says ~~Homeostasis and Microorganisms~~ and also Chaucer & Middle English Poetry. Nobody would ever think to snoop around in there so she feels safe to take the box out into the living room and open it up on the big desk.

It doesn't take long to find the letter she's looking for. It's that very first letter Asta ever read in full, the one from the auntie's house, where Ela talks about herself in the third person.

Charlie's with Ela Hennessy now so you'd better all keep your mitts off!

She reads it quickly and remembers how she had to look parts of it up as she had no idea what Ela was talking about. Well, she had some idea, but wanted to know exactly.

Butter wouldn't melt in his mouth: to look innocent yet be capable of bad action.

Flea in his ear: to reprimand strongly.

These were the expressions Ela used to describe that awful Miguel Garcia who abandoned the pregnant Sali but they are also what Elaine said when she was talking about The Guide Dog Who Wasn't.

Why is this getting her Spidey sense tingling?

Because if Mr Feather's mother is Ela, it means that Ela ended up having a baby with George. The same George who was such big buddies with Grandpa Charlie and also happened to be his stepfather for a bit. It's all very complicated and even if it doesn't officially qualify as incest, it probably should.

She sucks the end of her Fudenosuke and then starts doodling idly, repeating the calligraphy words she uses to practise the basic strokes.

Magnificent
Flourishing
Minimum
Josh Palazzo

WTAF? Well, Palazzo is a good practice word.

Palazzo
Ela Hennessy, where are you?
Elaine Feather, who are you?
E-L-A?
E-L-A!

Could Ela be short for Elaine? She knows it doesn't sound like it could be but written down, it's possible, isn't it?

Anything is possible.

As she walks to school in the pouring rain, an unfamiliar car pulls up and the driver gestures for her to get in.

The only person in the world she knows who would stop like this is Josh!

But it's not Josh. It's Mr Feather.

'Get in Asta,' he says. 'It's pissing it down.'

'What?'

'I said it's tipping it down with rain.'

Asta thinks about the absolute mortification of being seen getting out of his car once they get to school. She doubts he would agree to drop her off in the next street.

'I can't, Sir. What about safeguarding?'

'My mother has shown you a photo of me being potty-trained while holding a teddy bear,' he says. 'So I think we'll be OK and . . .' He throws a glance to the back seat of the car where the old woman from the staff room – his 'girlfriend' – is sitting, nose deep in a folder of documents.

Asta looks at the road up ahead of her. The drain is blocked again and for the next thirty metres, the double-yellow lines have disappeared under a lake of opaque rainwater. Anyone unfortunate enough to be walking on the pavement there would be drenched from the waist down every time a vehicle splashed through it.

She gets in.

'Pam, I mean, Miss Williams,' says Mr Feather. 'This is Augusta, I mean, Asta.'

The woman looks up from her folder and tips her head in the way old people think is an adequate replacement for a verbal greeting. Asta reciprocates with a watery smile but only after she's glared at Mr Feather for getting her name wrong.

'She is one of my A level students.' Mr Feather checks his mirror and pulls off. 'Her parents practically moved here from way out west so they could reap the benefits of our sixth form.'

'Oh yes?' says Miss Williams.

'Miss Williams used to be the headmistress of Cawsmenyn High,' Max tells Asta. 'She retired fifteen years ago and then she became a school governor and has been ever since.'

'Oh,' says Asta, who doesn't really understand. As far as she is concerned, the headmaster rules the school; the thought of the headmaster being ruled by a higher authority has never even occurred to her. It probably does mean that Miss Williams is not Mr Feather's girl-friend though.

'As Miss Williams used to be an English teacher, she's decided to shadow me from time to time to make sure everything is going well and that we're maintaining the high standards our students deserve.'

Asta looks over at Mr Feather. He looks back. He mouths very carefully and slowly so Miss Williams in the back seat can't see him.

'Help me!'

Asta has to try hard not to laugh. She decides that from now on, she will call him Max when they meet outside school after all.

On a train, somewhere between Cardiff and Bristol
9th February 1964

Dear Charlie,

Please forgive my wobbly handwriting. I'm balancing
the writing paper on a book and the book is balanced
on my satchel. I'm also having to stop every few minutes
because both of the men sitting opposite me are smoking pipes. At first, I was quite fascinated by the ritual
of tapping out, topping up and tamping down all the
shredded bits of tobacco but now that they've lit up,
their smoke is making it quite foggy in this compartment!

I'm glad your parents liked the bits and pieces I
brought back from Chinatown in London. I say Chinatown but for now, it is Chinatowns as everything
seems to be on the move between Limehouse and the
West End. Neither is very close to where I live but I do
have to go practically to Soho to get to Paddington so
it's no trouble. I know you said Ada tries to get some
things sent from Liverpool but often gets let down. If
you ever want anything else, I can send them to you
in the post myself if I am not due to travel home yet.

It seems like only yesterday I was on this train coming home for reading week. Wherever did the time go?
Don't they say time flies when you're having fun?

Thanks so much for our lovely walk on Wednesday. All we would have needed to make it perfect would have been a dog. I can't believe we were gone for two and a half hours and walked all those miles. If you'd told me before we set off, I wouldn't have thought it possible. The time just flew by but next time, we really should try not to get lost down by the riverbank. I used to be able to count the number of fields, how many hedgerows we passed, tell how far we had gone by looking at the canopy of sycamores, but now so much land has been sold off and made ready for the new houses to be built I must have lost my bearings.

You did tell me it had been raining hard for most of January and I'd brought the sun back with me from London. Too much the Londoner now, I forgot how Cawsmenyn has the biggest of puddles and the muddiest of footpaths long after the rain has stopped.

I was trying to show off that I knew the way so it served me right I ended up splat so close to a cow pat! You were such a gentleman trying to help me up; it's not something I'm used to which probably explains how I ended up pulling you down for a mud bath too. Mam was shocked when I got home looking like a creature from the Black Lagoon!

I am going to stick a stamp on this one and send it from the postbox at the end of the road when I get back to Rupert Street. Please write back almost as quickly!

Your friend,

Ela

Chapter Seventeen

Everything happens so much.
Now breathe.

Asta doesn't mind that most of the orders she gets on Write4U urge her to *Carpe Diem* and to *Be Kind*. She quite likes telling people called Sian, Winston, Ania and Marek to have *Many Happy Returns* but she has never been asked to write this particular phrase before. In fact, she's never ever come across it, so she asks the customer if she made it up herself.

> Oh no, I wish I had. I saw it online somewhere. I added the 'Now breathe'. My friend's having a difficult time lately – all the shit hits at the same time, you know. I want her to know I'm thinking of her.

Asta knows how the friend must feel.

Trapped in a dimly lit room with a strange man who keeps staring at you and bossing you around while being forced to wear the kinky head gear he's put on you.

Asta hates going to the optician and it's even worse this time because he is on the 5:2 diet and she finds it very hard not to giggle while he leans in and out from her face, looking deep into her retinas, all nasal hair and minty breath, his stomach growling like a grizzly bear. Fortunately, she's declared optically fit for another two years, although she may want to consider wearing her glasses for more than reading if things get worse. Does she do a lot of close work?

No, she lies, and starts thinking of putting her Write4U earnings towards some contact lenses.

When Asta gets home, she spots the Palazzo & Son Builders' van in the service yard. What are they doing here? Again. The living room has been done. Her parents' bedroom and Felix's too. Her bedroom, the kitchen and bathroom are staying as they are for a bit so that leaves only . . .

She races inside, hurtles up the stairs and runs along the landing into Grandpa Charlie's old bedroom. Most of the furniture is huddled into the middle of the room but there is no sign of the bed. His black-and-white framed photo of The Beatles that took up most of the wall with Paul – his brother from another mother – front and centre – is gone. So are the books – the Dexters and the Christies – from his bedside table. What about his collection of tourist trinkets – the miniature Big Ben, tiny Stonehenge, Liverpool snow globe and Cardiff Castle replica. Have they all been chucked out?

Vince and Josh turn around from where they are respectively cleaning and stripping separate corners of the room. Asta takes one look at them and has to run out again quickly. She doesn't like anyone seeing her cry.

Now she wishes she'd gone and composed herself in the toilet where there is ample tissue and you can lock yourself inside. Instead, she'd gone back to her bedroom and now there is a knock on the door.

'I'm fine,' she lies. 'You can go back to doing what you were doing.'

She hears footsteps disappear along the hallway which is good but then two sets of footsteps return which is not good.

The door opens straight after the knocking this time.

'We haven't thrown anything important out,' says Vince, looking uncomfortable on the threshold. 'Only the broken bed and the bedside table with the wonky shelf.'

'We had to throw out lots of chocolate wrappers though. They were under the bed,' says Josh.

'And down the back of the drawers,' adds Vince.

'And stuffed between the wardrobe and the wall,' says Josh.

Asta smiles. 'He was only here for a few months.'

'But it looks like he managed to squeeze in a year's worth of chocolate,' says Vince with a smile. 'Good for him.'

'Your mum and dad packed almost everything away before we got here,' says Josh. 'It's all in that other bedroom.'

'Oh,' says Asta. 'I didn't think. I was just surprised.'

'What's going on here?'

It's Tim, who looks understandably concerned to see two builders looking sheepish outside his daughter's bedroom. Vince and Josh mutter things like, 'just making sure . . . ' and 'best get back to it then . . .' before melting away.

Tim takes their place, propping the doorway up while Asta gives a big sniff and rubs the back of her hand along her nose. She pulls her sleeve down to cover up the slug trail of bogey.

'What's going on?' he asks.

'Nothing.'

'Why aren't you in school?'

'Optician's appointment.'

'Do you want a lift in, then?'

'Yes, please.'

The two of them clatter downstairs. The walls are ever so thin in this flat, the soundproofing even worse when a room has been stripped of its curtains and soft furnishings. Vince looks out of the window where he's sanding the sill down and sees Tim and Asta getting into the car. He shakes his head, purses his lips. It's amazing how people confide in their builder without even noticing they're doing it. He hopes they can talk it out. It's what he always does with Josh, after all.

Asta sits with her chin in her hands, elbow against the velour ledge, staring out of the window. Local scenery flashes past at twenty miles per hour – a mum negotiating a wilful infant, a baby in a buggy and two French bulldogs all at the same time; a couple of young men who walk as if they have springs in their shoes bouncing along the pavement; a traffic warden snapping a photo of a parked car that's overstayed its allotted time. She has angled her entire body away from Tim, twisted like a pipe cleaner. You could fit a breeze block between her and the handbrake. She doesn't know she's doing it; it's just a default position for when she rides shotgun with her dad. Either that or she spends all her time fiddling with the sound system, trying to get away from all that nineties pop. She's not bothering with that today.

Even though Liam Gallagher is urging everyone to 'roll with it' from both the front and back speakers, the silence is deafening. Eventually, Asta can't take it any longer.

'Why are we changing Grandpa Charlie's room? When you said we were redecorating, you said we'd leave his room alone for a bit longer?'

'It's your mother's idea. I'm just going along with it for a bit of peace and quiet.'

Tim taps the stem on the steering wheel until Liam shushes for a bit.

'She said it's been three months since . . . and he wouldn't want us to keep his room as some sort of peculiar shrine to him.'

'Yes, he would,' says Asta.

'Well, yes and no,' says Tim. 'Do you remember that photo of his mother, my gran, that we used to have in the living room back home?' He corrects himself quickly. 'Back in the Sun House?'

'The one where we used to put the fruit and flowers all the time?'

They'd kept a photo of Charlie's mother on a little armoire. There was always a fresh supply of fruit in a bowl next to it and bananas hanging from one of those special banana holders. Flowers too, usually an orchid or a pot of chrysanthemums. Bunches of roses or lilies were placed there in April for Tomb Sweeping Day and October for the Double Ninth Festival, also on her birthday and the anniversary of the day she died.

'Do you notice how we haven't put that back up here?' says Tim.

Asta shakes her head. She hadn't but then she hadn't noticed her parents had ditched the Nespresso machine either.

'Your Grandpa Charlie said we didn't need to any more. And that he didn't want us to do anything like that for him when his time came.'

Tim puts on the Scouse accent he always uses when quoting his own father. Asta wishes he wouldn't because he's not very good at it.

'Yer gorra look forwards, not backwards. Just cos we're not putting yurr Nan's photo back up doesn't mean we've forgotten 'er or don't think of 'er. It's all gonna be 'ere and 'ere.'

Tim taps his forehead and the left side of his chest with his right hand before quickly putting it back on the steering wheel.

'Well in that case, why didn't we throw all his stuff into a skip straightway?'

Asta tops this bit of teenage logic with a stroppy folding of her arms and even though the seat belt is now cutting into her, she refuses to unfold them.

'Because I didn't want to,' says Tim. 'I wanted to keep a bit of him with me for a little bit longer. I didn't go into that room for weeks after he'd gone. Your mother went in and kept on top of the dust and things. Then we went in together and got rid of the everyday things like medicine, newspapers, all that sort of thing. That was about all I could manage.

'Then when the builders came around to do the stairs and everything else – we'd booked them ages ago – your mother said it would be a good time to look at your grandfather's room too.'

'It's different for her,' says Asta.

'No, it's not. He meant a lot to her too,' says Tim. 'I know it's hard but he was my actual dad. If I can get through this, so can you.'

'I've got through it just as well as you have! Better, even. I can think and talk about him all the time and it's just fine. I use the past tense and everything. It's not my fault I haven't found the right Ela . . . '

Asta stops herself from doing a blab and it seems to be okay because Tim has started up again, almost as if he was doing a monologue all along.

'All the reminders of him around the house. Not even good ones. After they put that staircase up and got rid of the bit of skirting board that got knocked loose after he fell over that last time.'

Asta frowns.

'What last time?'

'It must have been while you were away with the cousins. When he fell on the landing. Felix and me found him on the floor when we got in. He said he hadn't fallen and he knew what he was doing, was planning to get up again by crawling into the living room and hauling himself onto the sofa but a draught had blown the door shut. He was looking for something and when we asked what it was, he wouldn't say. We couldn't see anything he might have dropped so I reckon he was just saying that to save face so we wouldn't think he was a wobbly old man.'

Tim has to stop talking for a bit. He swallows hard before carrying on.

'That's when we took him to the doctor, to give him the once-over and that's how we found out that everything we thought was under control, well, it wasn't any more.'

'He didn't fall over,' says Asta.

'Yes he did,' says Tim.

Asta frowns because her father hasn't picked up that she is making a statement. She is *literally* not asking a question.

All this time, she's thought Grandpa Charlie had forgotten all about the letters. Perhaps he was hoping to find Ela again himself. All the more reason why Asta should do it for him now.

18 Rupert Street
London
SE1 8AW
12th May 1964

Darling Charlie,

I just got off the telephone with Mam. As you know, phone calls between London and Cawsmenyn are a monumental task of technology, coordination and whether she can get to the phone kiosk at the Post Office before someone else has settled in there with a sackful of shillings.

I could, of course, call her from the phone Mrs Adams has in the hallway. I reckon there are a handful of offices and shops in town who rate Mam, and Daddy, enough to let her sit and wait for me to call her. Mrs Adams keeps it locked though and the key on a chain around her neck. She produces it only for 'matters of life and death' and listens in to confirm it is so. I don't think my chat with Mam today would have passed muster.

She was only phoning because it's Daddy's birthday and we like to remember him on this day. Mam got a bit tearful and repeated the story of how they met, how he proposed, how happy they were — as if we were strangers and she was telling me for the first time! I've heard it hundreds of times, of course, and I think you've heard most of it dozens of times.

Mam is happy that she went to take flowers to Daddy this morning and that we got to talk about him too.

'It's been a long time since I last seen him properly,' she said to me. 'I know he's gone but I am still here. No matter what happens, I love him so much.'

I know what she means. She still keeps his watch on her bedside table and winds it up every night. His cigarette case is on the mantelpiece even though none of us smoke.

It's nice to feel he's still around. I know you will know what I mean. We both lost our daddies when we were young. Not everyone understands that. It infuriates me when I hear the other students complain about how 'the old man' is bothering them. At least you still have your father and he has got to be an old man!

Oh dear, this is getting worse, not better. Sorry it's a grumpy old letter this time. I promise, hand on heart, to do better next time.

All my love,

Ela xxx

Josh: How you doing?

Asta: OK now. Sorry about before. It was a shock seeing Grandpa Charlie's stuff gone that's all

Josh: I geddit.
I know what it means to you.

Asta: Thanks. How's you?

Josh: Fine bit busy. I'm gonna have to go soon. Got to put another coat on.

Asta: In this weather? Won't it get hot?

Josh: A second coat of paint

Asta: I know I was deadpanning you.

Josh: I know you knew. I was deadpanning you back.

Asta: ☺

Chapter Eighteen

Max comes into the living room, blinks hard and leaves. Then he comes back in again.

'Sorry, am I in the wrong house?' he asks. 'What are you doing here? What are you *both* doing here?'

Steve is lying on his back, kicking his legs in the air and making a joyous growling sound. He clearly likes Elaine's living room. Or more specifically, her chenille rug. He twists his neck from side to side, tongue lolling and flashing a dazzlingly white fang-tastic smile.

'Steve and I were going past so we thought we'd call on your mum,' says Asta. 'And then she's walking over with me when I take Steve back to his place.'

'You were walking past?' says Max, 'all the way from the main road right to the end of the cul-de-sac?'

'Yes,' says Asta.

'And Mum is walking the mile and a half back to Steve's with you? And then again when she comes home?'

He narrows his eyes suspiciously at her while Asta widens hers innocently.

'It's not the first time we've done it,' says Elaine as she comes in. She perches on the front of an armchair, slips off her mules and crams her feet into a pair of trainers. She snaps her fingers. 'Tie my trainers up for me, Max dear.'

Max dutifully bends down to tie them. Double knots.

'I don't know why you bother going to that yoga class if you can't even do up your own shoes,' he mutters.

'The way I see it,' says Elaine, as she uses Max's shoulders to lever herself out of the chair, 'is you don't have a dog and bark yourself.'

Steve lifts his head and woofs twice.

'Exactly,' says Elaine. 'Asta, Steve, let's go then, shall we?'

'But I wanted to ask you about something,' whines Max.

Asta's getting a completely different picture of what teachers are like in their other, non-teaching lives. They're practically human!

'How about I give you all a lift to Steve's house in the car?' says Max, looking around at the three of them hopefully. 'We can talk about it then.'

Asta and Steve are having to fight over who gets to stick their head in between the two front seats, where Max and Elaine are discussing the problem.

'Come on, Steve,' says Asta. 'Budge up. I'll even open the window for you a bit so you can a get whiff of the outside.'

Steve hops over Asta's legs and plants his black pastille of a nose into the exposed two inches of fresh air. Drool starts to run down the inside of the glass. Asta looks away quickly, tries to listen in on the discussion going on up front.

'. . . much more often than before,' Max is saying. 'She always used to come in from time to time and I think the other headmaster before the one we have now used to encourage it. Got some help with continuity back then, the old Head showing the ropes to the new Head. That doesn't apply now though, a lot has changed since she was in charge.'

'Schools are still schools, children are still children,' says Elaine. 'Aren't they?'

'Yes, but teaching them is completely different. I swear she's still looking for the blackboard and some chalk when she comes in sometimes.'

'Perhaps she's stuck for things to do? There's no husband or partner, is there?'

Max slows down and flashes his headlights to let a bright orange Berlingo out at the junction. It flashes its tail lights back at him.

'No, don't think there ever has been either,' he resumes. 'Not that it bothered her. I heard she was a proper little globetrotter before she broke her hip in Rome last year. She decided to pack in the international jet-setting after that.'

'It sounds like she's a little bit lonely,' says Elaine. 'That's all.'

'Well, why doesn't she get a hobby then? One that doesn't involve lurking around school all day.'

'And she wants to be useful too, I expect.'

'Well, she's not *not* useful, I suppose. She's a good listener but you can have too much of a good thing. She's really only supposed to be observing lessons and reporting back to the other governors – not that they're that interested from what I hear – but now she's getting involved and making demands. When she was only visiting the school every so often, it was fine to have a chat with someone who's seen it all before. She could be helpful and wise, if a bit old-fashioned. But now, she's spending too much time with us and it's not just me that says so. The other English teachers feel like we're getting it in the neck more because she used to teach English. Either everyone is too scared to say anything or too kind to say anything. *She's just a lonely old lady, etc., etc.* It's starting to wear us all down. Didn't you say you knew her when you lived in town before?'

Elaine lived in Cawsmenyn many years ago, moving away before Max was born and only returning when he'd grown up.

'Everybody knew of her. Everybody seemed to like her. I know there was a young widower who took a shine to her. She was quite attractive in a "Oh Miss Williams, take your glasses off and let down your hair" sort of way.'

'We should find her a boyfriend,' says Max. 'Or a girlfriend if that's what she wants.'

'Is that *really* what you wanted to ask me about? To get me to find an attractive pensioner for Pam Williams?'

Max sighs.

'Not really. I just wanted someone to vent to before I explode.'

Asta leans back in her seat. Steve spots his chance and quickly replaces her in the gap, tongue lolling out, gleeful at bagging the good spot. She can see Max give him an appraising look in the rear-view mirror.

Asta doesn't quite get it. Max had a problem and he chose to go to his own mother? Even she would never burden her mum with something like that and Max is a fully grown man.

Isn't it all too weird?

18 Rupert Street
London
SE1 8AW
29th January 1964

Dear Charlie,

Thank you for your entirely unexpected letter. It was such a pleasant surprise to receive it, especially after a full day of rather trying lectures and practical work.

You ask if I would consider us becoming pen pals. Aren't they really meant for the exchange of international cultures? In any case, I am grateful for all your updates about what is going on back home. If I had to rely on what Mam and Sali tell me, I would have an accurate idea of meteorological developments in the local area and little else!

Am I saying yes? I think so.

I can't really help you with the problem you mention because, of course, my mother has never remarried after we lost Daddy. Although I think I might have got the wrong end of the stick. Even when I re-read the tone of your letter, I was very much of the impression that George is your natural father and that Ada is your stepmother. It is, in fact, the other way around, isn't it? You can see how I made the mistake because your mother seems so strict and harsh about everything while it is your stepfather who seems to be more accommodating. I agree with you that it is not entirely usual for mothers to stop their twenty-six-year-old sons from going out!

I will temper that sentence with saying that if you will keep on getting into fights (which, yes, I know, you 'did not start') you can see why Ada is being practical and doing her best to keep you out of trouble. Sometimes it's just easier to stand down. George has a point too though, in that he has managed to live in town for all these years and never had a punch thrown at him and he is very sociable. I can't think of anyone who has ever had a bad word to say about him except for the OIs — the obvious idiots.

It's the OIs who start those fights with you and Miguel, isn't it? Their problem is that their bloodlines are all just that little bit too close together, if you know what I mean. Haven't you noticed how they all look so alike! Whereas you and Miguel are different and (sort of) the new boys in town. Easy targets to pick out and pick on.

Perhaps your mother does have a point when she says you should be settling down with a nice girl. Parents do seem to like marrying their children off still. It's 1964! I'm fed up with the number of times my mam and Auntie Gaynor tell me they were settled down with a husband and baby on their hip by the time they were my age. I know Mam is proud of me going to university but she'd be even prouder if I lived up the road from her with a whole litter of grandchildren for her to cuddle and cwtch up to. I expect your mother feels the same way.

Yours sincerely,

Ela Hennessy

Chapter Nineteen

Asta sighs as she reaches to wash her hands.

Today, it's a small, prickly sort of creature. Not a hedgehog, too small for a porcupine, she opts for an echidna – Knuckles from Sonic. Before, it was just his obsessive cleaning – the constant smell of pine, lemon and bleach; the hand-held vacuum constantly on charge; all carpets hoovered into that clean triangle pattern – that was a problem, but ever since his insomnia kicked in, Tim's gone back to whittling animals out of soap too. What else can you do in the middle of the night when you have to keep quiet because everyone else is asleep? It explains that lemony smell that used to be in the living room all the time – slivers of Cidal inexpertly swept off the desk into the bin underneath.

He used to make animal soap carvings all the time for her and Felix when they were children, only stopping when they grew out of it. She longs for a smooth bit of white Dove, easy to use and without the uncomfortable sensation of sending a cat, a turtle, a dolphin into bubbly oblivion.

Asta crosses the landing from the bathroom into Felix's ex-bedroom. Her nose twitches as she steps into its murky darkness. Strange, the curtains aren't usually drawn in here. She can't get to the light switch without knocking over a stack of books dumped in front of it while the endless renovations continue in the rest of the flat.

It looks like Paradise or Purgatory in here; depending on whether you are the hoarder or the hoarder's sister-in-law. There is no flat surface which does not have a teetering pile of stuff all over it. The floor is barely visible, furniture and cardboard boxes masking its laminate planks. Asta has to lift her knees up and be very careful about where she places her feet as she makes her way over to the window to open the curtains.

There's a funny smell too. Asta is used to the distinctive aroma of a teenage boy's lair – sour, cheesy, sweaty smells masked with liberal squirts of Lynx and Febreze. It was always wafting down from Felix's attic bedroom in the old place. What she didn't realise was that it could still be so concentrated months after Felix skipped off to Bristol to contaminate yet another room with stinky socks and Dior Fahrenheit. Surely it should have dissipated by now. Grandpa Charlie's things are here too, which explains the faint whiff of Imperial Leather and mint-flavoured chocolate.

What is she looking for? She'll know when she finds it. Wouldn't it be brilliant if she found all the letters he'd written to Ela? He would have had to make copies of them though and realistically, she knows that won't have happened. But what if he had! Or maybe Ela returned all her letters to him, like giving back the engagement ring after you've been jilted at the altar or Willoughby returning Marianne's lock of hair. She realises she's doing a digression, letting her mind drift away from the matter in hand. The next thing she knows, she's in that imaginary place again, the one where people notice her and when they do, it isn't for all the wrong reasons. Where she doesn't get picked last for the team. Where the bus doesn't have to double-back because the primary school teacher managed to leave her behind on a school trip. Where someone in the doctor's surgery doesn't literally sit on top of her because they didn't see the seat was already taken.

She's enjoying going off on a tangent like this. She'd like to stay a bit longer but she knows it's her Mirror of Erised. She shakes her head like Steve after a rainy day walk. What she needs is some solid clue to help her find Ela, anything that is more than the gut feeling that points to Elaine.

Her other, more achievable, mission is to claim something of Grandpa Charlie's as a keepsake to take back to her room. She worries that when the things are 'gone through' before it all gets moved back after the redecoration, most of it will have disappeared. She walks straight into a cardboard box, freshly marked in green Sharpie with her mother's handwriting. It says *Charity Shop*. She hurriedly undoes the neatly folded flaps only to find a selection of shirts, trousers and jumpers. Most of them horribly old man-ish. Mandy is right, they are fit only for giving away, a cheap thrill for the over-seventies of the community.

There is a box marked 'Keep' and Asta is displeased to see it contains only one thing – a toilet roll. She lifts it out and looks at it, peers into its cardboard middle to see if there are any hidden messages scrawled inside, examines it for any sort of 'keep' significance at all. But there is none. It's just a toilet roll in an enormous box.

She squats down to dig deep into the box marked ???. It's outrageous, surely most of this should be in the 'Keep' box. She sees a knick-knack container she made for Charlie in primary school out of a cottage cheese pot and garishly polka-dotted in acrylic paint. There's his collection of souvenirs from around the world too. A miniature Statue of Liberty, a tiny Colosseum, a little bit of stone that claims to have been part of the Berlin Wall. A vast number of birthday and Father's Day cards demonstrating the writing abilities of herself and Felix. There are an awful lot of them and as she thumbs through, she can see the oldest ones – with vintage cars and men holding fishing rods – are signed with an infant's scribble of the three letters: T-i-m. She sniggers as she flicks through some later ones signed 'Timmy' and two years of adorable fountain pen scrawled 'Timothy' ones. These must have been the anal years because 'Timothy' has added 1983 and 1984 into the bottom right-hand corner.

She used to think Grandpa Charlie had moved back here not even remembering about Ela or her letters from all those years ago. Why didn't he ask her or Felix to fetch them out from under the floorboards rather than grubbing around for them himself? She wracks her brain to think about why he didn't just take them with him when he moved out all those years ago. She kicks herself for never having paid more attention to his back story. She probably knows more about Captain America's back story than she does about her own grandfather's.

When she gets up, she steps on something with all her weight. She sucks air in through her teeth and scrunches her face up and it's enough to stop her doing a swear. Lifting a foot, she can see a small wooden rabbit lying down and facing forward, tucked up and looking cosy. It's nice and warm to the touch. She's never seen it before amongst Grandpa Charlie's things or anywhere else for that matter. She likes it so she puts it in her pocket.

Finally, she reaches the window, without knocking into or stepping on anything else and pulls the curtains wide open. It makes a funny sound, not the clack clack clack of the hoops against the pole or even a swoosh of fabric. It's more like a low rumble, a sort of groaning of the sort Marley probably makes when he visits Scrooge for the first time. She closes the curtains again. Silence. She re-opens them and there it is again – a tortured, groaning sound. Behind her, she feels a spooky sense of movement. Something among these teetering piles of displaced objects is going to fall, trapping her inside, blocking the way to the door. She'll have to crawl over mountainous landscapes of crap to save herself. Instead of turning around to face her fears, she stares out of the window, looking down onto the alleyway that is a short cut into town, but she keeps getting distracted by the reflection of the room behind her. The rack of coats, jackets and dresses, temporarily removed to the end of Felix's bed, are moving as if being shaken by spectral forces. Then a ghoulish manifestation of something terrifying rises out of the bed.

It's Felix.

'What are *you* doing here?' she asks her brother, who is slapping the sheet off himself and revealing that in Bristol, he clearly has no access to a brush, comb or any form of shaving kit. His hair halos out from his head and small dots of stubble adorn his upper lip and chin.

'Mum asked me to come home,' he says. 'She told me we need to talk about Dad.'

It's Saturday afternoon and Tim is hunched over the desk in the living room, his shoulders rounded, his head drooping towards where his hands are, gently sculpting another lotus leaf flower into existence. Lately, it's been almost all lotus flowers and white rabbits standing to attention. Mandy has put her foot down and Tim is now only allowed to use the cheapest of '4 for £1' bars for his craft work. Ever since that incident with the Estée Lauder cleansing bar and a gorilla.

He doesn't suspect a thing.

Asta appears to be lolling about on the sofa, her shoulders propped against the arm, legs stretched almost to the third seat cushion. She digs her toes into the calico, then wiggles them, watching the stripes on her socks rippling like a cartoon sea. She's pretending to be scrolling aimlessly through her phone, when she's actually keeping a beady eye on her dad, to make sure he doesn't disappear into the weekend afternoon of Wales's greatest shopping destination. If you don't count Cardiff, Swansea, Newport and Wrexham. Never one for mooching around shops before, it's another of his peculiar new pastimes. It wouldn't normally be a problem but he has been known to return only in the nick of time for opening hours. Not such a problem on a weekday but Saturday and its inherent busyness – Ant and Dec didn't call their show *Wednesday Evening Takeaway* for a good reason – means the Saturday service has to be a precise, tightly-organised machine.

There's another reason why they need to make sure Tim stays in this afternoon. It's the reason Felix was hiding in the bedroom. His return will have maximum impact if it is sprung on Tim to be a surprise, and it's the reason why a week's worth of rancid washing has been stinking out his old bedroom rather than crammed directly into the washing machine.

Asta looks down at the video call where she can see her mother and brother milling about in the kitchen, putting the tea things onto a tray ready to bring in with them. Mandy turns to collect her phone from where it's propped up against the toaster. She pinches her thumb and first finger so they form a circle. *OK, we're coming in.* Asta goes to give a message back but just then, Tim shifts in his seat. Even though he doesn't turn around, Asta quickly converts her thumbs-up into a nose scratch.

'Look who's here,' says Mandy, as she opens the living-room door.

'Who?' says Tim, not looking up, but he senses something. He straightens up, unfurling himself like a flower in the morning sun.

'It's not my favourite son, is it?' he shouts out. 'What are you doing home?'

Felix hasn't even come into the room yet. He brings in the tray of tea things and waits while his father clears a space for him to put it down.

'Just checking in on Mum's current husband,' says Felix. 'That's still you, isn't it?'

He pulls a chair up to the table and sits at ninety degrees to his father. Mandy begins pouring out strong cups of nut-brown tea before adding splashes of milk that turn them a pale biscuit colour. She hands one to Asta before joining her on the sofa, while Felix adds two sugars into his tea; he's clearly not sweet enough. Tim adds three spoonfuls to his own and stirs furiously.

'So what did I miss,' asks Felix, 'while I've been away?'

Asta opens her mouth to relay a minutely detailed novella called *Steve and Asta: The Reunion* – when she feels her mother squeeze her knee. She decides to shut up.

'Not much,' says Tim.

'What's all this then?' asks Felix, picking up a soap rabbit with each hand, leaving the other three bunnies staring into space on the table. 'It's like a fluffle in here.'

'A what?' says Tim.

'It's what they call a load of rabbits. Like a herd of cows or a flock of sheep. A fluffle.'

'No, they don't.' Tim tries this made-up word out. 'A fluffle of rabbits? Really?'

He laughs.

Sometimes you don't see someone for ages, and it's only when you clap eyes on them again after an absence of nearly four months, that you realise you've missed them. That's what it feels like for Asta to hear her father laughing again. A proper laugh, not a polite one or a sarcastic one or one you do just to fit in with the crowd.

'I've been to the bathroom too,' says Felix. 'It's like a zoo in that bathroom cabinet.'

He picks a chocolate brownie up off the tray and takes a bite.

'Mum, this is amazing. When did you learn to bake like this? You did make it, didn't you? I can't taste any E numbers.'

He turns it over in his hands as if expecting to find a bar code.

'Oh no,' says Mandy, 'I'd never be able to make anything as nice as that. They're a present from the builder's son. He's taken up baking and brings his trial cakes and extras around for us.'

Asta nearly chokes on her tea. She's been helping herself to the slices of lemon drizzle, fruity muffins and bits of millionaire's shortbread she's been finding around the kitchen for weeks. She thought they were from a shop. It never occurred to her to think anything else but it turns out Josh made them.

No wonder they were so yummy.

'Have you tried it yet?' Felix asks.

He offers a brownie to Tim.

'Not yet,' says Tim. 'I've not really felt like it but as you're having one.'

He reaches forwards and takes a bite. 'That builder's boy is wasted as a builder. He could be the next Paul Hollywood. I'll have to have a word with Vince about not letting his talents go to waste.'

'He told me he's only taken up baking in the last few weeks,' says Mandy, 'but it looks like he has a natural talent for it.'

'Rubbish,' says Tim. 'His mother must have helped him.'

Dad's doing a sexism, thinks Asta.

'I don't think he's still got a mother,' says Mandy, 'or one who can help him bake a cake at any rate. Don't you ever talk to them about anything when you're in there with them for all that time?'

'Not the personal stuff,' says Tim. 'We talk about football, chainsaws, lawnmowers and that.'

Mandy rolls her eyes. 'He said he needed to keep himself busy when he's not in work. I asked him why and he said there's something bothering him and he needs to distract himself from it.'

Everybody looks pointedly in Tim's direction, taking in the man, his newly loose clothing, his sunken cheeks, his forearms spotted with curls of cheap white soap. Even the fluffle in front of him seem to be sitting up so they can gaze at him with sympathy. Tim's eyes look just that little bit shinier than usual and when he notices everyone's looking at him, he turns and looks over his shoulder. There's nothing there unless you count Vince and Tim's superb brushwork from when they painted one wall teal and the other jade.

'What are you all looking at me for?' he says, turning back. 'I'm fine.'

'Of course you are, Dad,' says Felix. 'Course you are.'

TODAY
MF created group 'Fung Family 2'
MF added you.
MF added Felix.

Asta: I don't get it. What's wrong with the other Fung Family Group?

MF: Your father is not in this one so we can talk about how it went this afternoon. What did you two think?

Asta: . . . (typing)

Felix: . . .(typing)

MF: Anytime, feel free to reply anytime. No rush for me to get to bed. I've only spent the whole night working at the wokface and then up to my elbows in industrial-strength detergent for another half-hour.

Asta: I don't know what you want me to say.

MF: I don't want you to say anything.

Asta: That doesn't make sense.

Felix: She means she doesn't want you to say anything just to make her feel better. she wants to know what you think about Dad.

MF: What do you think Felix?

Felix: He seems worse not better. Sad in a different way.
Has he been on a diet? He's gone a bit skinny.
Did something else happen while I was away?

MF: Not that I can think of. Asta?

Asta: no well yes but no . . . OK yes.

Felix: what?

Asta: When you went to Bristol it meant he lost the
other favourite man in his life.

Felix: Oh

Felix: . . .

Felix: Perhaps I should come back more often?
For the weekend?

MF: There's no need for that. You should be in Bristol
being a student. I just wanted you to come back this
time to find out what someone who hasn't seen him
for a bit thought.

Felix: Just look at him though . . . he's bound to be sad.
I know we try to cheer each other up but sometimes
you just can't be cheered up.

Asta: Really? We won't be able to fix him? Not even if we try really hard?

Felix: You can't fix everybody straightaway, not yet anyway.

Felix: What's wrong with you now?

'Nothing,' Asta says out loud.

'Nothing what?' says Tim.

He turns away from *Match of the Day* and looks at the rest of his family splayed out around the living room. They all look back at him and then quickly look away. At one end of the sofa, his wife, as familiar, close and essential to him as his own right hand. At the other end, his son, the student dentist who has a hole in his sock. And bunched up on a beanbag, sheeny black hair covering her face, is his daughter, the sulky bloody teenager. All three are nose deep into their mobile phones. Tim knows someone who'd be enjoying Man City v. Liverpool as much as he's trying to, who wouldn't be surgically attached to an electronic screen, but he's not going to think about him.

Fortunately, there's a distraction.

'Where are you all going?' he asks.

'Bed,' says Felix.

'To the toilet,' says Mandy.

Tim waits for the selectively mute Asta to say something but she doesn't.

'Are you crying?' he asks her.

'No,' says Mandy and the three of them hustle out of the room.

Chapter Twenty

Asta gets back from school to find a splash of things chucked onto her duvet cover. She knows the drill. Mandy is returning what she found in Asta's pockets when she came to do the washing. Asta always means to empty them herself before she puts her discarded clothes into the overflowing dirty laundry basket, but she just doesn't seem to get around to it.

There's the usual mix of clean-ish tissues, tube of lip balm, the long spiral of paper an empty packet of Rolos makes after you've eaten the last one yourself. There's even a pen! That would have been the cause of much shouting if it had made it into the wash. And what's this? The small wooden rabbit she trod on in Felix's bedroom. She thinks of Bugs, Peter, Judy. Charismatic rabbits all, this one looks nothing like any of them. It's a rabbit rabbit, not one that's pretending to be a human. Looks like her mum didn't recognise it either or she would have said something. Perhaps it wasn't ever Grandpa Charlie's at all and belongs to Felix? Not his usual kind of thing. Anyway, it's hers now so she shoves it onto the dressing table shelf between a box of tissues and a bag of cotton wool. It stares morosely at the soft round puffs that make a mockery of its own hardwood, rendered tail.

Asta's exhausted. On Thursdays, after English, she always has a free lesson which she likes to spend doing her own thing in the sixth form common room while Sophie, Paige and the others provide the soundtrack of what normal teenagers get up to, but today, Mr Feather stopped her.

'Miss Williams is interested in talking to a current A-level student,' he said. 'I suggested you because I thought you'd be able to give a fresh perspective, seeing as you haven't come up through the school from Year Seven.'

'She hasn't had a chance to get as jaded and cynical as us, Sir,' says Callum, who's bumping past them as he leaves the classroom.

He gives Asta a wink. Asta is astonished to be noticed by confident, average-looking Callum. She feels a pink flush rise up her cheeks and pretends to look for something in her bag so she can hide behind her curtain of hair.

'And she's waiting for you in Room Eleven if you wouldn't mind popping over to see her?'

'What? Now?' asks Asta.

'There's no time like the present,' says Mr Feather.

Asta knocks on the door of Room Eleven.

Nothing.

She pushes her face against the long narrow window in the door. She can't see anything so she knocks again and then presses an ear against the glass to catch anyone telling her to come in. That's when someone opens the door and she topples into the room.

'Sorry,' she says to Miss Williams, who has already turned around to go back to her desk. She follows the tiny ex-teacher and sits down at a desk in the front row.

'Don't you wait to be asked to sit down?' says Miss Williams.

Asta jumps up again before she can think about it.

'Please take a seat,' says Miss Williams.

Asta sits down again.

'Thank you for coming along to see me,' says Miss Williams. 'I don't know if Mr Feather explained to you. I'm on the board of school governors and I used to be the headmistress of this school.'

Asta nods.

'And as such,' Miss Williams continues, 'I wanted to interview a student about how English is taught as a subject. I taught English here you know, before I became Head. Of course, it was an all-girls school back then and the boys had their own school on the other side of town. Both grammar schools in those days. The secondary modern was already a mixed affair. Five years after I got the job, we went comprehensive, mixed abilities and boys and girls all bunched in together along with the multiple distractions that brings.'

'What's wrong with teaching everybody all the same in the same school, Miss?' asks Asta.

'Nothing,' says Miss Williams.

Asta wasn't expecting that. There is still something about Miss Williams that is quite literally old school though. She smirks to herself about her correct use of literally.

'Would you like to share the joke?' Miss Williams asks.

'What joke?' asks Asta.

'Then why are you smiling like that?'

Asta's jaw drops open. She is not used to being spoken to like this by a teacher. She normally goes unnoticed at the back of the class, which she used to think she didn't like very much.

Miss Williams embarks on a series of questions about *King Lear*, Thomas Hardy, Keats, Shelley and Coleridge. She presents Asta with a poem and asks her to mark up its scansion using the correct symbols.

It's almost like the exam of Asta's nightmares where you revise the wrong thing and can't answer any of the questions. The only difference is that none of these are on the A level syllabus so she hasn't read any of them. She's also never scanned a poem in her life. Well not like that anyway. She explains all of this to Miss Williams.

'And you're doing English A-level?' asks Miss Williams. 'You do know you should be reading around your set texts, don't you? To get a better knowledge of as much of the canon of English literature as you can. We want to make you into fully rounded scholars, not exam-passing machines.'

She looks down at the poem Asta has marked up where she's put a tiny smiley face, sad face and neutral face emojis against each beat.

'Now this isn't too bad. I'm presuming you've never studied this before either.'

Asta shakes her head. So does Miss Williams.

'I don't know,' she sighs. 'Thank you though, Asta. This lesson has been as much of a learning experience for me as it has been for you. Whatever happened to the three Rs?'

'The three Rs?'

'Reading, writing and arithmetic,' says Miss Williams.

'Arithmetic?' says Asta, 'that doesn't start with an R.'

'Neither does writing,' says Miss Williams.

Even though they've met more than once, Asta has never seen Miss Williams smile before and that's unusual. Unless you're meeting the prosecution, jury and judge for the first time in the dock, most people smile when they meet each other. Miss Williams never seemed bothered about this and Asta is surprised the old lady's face has not snapped in two with the strain. No, she actually looks like someone who knows how to smile and to have a good laugh. When she was much younger, of course.

'Why are *you* smiling?' Asta asks.

'Because it's an old joke. I'm thinking about all the troubles I had with some of the more mature colleagues I inherited after we moved from being a grammar to a comprehensive. They couldn't grasp the fact that things were changing. "What about the three Rs? What about the three Rs?" It was I who had to explain to them that it is, in fact, our business to prepare our students as best we can for what each tomorrow brings. Although the three Rs are an important part of achieving that, you can't simply lash a child to a textbook and expect them to become expert in all three. I used to think they were old dinosaurs but it now appears that *I* am the old dinosaur.'

'Oh no, you're not, Miss,' says Asta politely.

'Oh yes, I am,' says Miss Williams with a twinkle in her eye.

The bell rings and Asta leaps up out of her chair like everyone always does at the end of a lesson.

'I don't recall saying class is dismissed,' says Miss Williams.

Chapter Twenty-One

Tim's got a migraine. At least, Mandy thinks it's a migraine. Tim just thinks it's a brain tumour.

'Whatever it is,' says Mandy, 'I can't have you working down here looking like that. It's enough to put anyone off their dinner and that's not a look we want our customers to see. Get upstairs and get into bed. It's nine o' clock on a Wednesday night, not six o' clock on a Saturday, we'll manage perfectly well without you. Won't we?'

She directs this last bit towards Asta, who is on the shop side of the serving hatch, looking anxiously into the kitchen. Recognising a cue when it's been given, she nods, she's not quite sure at what. She watches as her father walks out of the kitchen, through the vestibule, to the bottom of the stairs. He looks the same as usual to her, well, the same as he's done since Grandpa Charlie, but if he's willing to leave work and go home, he must be feeling poorly.

This is the first time Asta has had to work here in the Yau Sum. Back in the Sun House, she'd been given the crucial kid-in-a-takeaway job of sitting out front until a customer came in. Then she'd have to pause her GameBoy, hop off the high stool and get someone out from the kitchen to serve. She'd tried to do some serving once and the customer had kindly read out the numbers to her instead of ordering the meals by name but she'd still managed to get it wrong somehow. 15 and 50. 16 and 60. They all sounded the same.

That was in her younger days. As soon as she'd been old enough to work in the shop in a genuinely useful way, her parents had put a stop to it. It was really annoying because she'd learnt all the meal numbers off by heart in an attempt to impress them. She'd even appealed to Grandpa Charlie. It was one of the great things about having your grandfather living with you. Even when it didn't work out playing good cop, bad cop with your parents, there was always a High Court judge in the form of Grandpa Charlie you could appeal to.

'They don't want you working the shop because they don't want you to get a hankering after it,' said Charlie.

'Huh?' said Asta.

'Me mam, me, yer dad, that's three generations you've got there of takeaway family. Three's bad enough and your parents don't want to make it four.'

Asta is woefully unprepared for this emergency shift. She can still remember all the numbers of the meals in the old place but that's no use on the menu here. She crosses her fingers and hopes for a quiet night.

And to begin with, all is well. Nobody seems to order a banquet, just a few people fetching something small in just for themselves or their other half too, often still in their work uniforms, with the name of a shop or a care home embossed on one side of their chest. She finds she can answer the phone and negotiate looking up the numbers on the menu and scribble the orders down all at the same time. She does despair though of the customers who insist on spelling their names out to her when they really don't have to.

J-O-N-E-S

S-M-I-T-H

'You think that's bad,' says Mandy, when Asta complains. 'I still get compliments on how good my English is and I am actually English.'

'What am I supposed to say if anyone says that to me?' asks Asta.

'Just thank them nicely and tell them theirs is good too.'

But as is so often the case, the only thing Asta has to fear about her unexpected shift in the shop is fear itself. Even when her mother goes upstairs for five minutes to check on the patient and she is left on her own downstairs, she copes. Not having a customer come in helps. She congratulates herself as she looks out beyond the counter, until she catches her reflection in the black mirror that the front window becomes after dark. She twists her mouth, bites the inside of her left cheek, wonders what it must be like to wake up every morning looking not like this but like someone else. She turns away quickly and heads into the kitchen instead.

It's warm and welcoming in here with so many things bubbling or sizzling quietly away in the background – the background hum of the extraction system, pots of curry, sweet and sour, BBQ and gravy sauces clinking gently as they tremble in the bubbling water of the bain-marie, the chip fryer waiting for a basket of chips to transform from pale and pasty to a crisp golden brown.

'I'm in charge of all of this,' she thinks, as she does a quick recce of both of the storerooms and checks the back door is still locked. As she retraces her steps, she stops to breathe deeply in the dried goods storeroom, to fill her lungs with the citrus scents and spicy smells that make the curry. She punches a bag of rice, feels the crackle of the plastic sack and the puny grains inside give way to her mighty fist.

Out of the darkness of the storerooms, back into the LED stainless steel dazzle of the kitchen, she stops to drop a pea into the chip fat, to watch it splutter and float to the top. She used to get told off for doing that but now she can because she is in charge. Right now, she is the manager. She owns this. She can do whatever she wants and if she wants to swing her hips and do a little shimmy as she swaggers out of the kitchen door and back over towards the counter, she will.

'Hi Asta!'

She freezes like a deer in the unexpected headlights of her English class – Paige, Callum, Sophie and a small Tom Cruise lookalike who must be her boyfriend Lambert. Later she considers her use of the word small to describe Lambert as redundant. Tom Cruise is already quite tiny.

'Oh hello,' she says back weakly.

'I didn't know you worked here,' says Paige, before tipping her head down to look at a menu.

'Nor me,' mutters Asta.

'What did you say?' asks Sophie.

If in doubt, change the subject.

'Was the film good?' Asta asks.

She'd heard them all talk about going to the cinema together.

'Yes, really good,' says Lambert.

His voice has the crackle of a thousand cigarettes even though he's never smoked one in his life, a form of protest against his ludicrous name. Sophie's right. Everything about him is perfectly formed, even his bloody voice.

Asta decides to hate him.

'You should have come with us,' Lambert adds. 'You'll have to come with us next time.'

Asta decides not to hate him after all.

The other three murmur assent. Callum even slaps the palm of his hand against his forehead. It all seems quite sincere. For now.

'Anyway, what shall we have?' says Paige. 'Who likes sweet and sour chicken balls? Special fried rice?'

'I can't have any of those,' says Sophie. 'What have you got that's carb-free?'

'Is your chicken halal?' asks Lambert.

'My mum says I can't have anything with MSG in it,' says Callum. 'Can you leave it out for us?'

It's like taking the curtain call at the end of an unpopular show and being pelted with ripe questions.

'I'm not sure,' says Asta. 'How about some plain boiled rice?'

'Isn't that a carb?' says Sophie. 'I could always take the pastry off a pancake roll, I suppose. What's in your pancake roll?'

Asta opens her mouth even though she doesn't know the answer. Before she can make a sound, Sophie changes her mind.

'How about some stir-fried vegetables? What vegetables are in it?'

'Onions, peas, bamboo shoots, water chestnuts, peppers, mushrooms . . .'

'Blimey Asta, you said that without moving your lips,' says Callum.

Asta turns to see her mum coming out of the vestibule, retying her apron strings.

'. . . beansprouts, baby sweetcorn,' concludes Mandy.

'Oh yes,' says Sophie and pretty soon everyone has piped up with their own particular dietary requirement and Mandy is able to suggest a selection of things that with a few tweaks, additions and omissions, will be suitable for the four of them to share.

'You are all going back to the hall of residence to eat it, aren't you?' Mandy asks. 'Or does it need all need to be packed separately?'

Callum splutters.

'No, we're not students. We're still in school. Asta's in our class.'

Mandy's face lights up.

'Well,' she says, flipping the back of her hand against Asta's arm. 'Why didn't you say so?'

When Mandy rings the food up, she presses the discount key on the till and the four customers are thrilled at the extra change they aren't expecting. Even more so when they realise there are Beatrix Potter fifty-pence pieces too.

All Asta has to do when the two of them get inside is to man the deep-fat fryer while Mandy cracks on with the real culinary skills, all flames and vegetables flying through the air as she wields the wok one-handed, throwing everything about so it all heats evenly. Asta can't even do a pancake without using the flipping thing to turn it over.

Asta shakes the chips about needlessly, watches a few sesame seeds detach themselves from the prawn toast and float to the top of the oil, worries if the chicken balls are moving past a crispy golden brown into an acrylamide-stuffed charred brown. Not yet, but they will be soon. She doesn't want to plot a slow future death for the others so she fishes them out and drains them before putting them into their foil tray.

Once it's all packed up and ready to go, Asta takes both bags out and puts them on the counter. None of the others notice she's there, they're all engrossed in something Callum is scrolling through on his phone.

'Do you think we should go?' Paige asks.

'Don't see why not, just for a bit,' says Sophie.

'Be rude not to,' says Callum.

Lambert looks up and spots the arrival of their meal. He leaps up and comes over to the counter.

'Are you going to the party?' he asks.

'What party?' says Asta.

'This Saturday,' says Lambert. 'I dunno who the guy is, someone still in school with you, is it? His eighteenth.'

'Yeah, Asta,' says Paige. 'You should come. We've never seen you out.'

Asta gulps. Even though she's always wanted to be asked, now that she has, all kinds of nightmare scenarios – wearing the wrong clothes, saying the wrong thing, sneezing into the cocaine if she gets offered any – run through her head like a film flashing before the eyes of a dying man.

'I don't know,' she says, before embarking on a brazen lie. 'I might be needed here.' She gestures humbly all around her.

'Oh good, you haven't gone yet,' says Mandy, running out of the kitchen brandishing two bags of prawn crackers. 'I forgot to give you these. They're good for all of you to eat, no forbidden ingredients of any kind.'

'Mrs Fung,' says Paige. 'Can Asta come to a party with us on Saturday?'

'Of course she can,' says Mandy.

'That's sorted then,' says Callum. 'See you tomorrow.'

As soon as the door has closed behind them, Mandy says, 'They seemed nice. I didn't know you'd made some new friends.'

'Neither did I,' says Asta.

Chapter Twenty-Two

Steve's having his five minutes of fun on the chenille rug in Elaine's living room. He wishes they had one of these at home. They've been coming here almost every day this week.

He misses his off-lead romps along the riverbank and into the fields and meadows but still, there are good smells on almost every street, what with lampposts, broadband cabinets, bins, even those trees that have been naughty and are encircled in their little metal cages.

He growls joyously, kicking his legs about until the rug has half flipped upside-down on top of him, then he looks up.

Where is everybody?

Elaine and Asta are upstairs in Elaine's bedroom. Elaine is dabbing something from a pot on to Asta's face. Asta is supposed to keep her eyes closed but she can't help opening one just a little. In the mirror, she can see the concentration on Elaine's face, feels the feathery touch of her fingers as she dabs and strokes upwards and outwards.

'I still don't understand why you had to call my mum,' says Asta, 'to tell her I was here instead of at Steve's house.'

'Asta!' Elaine stops what she's doing. 'Don't you think you should tell your parents if you're going to be somewhere else than they expected? And going to get home later than you said?'

'Not really,' says Asta. 'Am I supposed to?'

'You always call Mrs Li at home if you're going to be late picking up Steve.'

'Well, that's just good manners, isn't it?'

'And doesn't your mother deserve some of your good manners too?'

Asta opens her eyes to see the look on Elaine's face. 'I suppose so,' she says eventually.

'I'm pleased to hear it too,' says Elaine. She goes back to doing whatever she was doing to Asta's skin for a bit before leaning back to get a better look. 'I don't know why I'm using this, to be honest. Your skin is practically perfect. It doesn't look like you've ever had a spot in your life.'

Asta shrugs. 'Felix got the zitty gene in our family.'

'So even, so smooth,' says Elaine. 'We probably don't need any base at all except it does help everything else sit nicely on top. Let's move onto the eyes now.'

This is what Asta was hoping for. She's seen photos of Elaine, she's even seen the woman herself on her way to or from one social engagement to another and that's when she has that amazing eye make-up, a thick line of black that flips up into the most perfect cat's eye. Whenever Asta tries to do it, she looks like she's gone fifteen rounds with Anthony Joshua.

'Don't squeeze your eyes shut,' says Elaine. 'Just close them as if you were going to sleep. Relax.'

Asta tries but it's hard for a teenager to do what they're told when they could just do the opposite instead. All the tension previously squeezed into her eyelids is now creating a very wrinkled nose. Elaine sighs. It will have to do.

Asta can feel Elaine's warm finger pull tightly towards first one of her temples then the other. She's expecting a firm stroke, a toddler putting a paintbrush to the easel for the very first time, but all she can feel is a light feathery touch along her upper eyelid. It's almost ticklish but she bites her lip and tries really hard not to flinch. It's easier than she thought because once you get up so close to Elaine, she smells so calming and relaxing. It's her perfume, of course, but Asta can't help thinking that Elaine is a fabulous person and she can see why her grandfather liked her so much. If she is Ela, that is.

As soon as Elaine's finished, Asta opens her eyes and tries to turn around and look at herself in the triptych of the dressing table mirror.

'Ah ah ah,' says Elaine, carefully guiding Asta back to face her. 'Not until I've finished.'

Elaine produces a tube of mascara, brings the wand to Asta's face before shaking her head and putting it back.

'I know,' says Asta. 'I've only got five eyelashes on each side.'

'Mascara is overrated anyway. I wish I had some falsies we could use,' says Elaine kindly. 'We'll just use a bit more eyeliner for now. Perhaps we can get some false eyelashes in time for the weekend.'

Big fluffy brushes are produced and applied along Asta's cheeks and forehead. Smaller brushes and cotton buds appear and poke about above and below her eyes.

'Symmetry,' says Elaine, as she bites her bottom lip with concentration. 'That's what we need.'

She brandishes a lipstick and applies it to Asta's mouth.

'Now do this,' she instructs and pulls a pouty moue. Asta does the same, eyes cast down to watch her lips puckering in front of her.

Finally, Elaine splits a tissue in two and presses it against Asta's mouth.

'There, what do you think?' Elaine asks.

Asta's scared to look but once she does, she turns from side to side, seeing what she looks like from all angles.

'But I look really nice,' she says finally.

'Of course you do, silly,' says Elaine.

'I thought I was going to look like one of the Real Women of Somewhere like on those programmes you and Mrs Li like to watch.'

'Oh, they just put that on for the television. Those women probably look like me and Mrs Li when they're at home.'

Asta doubts this is true.

'Right, so this is the one you want to look like for your party, is that right? Or we can try a few other things?'

Asta shakes her head, watching herself doing it in the mirror.

'No, I like this one. It's lovely. Thanks very much.'

'Well, the problem now is that you had your eyes closed for most of it. We'll have to take it off and put it back on again together.'

As Asta wipes the oily balm onto her face, she asks Elaine how come she knows so much about all of this. 'It's a good job I thought of asking you how to get ready for this party.' She throws the final bit of cotton wool into the bin.

'Well . . . I am experienced in having daughters, step-daughters and temporary granddaughters, you know.'

'Temporary?'

'They don't often keep in touch once their father's relationship with Sarah, Nancy or Jessie is over. Teenagers though, just like you. And I knew my own daughters, what they were like when they were your age. Not a lot changes in the world of teenagers, you know. Little things like magazines, mobile phones, one-pound notes for pocket money. But the big things stay much the same.'

She cups Asta's face in her hands for a moment, before tipping some lotion onto more cotton wool and swiping it all over Asta from hairline to collarbone.

'Right, I think we're good to go again. Start with this one. I'll do it on me at the same time. I'll explain to you when you need to do it differently due to your lack of wrinkles.'

Asta likes the way Elaine makes it sound like having wrinkles is a good thing.

'What do you think I should wear to the party, though?' she asks, as they sit side by side at the dressing table.

'I've heard that jeans and a nice top are good for almost anything like that,' says Elaine.

'Do you think my grey hoodie counts as a nice top?'

'No, Asta. I don't. I think we may have to pop onto a couple of websites after we've finished doing this.'

18 Rupert Street
London
SE1 8AW
27th February 1964

Dear Charlie,

No, I think you're doing it wrong and you're pulling the thread too much. What you have to do is put
a matchstick between the button and the material.
Then you can sew the button on as tight as you like
and when you pull the matchstick out, there will still
be enough give so you can do the button up properly.
It will be easier to thread the needle if you wet your
finger and pinch the end of the cotton first.

It is a better idea to sew the button on yourself,
never mind what Miguel says about girls and sewing.
He's an idiot. You might just as well sew it on yourself
as wait for your mother to do it, especially as she has
to get you to thread the needle for her. Luckily for
Mam, she has Sali to thread her needles for her as
I'm not there. Otherwise, she would have to go out
into the street and flag down one of the neighbours'
kids to do it.

What do I think of Rosie Quinn, is that what
you're asking? And of Lynette Barrett? Well, I know

them, of course, from school, but I can't really give you any information as to whether they make good girlfriend material. I've never had to think about them in that way and I think it's unfair of you to ask. Just be content that if there was something truly dreadful about either of them, I would definitely tell you. As it is, you will have to work out what you think of them yourself.

Clemmie and I went out to the pictures earlier this evening. I should have known to expect something when she came downstairs with the biggest beehive I have ever seen. 'How did you do that?' I asked her. She tapped her nose and then asked me when I was going to get ready to go out. Bloody cheek! I told her I was ready and I didn't see the point of doing myself up to the nines just to sit in the dark with her for two hours. I also said I felt very sorry for whoever was sitting behind her in the cinema as they wouldn't be able to see the screen and she looked very pleased with herself.

That was because, as it turned out, she sat in the back with her Barry so nobody had to sit behind her and I don't think she saw much of the film. I sat in front of them so I could see the screen properly and here's the thing. She asked Barry to bring someone with him for me. I can't even remember his name. He was all wet, if you know what I mean? Or was he all dry? I don't know, I'm not a doctor, but he blinked a lot more than is usual and swallowed much more than is normal. During the film, he kept turning around to see what the other two were up to. When it got to an exciting bit in the film, he reached over and took my hand which would have annoyed me even if he hadn't made me spill my box of fruit gums! I took my hand back and kept it with me for the rest of the film.

It was awkward after the film finished but I told Clemmie I could find my own way home and I watched the happy couple and their third wheel spin off into Leicester Square while I made my way home to a mug of cocoa and this letter to you!

Your friend,

Ela

Chapter Twenty-Three

Asta's wishing she'd never come out now. She slumps at one end of the kitchen table, crushing herself into the corner of the banquette. She's made a small den for herself, piling the Ottolenghis, Rodens, Nigels and Nigellas up so nobody can see her. They can see a pile of cookery books, an arm, the top of someone's head, but nobody will know it's her.

The kitchen in this party house is bigger than her kitchen, bedroom and living room knocked together. The table and banquette are at one end of the room. At the other end is an enormous set of sliding patio doors that looks out onto the fairy-lit garden dotted with teenagers talking, swigging, dancing, vaping.

Between her and the garden sits an enormous kitchen island and it has one of those fancy boiling-water taps. She looks up from the recipe for Delia's sticky toffee pudding with pecan sauce to see two boys switching it from cold to boiling and back again. It is like watching man discovering fire for the first time and ends in probably much the same way with one of them burning himself and running off, closely followed by the other.

Asta's here because she needs a quiet nook to pass the time. She'd leave now if she could. She winces as she thinks again about her moment of humiliation.

Paige's mum had given them a lift to the party. Asta was surprised to get to sit shotgun next to Mrs Jones while Paige and Callum sat in the back together. She knows they're not a couple, just the best of friends who are not in any way romantically interested in each other. She thinks that's brilliant. After they were dropped off, the three of them walked up the steep gravelled drive that swept around to the front of the house. The digits one and eight were spiked into the grass alongside at regular intervals until they got to the top where someone had swapped the digits around to say eighty-one. Someone even more lark-ish had managed to spell out the word BOOB. Discarded cans of Fosters nearby proved alcohol had played a part.

As they got closer to the house, they could see solar lights strung from trees, sticking out of flower beds, edging each path and walkway. Some of them were already throwing out their dim glow while others waited for it to get darker still. They must have arrived in a lull between playlists because just as they reached the front door, Pharrell piped up to inform them how 'Happy' he was. Callum started swaying involuntarily to the music and Paige and Asta giggled as they watched him sashay into the house, swivelling around to show them his lip-synching skills.

After they'd dumped their contributions to the drinks tally on the long trestle table under the stairs, Callum wanted to take his jacket off so the three of them traipsed upstairs to find the bedroom that was also the cloakroom.

'No, you don't want to go in there,' he said, backing out of the first room so quickly he almost sent Paige flying.

'Nor that one,' he said, after the next door. 'Ah, this one seems more promising.'

The third door was covered in yellow and black caution-police-line-do-not-cross tape. Callum ignored it and tried the door handle. It was locked.

'Ahh, belt and braces. Like Branagh's Hamlet,' said Callum. 'Very good. Very annoying but also very good. I'll just keep my jacket on, I think.'

'Look at that,' said Paige, as they were heading back along the landing. She pointed to another flight of stairs that led up to the third floor blocked by a baby stair-gate, plastered in the same yellow and black tape as the locked room.

'Yeah,' said Callum. 'Monroe said the parents weren't mad enough to leave the house for the party. They've promised to keep out of the way on the top floor and not show themselves except in an emergency.'

'Monroe?' says Asta. 'Is that whose birthday it is? Should I go and say thank you for having me?'

Callum shook his head.

'Monroe should be thanking you for bringing the numbers up. It's a good turnout already though, isn't it?'

And it was. So many faces, a few of them vaguely familiar but most of them unknown to Asta. After a while, Paige and Callum split up and while she was wondering which one to go with, Asta realised they'd both completely disappeared. She meandered aimlessly from room to room, half-looking for them. In some kind of games room, she spotted Sophie and Lambert standing next to a pool table. They waved but were in deep conversation with two other couples. Asta didn't want to butt in. She'd now exhausted her knowledge of everyone else she knew at the party. There were one or two faces she recognised from the school corridors but nobody well enough to strike up a conversation with. She stood at the edge of a group of girls who were talking animatedly and was not noticed by any of them. When she spotted another girl standing awkwardly on her own, next to the table that the parents had laid out all the hot dogs, pizzas, toasted sandwiches and other alcohol-soaking carbs, she'd made a beeline for her, only for her boyfriend to turn up. They proceeded to snog so hard the girl practically fell backwards into some dip.

Asta decided to go upstairs and on the half-landing, a gangly boy clinked a Jägermeister against her J_2O and proceeded to discuss his belief in spontaneous human combustion 'which must be true because it happened to someone my cousin's neighbour did the accounts for'. Asta wondered if it was her chest that was about to spontaneously combust judging by the way he was leaning in towards her, eyes glued to about twenty centimetres down from her face. She carried on half-listening when what she really wanted to do was disagree, question the validity of this source, have a proper conversation. Impossible to do with someone so very, very drunk.

'I like your top,' he said.

He reached out a hand to touch the fabric, a piece of the fabric that was sitting snugly against her left breast.

'Thank you,' she said.

She took a step back.

He took a step forward.

'Nice and soft.'

He leaned over and breathed into her face, the rasping smell of alcohol that was working its way through his system. She could feel the balustrade pressing against her back and wondered if it would be better to fall and crush a few partygoers rather than stick with this guy.

'My grandfather's friend helped me pick it out,' she said.

Elaine had vetoed all the turtle-and polo-necked tops Asta favoured and practically forced her into this pink top, a bit tighter than she liked to wear ('You have the figure for it') and with something called a sweetheart neckline ('Your embonpoint will never be as smooth and firm as this ever again').

Asta sensed something untoward was about to happen so when he began to bend towards her, mouth parted like a freshly gutted king prawn, she was able to dip under his arm and slip away.

No need to be completely rude about it though so she shouted, 'There's someone I know over there,' as she made good her escape.

That was a lie but as she headed down the stairs, she did see someone she knew. Josh was standing in a small group chatting by the kitchen door. Did she imagine it or did he look away just as she spotted him? She stretched her neck, bobbed her head from side-to-side, gave a small chest-height wave, arm tucked in, just a few fingers waggling like an over-eager trumpet player. But if he was looking over at her before, he definitely wasn't any more.

She traipsed down the hallway, noticing a crack across the pretty azulejos floor tiles that wasn't there when they arrived. She went outside, weaving her way past clusters of strangers, and sat on the garden wall looking out. The house was an ideal location for an eighteenth birthday party, a detached house set back from the main road like all the other detached houses along this stretch. No neighbours close enough to hear you, to complain or to demand an invitation. Plenty of lawn and garden to sit down and catch some fresh air when you'd drunk too much. Not that those people down there were taking advantage of that. Quite the opposite as six or seven boys and girls were taking turns to roll down the steep grassy embankment, squealing, grunting and going 'f-u-u-u-u-u-c ...' before coming to rest in a sort of sunken ditch that divided the two halves of the lawn. After they'd all made it to the bottom, they were clearly far too pissed to get up and stagger back up for another go. 'Ha ha,' she heard one of them say over and over again until the others drowned him out by singing 'Oom-pah-pah' from the most recent school production of *Oliver!*

Asta wondered if she could be more like one of them – a confident thrill seeker who wouldn't feel guilty about vomiting on a stranger's lawn. Or maybe she could be the one who held the vomiter's hair back. Preferably not the one who's just skidded on the sick and fallen over.

It started to get dark and Asta didn't like it. She gave the solar spike closest to her a shake and it blinked its light once or twice before expiring. The next one along looked like it wanted to do the same. She got up ever so casually, sauntered toward the bright lights of the front door, only to find it blocked by yet another gang of people she didn't know or recognise. Still, the entire house was lit up like a circuit board so she edged her way around the building until she reached another grassy embankment. A set of stone steps led up to a small patio edged with pots of pink and purple flowers and, Asta was relieved to discover, a set of double doors that led back inside. The room itself was dimly lit but at least she'd be closer to the hallway and its glorious LEDs. She slipped inside.

It was quiet in here, party music muffled by the book-lined walls. A Chesterfield sofa, all bellybutton holes and metal rivets, was facing away from her. At right angles to it was the desk, an old-fashioned affair with a green banker's lamp casting a dim glow around the room. Colonel Mustard killed Asta Fung in the study with the lead pipe, she thought with a shiver.

She crept across to the door, outlined in bright light from the party in the hallway, when she heard some good-natured giggling coming from behind her. She looked back to double-check she'd closed the patio doors behind her and caught sight of two boys lying on the sofa, one at each end, top to tail.

'Sorry,' she said. 'Just passing through.'

'No problemo,' said one of them.

He was smoking a long thin cigarette that Asta knew from books, TV shows and films was a joint. A doobie. A spliff. It was the first one she'd knowingly seen in real life. Now it was being passed to the other boy who looked just like the first boy but without the beard.

'Do you want some?' he said, offering it out to Asta.

Well, it would be rude not to. Then she remembered the notices she'd seen, scribbled out in a mumsy hand, and stuck up all over the place.

No Smoking in the House please!

Would you mind using one of these ash trays?

Don't stub your fags out in my plant containers, you animals!

'No, thank you ... actually, I don't think you're allowed to smoke in the house. Maybe you should take it outside.'

She looked pointedly out through the patio doors where a girl was doing cartwheels. Somewhat ill-advised considering her choice of underwear. She looked back at the two boys on the sofa.

'What would Monroe's parents say if they knew you were smoking in here? What would Monroe say?'

'I know Monroe would be just fine with it,' said the boy with the beard. 'And so would his dad.'

'What makes you think that?'

'Because I'm Monroe,' said the smooth-faced boy.

'And I'm one of his parents,' said the preternaturally young-looking dad with a beard.

The two of them started laughing. Monroe kept saying, 'What would my parents say?' and giving his father a dead arm punch each time.

Asta had to unlock the door to open it. She dashed into the hallway, straight into a cobweb of police-caution-do-not-pass yellow tape that stuck to her face and hair.

'Shut that door,' Monroe's father called after her.

The kitchen is getting full now. The buffet must have all gone because people are coming in and ransacking the kitchen for more food. Asta sinks lower and lower into her seat, checks her phone again to see if Callum or Paige has replied to her text asking when they're thinking of leaving. They haven't even seen her message. She wonders if she can walk home on her own but the house is so far out of town and the council switches all of the street lights off at midnight. She thinks about the puny beam from her phone failing to light her way home.

Somebody sits down next to her and starts to eat a bulb of garlic as if it's a tangerine, splitting the cloves apart, popping each one into his mouth and chewing. He catches Asta watching him with astonishment.

'Don't think you're getting any of this,' he says. 'It's all mine.'

Asta can see the minced garlic swilling around in his mouth. What's more she can smell it too.

'No thanks, you have it for yourself,' she says, knocking over a pristine copy of *Persiana* as she gets up and out of sniffing distance.

Asta still can't see Callum or Paige anywhere. She drifts through the hallway, past the drinks table, where she sees someone's hair extension floating in a bowl of punch. A single stiletto is hooked on the edge of the table, the shape of each of its owner's toes visible, like a series of crop circles, inside the shallow vamp. There seems to be fewer people at the party now and she panics for a moment that Paige and Callum have left without her. She couldn't blame them if they had. She'd leave herself behind at the party too if she could.

She steps in through the nearest door to find it's a moodily-lit living room. In the corners, she suspects the primitive mating rituals of adolescent humans are taking place. A few people are standing chatting by the mantelpiece, while on the sofa, a girl lies flopped forward onto her stomach, arm dangling to the floor, sleeping it off. It's peaceful and everybody is keeping themselves to themselves and she tries to block out the occasional soft squelching sound coming from a nearby armchair. Practically perfect and you can't hope for more than that.

She settles herself onto the sofa, being careful not to sit on any of the girl's hair which has puffed out around her like a discarded mop. Asta blows out her cheeks and stares into space, pokes a tongue into the gap where a wisdom tooth is 'partially erupted.'

'Hello.'

Asta's reverie is interrupted by the sofa jolting as someone settles down on the arm.

'Hi Josh,' she says.

'I thought I saw you earlier on,' he says. 'I didn't know you knew Monroe.'

'I don't . . . or I didn't. I came with some friends but I've lost them.'

'Rewind that one a bit. You do know Monroe or you don't know him?'

A problem shared is a problem halved.

Where did she get that from? Ela, of course. It's good advice and even though it makes Asta wince to tell the story, she knows she feels better having got it off her chest.

Josh laughs just the right amount and in all the right places.

'A dad taking drugs with his son.' Asta shakes her head. 'That would never happen at my house. My parents won't even drink alcohol in front of us.'

'Neither does my dad,' says Josh, 'take drugs with me I mean. We drink beer together.'

'While your mum leaves notes telling you not to?'

'Well, she could leave us a note but she'd have to be at home for us to see it.'

'Does she work long hours then?'

'Might do,' says Josh. 'Don't really know what she does. She left us when I was still a kid. We're not aware of her current whereabouts.'

'Really?'

'Yes, really.'

'She's okay, though? She's not driven off Beachy Head or anything like that?'

'I wouldn't be that lucky.'

Asta is struggling to think of something sensible, kind and comforting to say when someone flips a switch by the door. All the overhead lights come on just as someone is coming out from behind the thick velvet curtains holding a suspiciously full bottle of what might or might not be beer at arm's length. Couples jump up from whatever they've been doing. Clothes are readjusted. Mouths wiped across forearms. Lipstick smears rubbed away. Badger eyes exposed.

An older woman with hair so artfully blonde it can only have come from beneath a series of foils is shouting into the room.

'Is that *marijuana* I can smell? *Who* is smoking inside my house?'

She sniffs deeply twice, realises the smell isn't coming from inside this room and leaves.

'Monroe's mum is much older than his dad, isn't she?' asks Asta.

'It explains a lot,' says Josh.

Romance has left the room as the couples disperse. Sadly, the beer bottle of urine has not. It's on the mantelpiece nestling amongst all the eighteenth birthday cards.

'I can give you a lift back if you want, if you can't find your mates,' says Josh.

Asta checks her phone again, being careful not to move too much in case of jolting the Sleeping Beauty next to her. She must be practically comatose to have slept through all of that.

Shit!

Josh seems to have noticed too.

'Do you think she's all right? Perhaps we should get her up, take her home as well.' He pulls a face. 'Unless she looks like she's going to spew.'

'Come on, wake up,' he says into the whorl of pink visible in the midst of the girl's multi-studded and hooped ear.

Asta gets up and leans over the girl, touching her shoulder gingerly. Nothing. She grips the girl's upper arm and gives her a shake. Still nothing.

That's when she feels it pressing against her hand. Something plastic and hard in the midst of all that soft wobbly flesh. She quickly rolls the girl's sleeve up and there it is – the white plastic of a blood glucose monitor sticking out of her arm.

'I think there's something wrong,' she tells Josh. 'Go get Monroe's mum back here.'

While Josh is gone and a few interested bystanders have started to mill around, Asta tries to remember what to do.

'Do any of you know her?' she asks.

Nobody does.

Asta gives the girl another gentle shake.

'Is she dead?' someone asks helpfully.

Asta grinds her teeth but says nothing, wonders if this girl is just very drunk, very low on blood sugar or a combination of the two.

The bystanders and rubberneckers that are crowding around begin to disperse, forming a guard of honour for Monroe's mother as she hurries over. Josh, Monroe and his dad are hanging back in the doorway. She visibly pales at the sight of an unconscious young woman with one of her sleeves rolled up at her son's eighteenth birthday party. The colour returns just as soon as Asta explains it's most likely a diabetic response to having drunk much too much.

'She's completely out of it,' says Asta. 'I think we need to take her to A & E.'

'I can't take her,' says Monroe's mother. 'I didn't think I'd need to drive. I've already finished the bottle of Pommery.'

While Monroe looks gutted his mum has drunk his birthday present, his dad puts up a hand like a child wanting to ask a question in class. His wife nods permission for him to speak. Asta and Josh exchange glances.

'I haven't had anything to drink. I'll take her,' he says.

'I don't think so, David,' says Monroe's mum. 'Driving while under the influence of drugs achieved equivalence with drunk driving in 2015. Don't you listen to anything I tell you?'

Josh puts his hand up now. Asta can't be sure if he's being sensitive to the mood of the room or sarcastic.

'I'll take her to A & E. I haven't had a drink,' he says.

'You come to my party and you don't get a drink, Palazzo?' says Monroe. 'What's wrong with you?'

'Me and Dad are installing a new kitchen tomorrow morning. Have you ever tried doing that with a hangover?'

The comatose girl with diabetes is called Jenna. Someone told Asta and Josh that as they made their way to the car.

When they got to A & E, that was the only name they could give, not even a surname. Such an evidently close relationship meant they weren't allowed to go behind the swing doors into triage with her, so they sit together to wait until someone comes out to say she is going to be fine.

An hour has passed and nobody has yet come out to say that.

'How did you know she was more than just drunk?' Josh asks.

'It was the white thing on her arm,' says Asta. 'Someone in my last school had one. We had a special assembly to tell us about it. Bit mortifying for him but I suppose if it's a matter of life and death? Hopefully not death, this time.'

'I can see how a death at your eighteenth would spoil things for lots of people. Monroe's mum and dad would probably have to get a new sofa for one thing.'

'Are you really installing a kitchen tomorrow? I mean later on this morning?'

'Yeah.'

'But you were the head boy?'

'I was that.'

'And I didn't think schools made the sort of boys who become builders into their head boy. It would never have happened at my last school.'

'Well, this one did.'

'Wow.' Asta is impressed.

'And it did not,' says Josh. 'Because this is my year off. I'm working with Dad to build up some funds for when I go to uni next year to do civil engineering.'

'What's that?'

'It means I'm literally going to build bridges.'

'Literally?' Asta has to check the word is being used correctly. 'Really?'

'Yup, wanted to do it ever since I was a kid. What about you? How are you getting on with school now? Bit better?'

'It's not as bad as it was. I got invited to this party, right? It's my English class, they were the ones who asked me.'

'Ah, that makes sense,' says Josh. 'Souls of poets in Mr Feather's English classes.'

'Hang on, how come you did English A-level? Is knowledge of iambic pentameter crucial to the construction of bridges?'

'They're both all about the meter? Not really. I just liked English and wanted to do it for A level. Books and Lego. They were my sole interests between the ages of three and ten. Bit obsessive, could recite entire chapters of *Wind in the Willows* and *Treasure Island* from memory. Like a human audiobook, I was. I could give you a burst now if you fancy?'

'Would you like to?' asks Asta.

'Would you like me to?'

There's a bit of stand-off as neither of them knows what the right answer is. Two heartbeats and then at the exact same moment:

Asta: 'No, thanks, you're all right.'
Josh: 'I probably can't remember how most of it goes anymore anyway.'

A man with an arrow through his head comes and sits down opposite them. He's accompanied by a policeman wearing the sort of old-fashioned helmet that Bertie Wooster liked to purloin. Asta and Josh stare at them, they can't help themselves.

Feeling their eyes on him, the man with an arrow through his head glares back, realises what they're looking at and takes the arrow off, hooking it over his leg. Now it looks like someone has speared him through the knee. At the exact same moment, the policeman takes his helmet off and is sick into it. His companion has to stop him from putting it back on.

'I think we should nip outside for some fresh air,' says Josh.

'Good thinking,' says Asta and they both head for the exit.

'Sorry,' says a woman, who practically crashes into them on their way out. 'Sorry. Sorry.' Followed by a small husband in glasses, she rushes up to the reception and can be heard saying, 'I think my daughter must be here? Her name is Jenna Wendt.'

While the receptionist is checking to see, Josh and Asta double-back on themselves.

'Does Jenna have brown hair down to about here?' Asta chops a hand against each collarbone. 'About our age?'

'Yes.'

'You're Jenna's mum and dad then?' asks Asta. 'We were the ones who brought her in.'

'Oh, you angels!' says the woman. 'The alarm went off on my phone to say she was having a hypo. She didn't answer when we called, of course, and when we called the friend who's supposed to have been with her, they'd had an argument and gone their separate ways.' Her lip curls. 'So we hoped she was here and not lying on the sofa in some hellish house party that reeked of drugs with bottles of urine lined up along the mantelpiece.'

'It was just the one bottle,' says Asta.

She frowns and rubs her shoulder where Josh has bumped it.

'You should go through now,' the receptionist calls across to Mr and Mrs Wendt, her thumb on the button that releases the double door.

Jenna's mum dashes through while the dad shakes both their hands hurriedly.

'I'm sorry, we have to go. We haven't had the chance to thank you properly. You must tell me your names.'

They tell him.

'Rather unusual,' he says, an understandable code for *foreign and not easy to remember even though my own name is German in origin*. He prepares to make a note of them on his phone. All the while, his wife and the nurse are waiting in the open doorway.

'Here,' says Josh and hands him one of Vince's business cards. 'Please let us know when she's okay.'

'I will do,' he calls out just as the doors swing shut behind him.

The Yau Sum is all shut up by the time Josh drops Asta off and the upstairs flat is in darkness. This is a good thing.

'Thanks for the lift home,' she says as she quickly scans the footwell and space between the driver's and passenger's seats for anything she might have dropped.

'Couldn't leave you in the hospital, could I? And it seemed stupid to take you back to the party. I'm sure it drew to a premature end after we left.'

'I don't know if there would have been much of a party to go back to,' says Asta. 'Monroe's mum was forcing people to go around with recycling bags and black bin liners while you were getting the van up to the front door. She even got the Hoover out.'

'I'm glad I missed that,' says Josh. 'I never know if you're supposed to recycle crisp packets or not. Instead of helping clean up, we helped to save a girl's life. Not bad.' He looks over at Asta. 'I think we could make a pretty good team together.'

'Yeah, I think so too,' says Asta. 'We'll save lives and solve mysteries in a builders' van. They'll write books about us and turn us into the next streaming sensation.'

She looks over at the dismayed expression on Josh's face.

'We don't have to if you don't want to, it was just a joke,' she says. 'There is a mystery I do want to solve, though. Even if we can't find my Grandpa Charlie's Ela because she's dead or disappeared . . .'

'Oh yes?' says Josh, brightening up.

'. . . I'd love to know what happened between them. You do know what I mean, don't you? You read the letters. You like them as much as I do.'

'Uh huh.'

'Obviously, in a very important way, I'm glad it didn't work out otherwise I wouldn't exist, but the letters, they loved each other so much. What went wrong?'

Josh shrugs.

'I think I have a good suspect for who Ela is now,' says Asta. 'But I'm scared to ask in case it isn't who I think it is. I really want it to be her because she is so nice to me.'

'What makes you think it's her?'

'A feeling?'

She can sense Josh's disapproval fill the van.

'It's not much to go on,' he says. 'Remember when I said I could help you find out who she is? Well, that offer's still on. If you want it.'

He turns to face her.

'Oh hang on, I might be able to help you right now.'

He brushes a finger ever so gently across Asta's cheekbone.

'There,' he says. 'I know with one eyelash you blow on it and can make a wish but I think with this number, you should be able to make as many wishes as you like.'

Asta looks down to see Josh holding one of her false eyelashes. She squeals and pulls the sun visor down to inspect herself.

'I look like a droog!'

She peels the other eyelash off and puts her hand out so Josh can give her back the first one. He has to stifle a chuckle as he hands it over. She flings both eyelashes into the gutter as she gets out of the van, then leans back in through the window to say goodbye to Josh. He's had the same idea and is leaning across the passenger seat so they end up practically headbutting each other. Or kissing.

They spring apart like two magnets of the same polarity.

'Thanks for the lift,' says Asta.

'Will I see you around then?' asks Josh.

'How else are we going to find Ela if you don't?'

As Asta creeps along the hallway to her room, someone opens the living-room door.

'You didn't need to wait up,' says Asta. 'I said I'd be back before one.'

'I couldn't sleep anyway,' says Tim. 'What was the party like?'

Asta shrugs.

'Do you want some hot chocolate?'

Asta nods.

'It should be ready by now. I was going to leave yours to microwave when you got in but you're here now so might as well.'

Asta follows her father into the kitchen. As she passes the living room's open door, she can see the television is on. Three freshly whittled soap elephants stand on the desk, trunks forward, watching the news.

Tim pours from the saucepan into two big mugs, swirls cream on top and flicks chocolate from a yellow Cadbury's wrapper on top. He brings them over to the table.

'Did you wait up for me?' asks Asta. 'Or could you not sleep anyway?'

'Bit of both,' says Tim.

'I like your new elephants,' says Asta. 'They were always my favourite. Felix's too. Grandpa Charlie used to like your rabbits best of all though.'

'Did he?'

'Yeah, he used to call you Michelangelo and he always called the rabbits David. Don't you remember?'

Tim shook his head.

'No, because he never said anything like that to me.'

'Well, now you know,' said Asta.

She watches the bits of Flake still bobbing about on the cream. They're getting fuzzy around the edges but refusing to melt.

'Sometimes, I can't help feeling guilty,' says Asta.

'What about?' says Tim. 'What did you do?'

Asta can see thoughts of being a grandfather before his time race across his face.

'Nothing like that.' She takes a hot sip so she can gather her thoughts. 'I feel guilty because I had a nice time tonight. Sometimes, I don't think about Grandpa Charlie all day and that makes me feel like I'm forgetting him.' The hotness of the chocolate must be making her nose run. Her eyes water too. 'I don't want to forget him.'

'Me neither,' says Tim. 'I think about him a lot and it makes me wonder . . .'

'Wonder what?' says Asta.

'Wonder what he really thought of all of us.'

Asta opens her mouth but her father keeps talking. She shuts it again.

'I know what he thought of you and Felix. Unconditional love and affection. Proud of everything you've achieved. He liked how good at school you both were. Felix obviously but he was impressed with your GCSEs too. Brainy kids, he called you two. Chips not off the old block.' He sighs. 'I don't know. It's different with grandparents and grandchildren, a lot less complicated. All the good stuff, none of the bad stuff. You could never disappoint him. Me, on the other hand . . .'

Asta would like to know what to say to this but she doesn't. She looks down into her mug instead.

'I think hot chocolate can help you sleep if you can't,' she says. 'It's the tryptophan in the warm milk.'

'It doesn't work,' says Tim. 'Or I'd be comatose every night.'

'Should we talk about Grandpa Charlie more than we usually do? Like we did just now?'

Asta's father shakes his head.

'Mr and Mrs Li and their family say we should talk about people after they've gone. It keeps the memory of them alive for us.'

'How did that topic of conversation come up?' says Tim.

'We were just . . . we were . . . '

'I don't think I'm very comfortable with you discussing our private family life with the Li family. Perhaps we should think about getting you your own dog so you wouldn't have to keep going around there all the time. I'm sure Vince could make a little kennel out the back, fence a bit off.'

'I don't care about any other dog,' says Asta. 'Steve's my dog, even if I have to share him!'

She gets up.

'You just don't get it, do you?' she says, loud enough to make her point, quiet enough not to wake her mother.

A bit of a waste, really, as she slams the door when she leaves the kitchen.

'What's going on?' asks Mandy, all bleary-eyed, appearing in the doorway of Asta's parents' bedroom.

'Ask him,' says Asta, before going to her room where she climbs into bed and pulls the duvet over her head.

Chapter Twenty-Four

Those American high school films where the guy scores the winning goal at the big game and the next day all heads turn as he walks to his locker, and people randomly high-five him in the corridors?

Well, it's not quite like that, muses Asta as she goes to her first class, but it is probably as close as she is ever going to get.

'You did good, Aldi,' mutters a boy walking past, the knot on his school tie almost as big as his head.

'That's not her name, you idiot,' his friend says. 'It's Pasta.'

'What? Like fusilli?' He pronounces it F.U. Silly.

She notices previously resting bitch-faced students smile at her. Others turn to notice her for the first time. It's a bit unnerving but makes a nice change. She doesn't think she could cope with it if it went on for much longer than today, though.

Before she can get to her usual seat in class, Sophie intercepts her with a big hug.

'You're a hero,' she says. 'You saved Jenna's life!'

'Did I?' says Asta.

'Yes, you did,' says Callum, turning around, 'and nobody in her school knows you so it's all been mysterious heroics as far as they're concerned.'

'There's another high school in town?' asks Asta, astonished.

She's hated this school for such a long time. The thought of having missed out on a perfectly good Hogwarts within a radius of five miles is upsetting even if she is starting to get the hang of things here.

'She goes to the Welsh one now, Ysgol Ffuglen,' says Paige, also doing a one hundred and eighty degree turn from the row in front. 'She was here all the way up until GCSEs though. That's how everyone here knows her. She never got involved in cliques or bitchiness or anything like that. A bit like you, I suppose.'

Asta suspects Paige has confused not getting involved with anything like that with not getting involved with anything at all. Still, it's a compliment so she'll take it.

'And you left the party with Josh Palazzo too,' says Sophie.

Asta flushes and is about to say something horribly incriminating like 'we're just good friends', when Sophie chips in again.

'Just teasing. He must have been the only sober person at that party. You missed it, Asta, but when it started winding up after you left, the queue of mums and dads coming to collect was like the Monday after Glastonbury.'

The room falls silent as Mr Feather sweeps in with Miss Williams in tow. They both stand at the front of the class, Mr Feather behind and Miss Williams in front. The teachers and the students eye each other with varying degrees of suspicion until the class spots Mr Feather mouthing the words 'get up' behind Miss Williams's back.

Stunned, everyone stands up, just as Miss Williams turns to look at Mr Feather who is now a figure of stern composure once more.

'Thank you, class,' says Miss Williams. 'You may sit.'

'I don't see why I have to do it, Sir, I mean, Max. I don't know. This is definitely an out-of-school conversation taking place on school premises.' Asta glares at a couple of Year Eights walking past, curiosity painted across their zitty little faces. 'Can't one of the others have a go for a change?'

'Well, not exactly,' says Max. 'You see none of the others have been stalking my mother with quite the same degree of vigour as you have. What difference does it make to you? You still get to indulge your, to be honest, quite remarkable fascination with the elderly . . .'

He starts to wilt under the heat of Asta's hard stare.

'. . . I mean, your unique talent and empathy with the older members of our community. Do me a favour and take Miss Williams off my hands after school today?'

'Can't you tell her to go away?' says Asta.

They look across the school hall where Miss Williams is eating a piece of chicken. Just as she gets the fork close to her mouth, the morsel of meat falls off and lands in her lap. She looks around to make sure nobody has noticed. Max and Asta both know not to look away suddenly – such a giveaway that you've been watching – but to gaze serenely out of the window just beyond where Miss Williams is sitting. She seems satisfied no one's spotted her so she takes the bit of chicken out of her lap and pops it into her mouth.

'Am I going to have to feed her too?' says Asta.

'It won't be for much longer,' says Max. 'She's being made to retire from the Board of Governors. They want some young new blood on there instead. We just need to keep her, well, not sweet but happy until she goes.'

'What for? Does it even matter if she's leaving?'

'It's a tricky concept, it's called, oh what's it called? *Being nice*?'

There's being nice, and there's being *Nice*.

It's on the tip of Asta's tongue to say she saved a girl's life at the weekend but stops herself just in time. 'There's no lid on good deeds,' as Grandpa Charlie said. You can't 'rest on your laurels', as Ela wrote.

'Why can't *you* take her?' she asks.

'I have a pressing personal issue that I can't reschedule.'

'Really? What?'

Asta wants to push this one a bit further but on seeing Max's face, decides not to.

'You can have my clothbound *Mayor of Casterbridge* if you do this for me,' he says.

'Chuck in a copy of *Tess* and it's a deal.'

Chapter Twenty-Five

'Keep the change,' says Miss Williams, leaning forward to pay the taxi driver.

'Cheers,' he says and when he sees the size of the tip, he hops out of the car and opens up the door for her. Asta jumps out to meet her too. It takes a while but soon enough, Miss Williams is upright and outside of the car, not inside. Asta notices how slowly she releases her gnarly grip from the top of the car door.

'Do you think you can come back in half an hour?' Miss Williams asks the taxi driver just as he's about to drive off again.

'If I can't, I'll make sure someone else does, don't you worry, missus,' he says, before pulling one tanned arm back into the car all the better to drive with.

'Mrs,' says Miss Williams, shaking her head.

'Would it help if I took your arm?' asks Asta.

'I normally manage just fine on my own.'

But Miss Williams still crooks out an elbow so Asta slips her arm through and together, they walk through the gates of Cawsmenyn Town Cemetery.

On a day like today when the clocks sprang forward a few weeks ago, the afternoon is still bright and sunny, the onset of the evening delayed by one more hour. The cemetery is looking peaceful, the grass trimmed before last week's thunderstorm so the slivers and stubble of green that stuck to the headstones have all been washed away. Many of the graves have fresh new flowers but on closer inspection, some are extremely convincing fakes. Others have none at all and when Asta leans in to make out the dates on the headstones, she sees there are probably no family members left to bring flowers any more. Or if they are, they are metaphorically, chronologically and literally too far away.

Entire families lie together in one plot, their stories spelt out lightly in faded gold on black granite. Husbands whose wives passed long after they did. Couples who joined an infant child. Young men lost at tragically young ages with no indication of how they came to their untimely ends, only the love and loss of their parents etched into the stone for eternity.

Asta skims these mini-histories with her sharp teenage eyes while she keeps slow pace with Miss Williams.

'I expect you're wondering what we're doing here?' says Miss Williams.

'A little bit,' replies Asta.

'I've come to check the dates on my predecessor as headmistress. I'm preparing a history of my tenure at the school for the archives. We've had a long and happy association – Cawsmenyn Grammar, Cawsmenyn High, whatever it happens to be called – but all of that will come to an end when they retire me from the Board of Governors. Not my choice but we all get led out to the knacker's yard in the end. It could be worse, I suppose. We should all hope to outlive our usefulness. Not everyone is lucky enough to be able to do that.'

They've reached a wooden bench, slatted on the back, slatted on the seat, slatted on the arms at each end. Helium balloons have been tied to it after a young person's funeral but they no longer strain skywards. Instead, the curly foiled ribbon that's tethered them to the bench has gone slack, the balloons hovering inches off the ground.

Miss Williams sits down and makes an audible sound of relief as she does it.

'This is as far as I go, I'm afraid.'

She looks up the steep incline the path takes to the next part of the cemetery.

'In the days when I could still get all the way up there, I always fancied the view. You do have your mobile phone with you, don't you?'

Asta flushes, thinking of Mrs Yates's face at the recycling bins. She nods.

'Would you mind going up to call on her? Llinos Bellamy. Do you see that bend in the path there? Just past that, on the left. Please could you take a photograph of her so I have a record of the dates?'

Miss Williams seems a little short of breath.

'Will you be all right while I am gone?'

'Yes, I'm just a little overdressed for the weather.'

Miss Williams plucks at her heavy tweed jacket, undoes the top button, loosens her scarf.

'All right then, I won't be long.'

It is a very steep incline. The reward is indeed the view from the top as Asta looks down over the graveyard and into the patchwork of the housing estate beyond – all washing lines, trampolines and postage stamp lawns. She can see the traffic milling about in the distance but up here, it is country quiet. The yew trees sway in the breeze with what Mr Feather would call 'onomatopoeic susurration' and birds are not literally going tweet but something quite similar. She tries to see if she can wave to Miss Williams but can't spot her from this angle.

Finding Llinos Bellamy is not hard. Asta is surprised to see the headstone has an actual photograph of her – a benign-looking lady with her hair pulled back and actually wearing pince-nez. She's also astonished to see that the headstone gives Llinos Bellamy's address, a house that Asta walks past most days with Steve. There are no flowers but the grave has been well thought out, pleasingly smooth with no inside corners or edges to attract feathers, fluff or stray bits of greenery. She takes a photo of the headstone, as instructed, explains briefly to Llinos Bellamy that Pamela Williams sent her and then heads back down the hill.

She has to hop off the path, step into the space between a row of identical graves as a Volvo estate hurtles up the path and disappears around the corner. Even cemeteries are not immune to bad behaviour. She looks at the graves around her, all in Polish, none of them new, all looking very military.

'*Przepraszam*,' she whispers, before continuing on her way.

She quickens her pace as she approaches the bench. Miss Williams's head is slumped forward, eyes closed, no visible signs of life.

'Miss Williams!' she calls as she gets closer and then, 'Pam!'

Nothing.

But when she kneels down in front of the old woman to look into her face, Miss Williams lifts her head and Asta can see the AirPods in each ear.

'Rather a good signal for Classic FM here,' says Miss Williams. 'There will be some people in town quite jealous of that. Did you find Llinos?'

For some irrational reason, seeing Miss Williams so hale and hearty when she was supposed to be old and frail makes Asta feel even more angry than usual.

'Yes, I did. Do you want to see the photo?'

Miss Williams fiddles about with her phone. 'Can you AirDrop it to me?'

Once that's done, Miss Williams checks her watch.

'That half-hour went quickly,' she says. 'There's just enough time for me to go and see my mother. She's over here. You don't have to come with me. It's nice and flat so I will be able to manage it on my own.'

Asta has already sat down and is scratching some sort of graveyard insect bite on the back of her knee. She tries to work out whether Miss Williams wants a private moment with her mother or is just being polite. The latter, most likely, so she jumps up and gives only the tiniest of chases to catch up.

As they walk along, an ever-so-white butterfly lifts itself up from the grass. Another one joins it and they flutter ahead before coming to rest on a grey tablet of a headstone. Unlike many of the other graves, this is all there is and this means that someone has been able to plant flowers on the grave rather than leave cut ones behind in a pot. The grave has a generous scattering of small blue flowers, each with a burst of yellow in the centre.

'Oh,' says Miss Williams, looking pleased. 'The forget-me-nots are out for you, Mam.'

Asta raises an eyebrow. She wasn't expecting posh-voiced Miss Williams to say Mam. Mater, maybe, but not Mam. She looks at the grave of Mrs Jane Williams. Her husband, Mr Henry Williams, outlived her by only a year and they are *reunited at last*.

Asta shuffles about for a bit and kicks her toes against the tarmac while Miss Williams spends time with her parents. She spots another grave further along, beautifully maintained with both fresh and artificial flowers. There is a photo of a distinguished-looking man on a plaque resting on the grave, entirely separate from the headstone. He looks very handsome with a well-tended moustache. Older, distinguished, a proud half-smile and a mayoral chain. Asta feels a leap in her throat when she sees his name.

Miguel Lopez.

There can be only one Miguel Lopez. It's Cawsmenyn after all, not Cartagena.

'Oh Miguel,' says Miss Williams as she appears next to Asta. 'He was a rogue.'

'Did you know him?' asks Asta.

'Oh yes, he was one of the Basque children, evacuated here during the Spanish Civil War. There was a camp outside town, you know, because a small and excessively opinionated selection of people in town were suspicious, even of children appearing from a war-torn place in search of some semblance of peace. *Plus ça change*.'

'But did you know him?' repeats Asta. 'Properly.'

'Everybody did,' says Miss Williams.

A car horn honks three times, the sound coming from the direction of the gates. The taxi driver has come back.

'Run on and tell him I'm coming,' says Miss Williams. 'In case he goes without us.'

Asta races ahead, looking back before she turns the corner to make sure Miss Williams is still upright. Not only is she still standing, she seems to be looking carefully at Miguel Lopez's grave.

Chapter Twenty-Six

When Asta and Steve turn up at Elaine's house, the front door is wide open. So are all the doors on Max's car which is parked on the drive, the tailgate too. Steve thinks it all looks not quite right so he raises his tail and barks and barks, stopping only when Max appears in the doorway. He tugs on his lead, wanting to greet #208 on his list of close human friends but Max is very rudely ignoring him.

'What's going on?' Asta asks.

Max doesn't say anything, just flings a black bin liner over his shoulder, gathers up two McCain-branded cardboard boxes into his arms. They clearly do not contain oven chips any more. He goes back into the house. Elaine appears and crosses the stubby daisy-dotted lawn towards Asta and Steve.

'Max is moving in with me for a bit,' she says in a low voice.

'Don't tell her about my private life,' snaps Max from the upstairs window Asta knows belongs to the front bedroom.

'I didn't,' Elaine calls up to him tetchily. 'But I think you just did.' She turns her attention back to Asta. 'It's probably best you not come in today. We might have to cut down on your visits until Max has settled in.'

Asta panics.

'But I wanted to say that I know a builder who can box the boiler in for you!'

She says it so quickly, she has to repeat it twice before Elaine can understand her.

'Oh well, that's very good,' says Elaine. 'I'm fed up with looking at it when I'm in bed and it should block out some of the noises it makes. I'll talk to you about it another time.'

Josh: What did she say?

Asta: We got a problem.

Josh: Why did she say that?

Asta: She didn't! The problem is Mr Feather's moved in.

Josh: ???

Asta: He is her son.

Josh: Ela is Mr Feather's mum!

Josh: Can't we just ask him about it?

Asta: If you don't want your head bitten off we should stick with plan a. There is no plan b.

Asta: anyway he won't know about his mum's first love. People don't, do they?

Josh: Speak for yourself.

Asta: Is that supposed to be funny.

Josh: yes and no.

'You're not going out dressed like that, are you?' asks Mandy.

Asta wishes there was still a way to get out of the flat without having to go through the shop during opening hours. She looks down at herself. Jeans and a nice top.

'What's wrong with it?'

'I can't see the bare skin on your knees, thighs or shin. You're not wearing a hoodie.' Mandy leans in closer. 'Is that make-up you're wearing?'

Asta bites her lip and feels her teeth sinking into cherry lip gloss. She nods.

'Well, you look very nice. Much less scowly. You should do it more often.'

Asta smiles, proving her mother's point.

'Where are you going?' Mandy asks.

'To meet up with a couple of the guys who came in for a meal that time.'

And the girl whose life I saved, she doesn't add. She hasn't even mentioned it to her parents. You've got to have a private life, haven't you?

'But where are you going?'

'Um, not sure yet. I'll be with the others.'

'And what time do you think you'll get back?'

'I'll be back by half-nine for sure.'

'Well, make sure you do. It's a school night.'

In spite of Callum's confident plans he could get them all into the pub using his brother's ID, they have been relegated to the beer garden. It's just as well it's a nice day for them to sit under the lopsided, beer-branded parasol close enough to the car park; you can almost taste the diesel. Even to be allowed out here, someone has to have a meal and Jenna has volunteered to have something to eat.

'I don't mind,' she says. 'I need the carbs around about now anyway.'

Everybody looks away politely as she lifts her top up, pinches a bit of her flat tummy out and spears it with her insulin pen just as the waitress brings the tray over. She quickly bangs the plate down and hurries away.

Jenna shrugs. 'Some people don't like needles.'

'Callum is one of them,' says Paige.

'Can't help it,' he mutters, his head down somewhere between his knees.

'You need some exposure therapy, Callum, you big baby,' says Jenna. 'I can give myself some more injections. Look! In the arm!'

Jenna's prodding herself in the triceps with her injection pen, pushing the miniscule needle in and out of her skin but stops short of pressing down to release anything.

Asta's wondering if she made the wrong decision. Perhaps she should have let Jenna die.

'Stop making it all about yourself, Callum.'

Jenna dunks a chunky fat chip into the tiny dish of ketchup and takes a bite, chewing loudly with her mouth open.

'I can't help it,' comes a muffled reply.

'He's right, he fainted dead away when he had to have his yellow fever injections,' says Paige.

'Let's hope he doesn't get diabetes then,' says Jenna. 'At least three jabs a day with Type One! You think the size of this needle is bad, you should see the one for blood tests. Like a biro it is. Every six months, you'll get to feel a bit of a prick in your arm.'

Asta should definitely have let her die.

'Chip anyone?' says Jenna, offering the plate around.

Callum immediately feels strong enough to rouse himself to get one.

'See?' says Jenna. 'He's fine.'

She winks at Asta, who turns around to see if anyone more wink-worthy is standing behind her. There is nobody there.

'The real reason we're here is for me to thank this one.'

Jenna lifts up her sparkling water and clinks her glass against Asta's.

'Thanks, you literally saved my life. I've never seen you around. Where you from?'

'Traeth,' says Asta. 'We moved here last summer.'

Jenna nods. 'Explains why you sound so posh.'

'It's not posh down there,' says Asta.

'It's the English dash to the Pembrokeshire coastline, isn't it? Buying it all up for second homes.'

Paige and Callum roll their eyes. *Oh no, not this again.* It turns out Jenna Wendt is quite the passionate nationalist with a teenage enthusiasm for Welsh independence.

' . . . and that's why I decided to go to do my A levels in the Welsh-medium school,' Jenna concludes. 'And I'm going to do my degree in Welsh in Cardiff too. Differentiation, vectors, matrices, all in Welsh. It's going to be bloody fantastic.'

Alliteration. Assonance. Metonymy. These are the A level expressions Asta is used to.

'What are you studying?' she asks, mystified.

'Maths, of course,' says Jenna. 'Don't tell me you're one of those?'

'One of those what?'

'*I don't do maths, I can't do sums. Where's the calculator on this phone?*'

'Come on now, Jenna,' says Paige. 'We've told you this before. Callum and I, Asta too probably, have the souls of poets and we're not interested in your multiplication maths hacks even if your Insta Reel did get three hundred and two views. Now, does anyone want another drink?'

18 Rupert Street
London
SE1 8AW
18th March 1965

Darling C,

Clemmie asked me to go into London town with her today and rather a smart part of it too. Her mother has promised her a nice bit of jewellery for her twenty-first and she wanted me to help her choose. She asked me what Mam gave me for my twenty-first; I showed her my watch and she said she liked it but she was going 'to eschew practicality for something pretty'. This from someone doing Pure Mathematics! No, I don't know what makes it pure either.

The thing about London is you can walk down some streets and every single shop sells the same thing in a way that never happens at home. In Cawsmenyn, you amble down the high street and it's butcher's, sweet shop, bakery, ironmonger, greengrocer but here, you go to one part of town to be surrounded by a dozen butchers, a shoal of fishmongers or a forest of florists! And it's the same with jewellery shops. What would Brian the Diamond think of having even one other jeweller in town apart from him?!

To begin with, it was amazing to see so much
silver and gold, so many rubies, sapphires and emer-
alds winking away at us from the shop windows.
Trays and trays of them and when you went inside,
glass cabinets filled with even more. Necklaces with
pearls of pink, silver and grey. Cameo rings with the
girl's profile always turning shyly away from you.
Gold chains, some so delicate you could hardly see
them, and others thick as the string you use to tie
up a parcel.

I tried to get Clemmie to narrow down what she
wanted. Did she want a brooch, a necklace or a
bracelet? She said she would know when she saw it
and until she saw it she would have to look at everything and she did mean <u>everything</u>.

We were peering into the window of the umpteenth
jeweller. She was just next to me, ogling a triple string
of shiny not-diamonds that looked more like it should
be around the neck of a poodle than a human. That's
when I saw it on a tray all on its own, not sharing
it with half a dozen other bits and pieces. A round
gold pendant with a plus sign picked out in tiny red
stones on the top and a minus sign in tiny white stones
beneath it.

'Look,' I said. 'That's the one for you. A maths pendant!'

We both pressed our faces against the window, smudging the glass, and of course we had to go in.

The jeweller explained it wasn't a maths pendant. He brought it out for us to look at and underneath the plus sign was the word *qu'hier* and underneath the minus it said *que demain*. I could translate the French: *than yesterday* and *than tomorrow*, but I still didn't understand. Then he explained it to us.

'It's from a famous French poem about love. The necklace says *plus*.' He pronounced it the French way. 'Which we should translate as more than or greater than. Something similar for the minus. It means *moins* or less than. The words "I love you" are implied from the original poem so the necklace is saying, "I love you more than yesterday and less than tomorrow."'

And it struck me then, stood there in a dimly-lit little shop hundreds of miles away from you, that this necklace knows all about me and knows exactly how I feel about you. What a clever thing it is!

Of course, Clemmie didn't like it, saying that the positive and the negative cancelled each other out. She is Pure in Mathematics but I have the soul of a poet and so does the necklace. If a necklace can have a soul at all!

She still hasn't found anything she likes so I suspect we will be back in Hatton Garden again before her birthday in two months' time.

Loving you more than yesterday, less than tomorrow!

E x

Chapter Twenty-Seven

'Well, I could just box the boiler in for you? Or I could make it a floor-to-ceiling cupboard so you can keep the vacuum cleaner and things in there too. Nice and tidy and out of the way.'

Josh taps the pencil against his bottom lip, puts it behind his ear again. Then carries on making a note of all the measurements on his phone.

Asta is sitting on Elaine's bed, wondering if there's anything Ela-related hidden under it. She scans the rest of the bedroom, the wardrobe, the drawers, the book-case. There's even a hatch to the loft in here. Could there be anything concealed in any of these places? Would she have time to investigate them all under the cover of banging, drilling and cupboard installation?

'How much will it cost?' asks Elaine, propped up in the doorway, narrowing her eyes, trying to imagine what it will look like.

'Oh, you'll get mates' rates, Mrs Feather,' says Josh, looking over at Asta.

'That's very kind. Do call me Elaine though.'

'Elaine?' Josh nods. 'Don't meet too many Elaine's these days unless they're going by shorter versions of their names. You know, Josh for Joshua? Asta for Augusta? Ellie for Elaine?'

'Ellie? Like Miss Ellie?' says Elaine, laughing.

Asta and Josh are mystified. He keeps going though.

'Any nicknames when you were younger?' he asks.

'They used to call me Snowdon on account of being so tall,' says Elaine. 'Always asking what the weather was like at the peak. Didn't like it much. Stopped that once Princess Margaret married Antony Armstrong-Jones and he got called Earl Snowdon. They just called me Beanpole after that.'

'I'll need to check on the cost of the materials and then I'll message you the price?' says Josh. 'How does that sound?'

'When do you think you can fit it in?' asks Elaine.

'I'm working with Dad in the day and in the evenings, it's only really Wednesday I've got free.'

'I'm not in on Wednesdays,' says Elaine. 'It's my yoga class.'

Josh already knows that and he could do it any evening really.

'I can come with Josh on a Wednesday so there'll be someone here as well. Just in case?' says Asta.

She hopes it doesn't sound too well scripted so Elaine won't suspect a thing.

'Oh no, Asta, it will be fine because Max will be here, won't he, now he's staying here for a bit.'

Asta agonises for an age on where to put her phone for the Facetime with Josh. It doesn't really make sense as he's probably seen the room lots of times when he's been working in the flat. But her room is one of the few that hasn't been revamped yet so maybe not? In any case, she experiments with different backgrounds. Against the window so you can see the pole of the street light? On the bed with the frilly flowery pillowcases? On the chest of drawers so she's against an expanse of plain magnolia wall?

In the end, she opts for sitting on the floor with her back against the door, MDF panels in plain sight, safe from any parents barging into the room. Josh said he'd call as soon as he finished installing Elaine's new cupboard but how long is that going to take?

Ages as it turns out. If 9.45 p.m. can be counted as ages.

'Hey,' says Josh.

'What happened?' asks Asta. 'Sorry, I mean, hi Josh. It's so nice of you to call. What happened?'

'Mr Feather's really nice, isn't he?'

'I don't want to talk about Max. Did you manage to find out anything about Ela?'

'I'm not sure. I didn't get a chance to have a proper snoop because Mr Feather – he did say I could call him Max now but it seems weird, doesn't it? – was with me almost all of the time. He was really useful, though, for holding things and passing me stuff. I said it was a case of me teaching him now.'

'So you didn't get a chance to look to see if there was anything? At all?'

'I asked Mr Feather if I could have a toasted cheese sandwich with Emmental and sliced tomato. He said they only ever have cheddar so I did my puppy dog look . . .'

Josh dips his chin and stretches his eyes up to the camera.

'. . . and he offered to go the shop and get some. That's when I looked in the drawer of the bedside cabinet, like you said, and there was a box with her passport and birth certificate in it, and other important looking stuff, but no sign of her ever having been called Hennessy. Her maiden name was Jones and she's only been married once and that was to Mr Feather's dad.'

Asta groans. She doesn't fancy explaining the complex and difficult story behind why the dead Mr Feather is not Max's natural dad.

'I couldn't find any letters at all so if your Grandpa Charlie sent any back to her, she hasn't kept them.'

'I suppose you don't, do you?'

'Oh, I don't know. If I ever got a love letter, I'd keep it. Unless we broke up horribly. Then, the shredder.'

'I don't know. It's not exactly turning out how I wanted it to. Did they even have shredders in those days?'

'I think you may have got this arse over backwards, Asta. You've decided Elaine is Ela and you're looking for the evidence that she is. What we should do is look at all the letters again and see where the evidence points us?'

'But my gut!'

'Why? What's wrong? Did you eat something that's gone off?'

'No, my gut feeling. What my heart is telling me. That's what they say isn't it. Listen to your heart. Go with your gut.'

Josh pulls a face.

'Where did you hear that? They're just organs in your body. One pumps blood and the other digests food.'

Asta explains they'd both been bespoke wall-art quotes she'd written up for Write4U.

'This is the problem,' says Josh. 'Your heart and gut want it to be Elaine but I don't think it is.'

'No,' says Asta. 'I should go to Elaine's and have another look on my own. Me and Steve could do it. How long is Max staying for?'

'That's the thing. Max has broken up with his fiancée. They're selling their house. He showed it to me on Zoopla. I think Dad might like to have a word with the builder they used for the extension. Anyway, he's going to be living with Elaine for now.'

Asta's not happy. How can she keep an eye on Elaine/ Ela if Mr Feather is going to be there all of the time?

'No, you can't keep barking up the wrong tree,' says Josh. 'Tell you what. You bring the letters around to mine. It's been ages since I read them and I only did it the once. Perhaps we can get more headway if we work on it together?'

'I suppose we do make a good team,' says Asta grudgingly.

Chapter Twenty-Eight

'Hello, young Asta. Come on in,' says Vince.

Asta steps over the threshold.

'Shoes off if you don't mind.'

Asta shucks them off and pads after Vince into the house. At the bottom of the stairs, Vince shouts up, 'Asta's here!' and there is a disturbing bump.

'Don't know what he does up there,' says Vince, leading the way into the kitchen. 'Gets onto the wardrobe and jumps off at regular intervals?'

'Oh really?' says Asta, uncertain if it's a joke or not.

Vince stares at her. 'I think it's more to do with his barbell.'

Vince puts the pods into the coffee machine. 'So, you're looking for the girl who wrote some letters, yeah?'

Asta's astonished Josh has told him all about it. She still hasn't mentioned it to her parents. She only wants to present it to them when she's found the solution, not turn up with another problem. Josh must have felt able to tell Vince because he hasn't got any skin in this game.

'I'd like to. Did you read the letters?'

'When he found them in your place? No chance. Fifty per cent of the team has got to do the work. He read a couple out loud to me but I couldn't really hear them over the sound of the drill. Now, let's see if there's any cake left.'

Vince goes into the fridge and brings out a solitary piece of millionaire's shortbread.

He scratches his head.

'You have it,' he says. 'Looks like we've run out. Josh was on a baking spree for a while back there. He told me he was having to take his mind off of a girl but it must all be sorted now.'

Asta has a different sort of gut feeling. She doesn't like it.

'Which is good, I suppose, but it means I'll have to buddy up with Mr Kipling again. Still, it was fun while it lasted. Go on, you have it.'

He pushes the cake towards Asta.

'No thank you,' she says. 'My appetite's gone.'

Vince shrugs and pushes it into his mouth all in one go. It is, to be honest, quite a small bit of cake. Not that small though. Out of nowhere, Bruce Willis shouts, *Yippee ki yay, mother—!* Vince checks his phone and shows the message to Asta.

Can you ask Asta to come up to my room please?

While she's looking at it, another message comes through.

> The worst of the mess is in the laundry basket in your
> room. I'll pick it up after she's left.

'Whoops,' says Vince. 'You probably weren't supposed
to see that. Take this coffee up to him, would you?'

Josh's bedroom is so enormous, it looks like what it
is – two bedrooms knocked into one. At the far end
are the embarrassing bits like the bed, wardrobe, bean
bag, PlayStation. This end, the one closer to the door,
is more of a hobby room with an enormous desk and
shelves crowding the walls around it. In the spaces
between books are fully constructed Lego kits but
instead of wonky houses in primary colours, they are
all the muted greys of the Lego Architecture not-for-
children collection – the Burj Khalifa, the New York
skyline, Brandenburg Gate.

Josh has brought a dining chair up to the room and
the other chair is a full swivelling, five-wheeled, high-
backed office number.

Asta puts the pile of letters onto the desk, then undoes
the bit of string that's holding them together.

'So, this is all of them?' asks Josh.

'Think so.'

'Not as many as I thought,' says Josh. 'I suppose I'd
better get reading.'

He opens a drawer in the desk and pulls out some
paper and a pen. He starts clicking and unclicking it on
and off in a way that sets Asta's teeth on edge.

'I don't know if I need to read them again,' she says. 'I almost know them off by heart.'

'Didn't Mr Feather use to say it's re-reading the text that brings you closer to the author?' asks Josh.

He's inscribing poker-straight notes in tiny hand-writing onto unlined paper. It's quite impressive! He settles back into reading, his elbow propped onto the table, his chin in his hand. Asta admires his profile briefly, imagines herself the heroine of a Jane Austen novel, etching her sweetheart's silhouette.

She sighs and reaches out for a letter. She starts reading.

18 Rupert Street
London
SE1 8AW
10ᵗʰ March 1964

Dear Charlie,

Thank goodness it's nearly the end of term and on Friday, I am coming home! For three whole weeks! I will, of course, miss your letters but hopefully we will get the chance to see each other in person?

It will be nice to see Sali again too and to catch up with her properly as she is not a good correspondent. She's just as bad on the telephone. Mam says she will go to the kiosk at the Post Office with her and is much her usual self all the time she is dialling the number (I'm afraid there are rather a lot of eights and nines in the telephone number here) and even up until the pips go and she has to put the shilling in. As soon as we are connected, she gets tongue-tied and I hear her breathing heavily as she hands the phone over to Mam. Honestly, you would never believe it from talking to her normally, would you? I think some people are just better at being with you in the here and now. She takes a terrible photo too, you know, always blinks at the wrong moment or looks away, but as you know, she is so pretty and chatty and gregarious in real life, the complete opposite of me.

Chatty and gregarious? That could be you so I'm sorry it's not worked out with Jeanette who is <u>also</u> chatty and gregarious. Perhaps it is, in fact, opposites that attract? You should immediately seek out the quietest, shyest girl for your next pursuit although the irony is: how would you find her?

As for me, Clemmie very much has got the hint about never attempting any kind of double-dating again without telling me first. Even if she tells me first, I won't go. I'll have to make sure I'm washing my hair that night, anything to get out of having to accompany her, Barry and A. N. Other to some dance party or nightclub. I'd much rather spend my spare evenings with John Donne or Andrew Marvell. Yes, they are poets, but not like Dylan Thomas. Dylan took his trousers into the laundry where Mam worked once and she said his legs were ever so short but he had the presence of a taller man.

Maybe there is time for one more letter from you before I leave London?

Yours hopefully,

Ela

18 Rupert Street
London
SE1 8AW
12th April 1964

Dearest Charlie,

So here I am again. Back in London, sitting at my desk, looking out of the window while working out what to write. That white cat with the silvery bits of tabby on its face and tail is out there on the roof of next door's corrugated steel shed. It is literally a cat on a hot tin roof except Elizabeth Taylor was not keeping an eye on the bird table and trying to work out when and where to pounce!

It's all the same but also, in the most important way of all, totally different. I miss you so much already and I can't believe we won't see each other again until the end of June when term finishes. Still, we have our letters. Did you mean it when you said you would write every day? Well, if that's what you're doing, it's what I'm going to do too! I realise our letters might overlap and we will end up talking to each other at cross purposes but this letter is half written now anyway.

I got in late last night and Clemmie was out with her Barry so I didn't see her until this morning and the first thing she said was, 'You look different!' I asked her in what way and she said a very good way, like I'd been bathed in sunlight and I wasn't anywhere near as glum as I used to look. I just smiled and looked pleased. I have decided to call it, 'The Charlie Tonic — banishes the gloom to give you a bloom'. Now what do my lecturers know, saying I haven't got a way with words! That's as good as 'Put a Tiger in Your Tank' and 'Drinka Pinta Milka Day'. The thing is they are both advertising slogans and I only really want one person to be able to enjoy The Charlie Tonic and that person is me!

Anyway, I didn't tell Clemmie why I looked so well until later on when we were strolling around the market down Petticoat Lane. It is a very special market, not least because it's open on Sundays. We didn't need anything but it's the sort of market that's more like going to see a show than going to see some shops. Traders selling sets of china by throwing plates and cups into the air and catching them. It makes your heart go into your mouth just watching! Toothless old ladies at the jellied eels stall, sucking the meat off of the curly fishbone and leaving it behind. A Pearly King and Queen, just standing around waiting to be noticed. They didn't have to wait long!

There was one thing I did spot, though, and that was all sorts of people from all over the world strolling through the market. You could hear it when you walked about, all the different accents and all the different faces and hairstyles. Lots of mixed couples like us too and nobody batted an eyelid. That would be nice, wouldn't it? Not that it bothers me. Staring at us is rude. Saying rude things to us is rude and we should just ignore it. I'm glad we're agreed on that. Still, for the most part, back home people know us for who we are. Lovely as it was down the market today to see so many different kinds of folk around, I wouldn't be surprised if I never saw any of them ever again.

I know it's annoying when everyone knows everybody else's business in Cawsmenyn but there really is something to be said for it when the chips are down. It's good to be anonymous and pass through the streets incognito too, but if I had to pick one over the other, I know which one it would be!

It's back to lectures again tomorrow and an early start on Mondays which I'm not fondest of. Best get on with Sunday-night preps, which Clemmie insists should include plaiting my hair before bed to stop its bird-nest qualities. Oh, that's her knocking on the door to come and do it for me now.

Lots of love,

Ela

Asta tugs at her own hair. It's naturally poker straight, sleek and shiny but she still runs her GHDs along each strand after she washes it.

'All right?' says Josh, next to her. He seems to produce an awful lot of heat for one mortal boy. 'Where you up to?'

'Ela's just gone back to uni after the second Easter and they're a couple now.' She wishes she knew how her Grandpa Charlie and Ela got out of the Friend Zone. 'How about you?'

Josh looks over at his notes, now onto their second page.

'Charlie's mum and stepdad have bought themselves a new takeaway in Traeth. That must be the one you used to live in, right?'

Asta nods.

'And they're trying to staff it up and do some Charlie matchmaking at the same time. *Killing two birds with one stone?* Is that what they used to say?'

'I think we just call it multi-tasking now,' says Asta.

18 Rupert Street
London
SE1 8AW
4th May 1964

Darling Charlie,

I know I've said this before but thank you so, so much for keeping writing your wonderful long letters these past few weeks even though you've not been getting anything nearly as good back. Those letters and the photo of you with Guto's horse pulling a jib have been the only things that have kept me going while I've been revising like mad for the exams. They're not even the final ones (also known as the ones that really count!) so I don't know how I will cope this time next year! Your letters have been a lifesaver. I have just one exam left now and luckily, the last one is the easiest one for me, so I think I will be all right to have half an hour to write and send this to you.

You made me laugh when you told me about that man coming down to see about the new chef job at the shop in Traeth and bringing his daughter with him! It's not even as if his daughter was a small child who needed looking after, even though you did have to chaperone her while Ada and George put the man through his paces.

No, it's not an insult to call a girl of eighteen a full-grown woman because that is what she is, never mind the age of majority. She is old enough to be married, after all. I expect that couple of hours you spent walking the street – not even streets! – and beach-with-the-tide-in of Traeth can't have been that bad. If her father gets the job, I suppose you will be seeing a lot more of her.

Your <u>loving girlfriend</u> (and don't you forget it!)

Ela xxxx

18 Rupert Street
London
SE1 8AW
22nd May 1964

Dear Charlie,

Mam said she bumped into your mother down the market the other day. They were both at the fabric stall. She thought it would be nice to say something to her, on our account, but Ada wasn't very friendly or pleased to see my mam. When Mam said it must be hard for us spending so much time apart (and it is, I can tell you), a funny look came across Ada's face and she said, 'Ah, one of Charlie's lady friends.'

So I have to ask you. Am I one of Charlie's lady friends because he has had several, past and present? Or am I one of Charlie's lady friends all at the same time, right now?

Yours,

Ela

18 Rupert Street
London
SE1 8AW
23rd May 1964

Dearest Charlie,

Well, of course, after your telephone call, Mrs Taylor and Clemmie rallied around me because any unscheduled phone call must be serious. It didn't help that I burst into tears, <u>with relief</u>, as soon as you rang off!

I think I understand your not telling Ada about us. I have told Mam and Sali, of course, and they are just fine with all of it. Rather pleased, in fact.

Perhaps when I come back for the long summer break, we can tell your mother together but not if it cuts into the time we get to spend together. I already have plans for us to have long walks, bike rides, day trips and picnics often.

In the meantime, please can you write by return with anything Ada or George might like from here in London that they can't find back home and I will make sure to get it.

Love,

Ela x

Photographic postal card company – London – Eros and Piccadilly Circus	
It's a long way to Cawsmenyn It's a long way to go It's a long way to Cawsmenyn To the sweetest boy I know Goodbye Piccadilly! Farewell Leicester Square! It's a long long way to Cawsmenyn But my heart's right there. See you very soon, E xxx	Charlie Fung Yau Sum 77 Joyce Street Cawsmenyn

18 Rupert Street
London
SE1 8AW
24th September 1964

Darling Charlie,

I miss you!

I miss you!

I could keep writing that over and over to show how much I miss you but then that would make for quite a boring letter.

What I don't miss is the strange cabbage smell here in Mrs Taylor's house. It's still here and I know you said I should move to different lodgings but I don't think I can afford to take any risks here in my final year. Peculiar as it can be here, I know how it all works and Clemmie is back for her final year too so we will struggle through it, the two of us together.

I almost made a mistake and missed the turning for Rupert Street off the main road and that's because, ta-dah, there is now a phone box at the end of the street! I did notice it there, thought I must have got my bearings wrong. It just looked so red and so shiny and so new. Not so new that it doesn't already have its array of 'business' cards stuck up inside but who cares? It's a telephone at the end of my street so I can call you whenever I like! It will have to be during the day, I suppose, as I can imagine your mother's face when she realises the business line is engaged.

The thing is I will have lectures at different times of the day and as I don't have my timetable yet, I can't tell you when I will be able to call you. As soon as I have it, I will write and let you know but for our very first phone call, how about half past ten, this Saturday morning? We can talk for a lovely long time at weekend rates and my purse will bulge with shillings as I jangle my way down the road!

I can't wait!

All my love,

Ela xx

18 Rupert Street
London
SE1 8AW
30th October 1964

Dearest Charlie,

I'll miss our telephone calls, of course, but I suppose it is quite right what your mother says when she says a business line is for business calls only. It is a bit of a relief because the phone calls are expensive and I suppose neither of us wanted to be the first one to say that. So Ada has done us a bit of a favour by putting a stop to it, I suppose.

I seem to have got a bit rusty at writing letters which is a poor show. I was going to hold off on sending this but then, I thought, a small, not-very-good letter is better than no letter at all.

Love as usual,

Ela x

18 Rupert Street
London
SE1 8AW
23rd November 1964

Dearest Charlie,

Yes, the engagement ring is absolutely beautiful. It fits perfectly too and in spite of myself, I do love it.

I won't be saying any of that in front of Harri, however.

I have no idea when exactly he started sniffing around Mam again and you can see why she didn't tell me until this fait accompli because I would have been on that train from Paddington in two shakes of a lamb's tail.

As it was, I only managed to get there for one night for the engagement 'party'. Thanks again for coming with me. I know that it must have been hard to ask your mother and George for the time off but I did need you there and after those things he said about us stepping out, about you, well, I wouldn't have blamed you if you'd said no and I love you for being big enough to say yes.

Harri did seem changed, didn't he? Do you believe him when he said he's given up the drink? There is no more of that awful lingering whisky, brandy, beery smell about him now and his apology seemed sincere enough. When he shook your hand, I thought he was never going to let go of you.

I could have done with less of the 'you don't have to call me Dad'. It hadn't even crossed my mind.

I did see the way he looked at Mam when he really didn't know I was watching. If I had to pick a word to describe it, it would be 'besotted', which, I suppose, is good?

I asked Auntie Gaynor what she thought Daddy would say about all of this and she said he would have wanted her to be happy. I can't believe she didn't let Sali come along. She used to love a get-together and I haven't seen her since the summer.

'Oh no, Ela love,' she said. 'Sali's a different girl since you-know-what. She'll be happy enough at home with a ball of wool and Mrs Dale's Diary.'

She made it sound like Sali is a kitten! I wonder if she would have tried to see Miguel if she'd come. Perhaps it's just as well she wasn't allowed.

I wonder now if I've been selfish, leaving Mam behind with a houseful of paying strangers while I waltzed off to London. Would she have accepted a proposal from someone like Harri if I'd been there to look out for her?

As for him, I blow hot and cold although there can be no doubt about how Mam feels. I know it because she looks on the outside so completely how I feel about you on the inside. I know there are those who don't think I should be allowed to feel that way about you so I don't think I should judge Mam for something that makes her so happy?

Honestly, they were even giddier than we are when we're together. Which is not nearly as often as it should be.

I am worried that it is all a bit hasty, getting married in the first week of January. That is for my sake, they claim, so I can go to the wedding and not have to come back again after term starts. Do you know what Mam said when I asked her if she didn't think it was all a bit rushed? She said at her time of life, she didn't have a moment to spare and she intended to grasp at any opportunity to be happy and to hold onto it tight.

I can't fault that but I will be keeping a beady eye on Harri and his activities when I come home for Christmas and for — I can't quite believe I am writing this — my mam's wedding.

You will come to the wedding, won't you?

All my love,

E xx

'That's a big sigh,' says Josh.

Asta looks up. She didn't even notice.

'I've reached the bit where Ela's mum is going to marry the lodger.'

'Ah,' says Josh. They exchange disapproving looks. 'Yes, I know.'

'I just don't get it,' says Asta. 'How can Ela's mum marry Harri after he hit her that time?'

'It sounds like he turned over a new leaf,' says Josh.

'A leopard can't change its spots,' replies Asta.

'Looks like he managed to do it,' says Josh. 'Better late than never.'

'Better safe than sorry.'

'Well, the early bird catches the worm?'

'That one doesn't make sense,' says Asta.

'I know,' says Josh. 'I couldn't think of any other old sayings that fit. Anyway, Ela's mum and Harri, well, he was in the wrong but she forgave him. Ela's in two minds though, Charlie too probably.'

Asta does another of her epic sighs. 'I suppose everybody deserves a second chance. Don't they?'

11 Seaview Cottages
Porthgynffon
South Glamorgan
1ˢᵗ January 1965

Beloved and wonderful Charlie,
   HAPPY NEW YEAR!
   I hope it was just busy enough in your shop last night and not at all like it has been for the past few years with the drinking and swearing and fighting. And that's just you, Ada and George!
   The funniest thing happened here last night. It was too cold to go out even if we wanted to so Mam and Auntie Gaynor got out the cherry brandy and the port and lemonade and soon they were talking nineteen to the dozen about people who'd died, people who'd nearly died, people they thought were dead but then bumped into down the shops and realised hadn't died at all. It would almost have been funny if Sali and I hadn't been trying to watch the television. We tried shushing them but they kept shushing us back.
   Anyway, by midnight, the old folk were the worse for wear while we young ones were trying our hardest to stay up just to see the New Year in. As soon as Big Ben binged his last bong, we all headed for bed.

Then ten minutes later, there was a loud banging at the front door. We tried to ignore it, thinking it was someone who wasn't very good at Knock Down Ginger but it would only stop for a bit, then start up again. In the end, we all met up on the landing in our nighties to see what to do.

Mam said we should call the police. Auntie Gaynor said it could be the police calling to tell us about something awful that had happened. Sali said the only people she knew well enough for the police to call to tell her about were standing right next to her. So I put my dressing gown on and went and opened the door.

And it turned out to be the doctor, the one we had to tell him all about Sali that time. He was three sheets to the wind, he was holding a massive lump of coal and kept shouting something about his foot. Anyway, it turns out first footing is a Scottish custom for tall, dark handsome men to be the first to call at the house each New Year because it brings you luck and it turns out Dr Carmichael is Scottish and he likes Sali very much and, more importantly, she likes him! She is a dark horse for never having mentioned any of this to any of us. The Sali of old would talk nineteen to the dozen about every boy who caught her fancy and she certainly would not have looked twice at a short, greying middle-aged widower. I didn't dare say anything about that making him a bit of a second footer!

Anyway, it was all so exciting and I'm wide awake now so I thought I would write and tell you about it even though I might get home and tell you all about it again before this letter even arrives with you.

It was so wonderful and romantic and unexpected! What with Mam and Harri's wedding next week, it looks like love is in the air for the brand new year!

Can't wait to see you again.

All my love,

Ela xxx

18 Rupert Street
London
SE1 8AW
18ᵗʰ January 1965

Dearest Charlie,

Well, here I am back in my little study room in Rupert Street after meeting up with Mam and Harri on their way back to Wales from Brighton. We had a lovely cream tea in town where the tiny cakes came on a three-tier stand and the sandwiches with their crusts cut off. Harri kept lifting his pinkie every time he took a sip of tea and insisted on using his 'posh' voice. Mam giggled like mad every time he did it and I tried to join in. Well, I had to.

Mam told me about this woman they kept seeing in their hotel. They were only there for a week but they saw her with four different men. All the men looked very shifty, she said, really uncomfortable and she thought the woman must be a prostitute and the men her clients. It turned out they were her clients but not in the way you expect. The men all wanted divorces but you can't get divorced unless you can prove adultery and usually, there isn't any, so then you have to hire someone to be 'the other woman'. She holes up in a hotel bedroom with them all night playing cards or reading a book and in the morning, Bob's your uncle. Or your soon-to-be ex-husband!

I wondered if it was a bad sign to bump into someone who specialises in divorce while on your honeymoon. Mam used to be very much into reading tea leaves, crossing palms with silver and all that sort of thing but no, I could see it hadn't even occurred to her so I didn't press the matter. She used to be so superstitious, always feeling everything she saw or heard was a sign of something when really it was just a snapped shoelace or a broken saucer. She puts on a good act outside the house but she's been a bit of a nervous wreck for as long as I've known her. Is it my imagination or was she never like that when my daddy was around?

The more I see them together, the more grateful to Harri I feel for making her so happy and that is definitely not something I could have said even five months ago. It just goes to show that you never can tell what will happen next.

Love,

Ela

18 Rupert Street
London
SE1 8AW
27th January 1965

Dearest Charlie,

It's a funny one, isn't it, and a bit of a tricky one too.

I am (of course!) with George on this one and advise you to take tea, or whatever it is that Ada wants you to do, with this succession of young 'cousins' who travel all the way from Cardiff, Liverpool and Manchester to see you. I find the lack of Y chromosomes amongst your wider family really quite remarkable. I suppose you must have male cousins and it must be their busy schedules that prevents them from visiting their 'auntie' and her rather fabulous son!

It probably is more trouble than it's worth to do otherwise and it's not these unfortunate young women's fault that your mother and their parents have sent them on a fool's errand all the way down to quiet Cawsmenyn.

Yes, I seem breezy while writing this letter but what else can I do? I can hardly hop onto the train and scratch at these girls' eyes and pull at their hair. I very much would like to but the fact that you tell me about them means I feel better about it all.

I am pleased that your stepfather thinks of us as a proper couple even though we spend so much time apart. Do you think he might be able to convince your mother of that too? I know I have nothing to worry about but in the wee small hours of the morning, or the slightly boring moments of a very dull lecture, I can't help thinking silly thoughts.

Clemmie has asked me if I will go with her to see Winston Churchill in his coffin at Westminster Hall and I have said yes. She feels she has to go with a name like hers and it is the least we can do.

Love,

Ela x

18 Rupert Street
London
SE1 8AW
17th June 1965

Dearest Charlie,

Thank you so much for coming to see me even
though it was just for one day. I know how difficult it
must have been to get the time away from your mother
and work and the shop.

Mrs Taylor does not suspect a thing about my not
making it back to my own bed last night and we have
Clemmie to thank for that. Oh, and if asked, I'm to
tell Mrs Taylor that I was with my cousin, Charlotte.
We have to get our stories straight, you see. I've done
it often enough for her and her Barry!

I'm starting to get the panics about the results of
my exams now. I know it's all done and dusted and
I can't do anything about exams sat weeks ago but I
can't help it! As well as that, I'm a little sad at the
thought of leaving London behind me. You asked
me if it was always my plan to come home again
after I got my degree and the honest answer is I
really don't remember. All I do know now is I must
come home because it's been so hard being apart

from you for weeks on end and the tutor tells me that, with my qualification (she seems quite confident I will pass!) I should quite easily be able to get a job anywhere in the country and that includes Cawsmenyn.

I had another argument with Clemmie (I will miss our squabbles!) when she said you and I have not been boyfriend and girlfriend for more than a year and only good friends for a while before that. 'No,' she said, 'you have just been stepping out for the few weeks you spent together during the vacations.' Apparently, last summer didn't count either because of the time I spent with Auntie Gaynor and Sali!

'What about our letters?' I asked her. She pondered it before deciding that if each letter equates to one hour, we would already be celebrating our golden wedding anniversary!

They say the exam results should come out any day now but we won't necessarily know about it until just beforehand. I will most certainly write by return as soon as I know the result and then, I will come home the very next day. Almost everything is packed up and ready to go to Paddington in a taxi. You could say I am living out of a suitcase!

I can't wait to get home and see Mam and Harri.
And you, of course, my darling. We will have the
whole summer ahead of us. What shall we do with it?

All my love,

Ela x

Chapter Twenty-Nine

Even though she's read the letters dozens of times, Asta always feels sad when she gets to this final letter. Charlie and Ela seemed so happy, so ready to ride off into the sunset. If her very existence didn't prove otherwise, Asta could believe the letters stopped because Charlie and Ela were together forever.

She looks over to where Josh is sitting. He has read the exact same letters she has but he's managed to fill two sheets of A4 with notes. She stretches her neck over to see what he's writing but although Josh has many fine qualities, neat legible handwriting is not one of them. She has to squish down a smile when he curls his arm defensively around his papers, as if protecting his work from being copied. When he looks up and sees her, he flushes with embarrassment.

'I've got to go to the toilet,' he says.

He turns his scribbled pages over so they face downward.

'Don't look at them,' he says. 'It's just mind mapping and scribbles, not for sharing.'

Asta nods solemnly. After he's left the room, she re-reads that last letter again. It is one of her favourites, so happy, so hopeful. Anyone would wish for Charlie and Ela to live happily ever after once they'd read that. It is completely clueless though. Or should that be clue-less as there is nothing there that will help them find Ela. She tries to think of any incontrovertible facts scattered through the letters, anything worth following up that would meet Josh's exacting standards.

What about this wedding between Ela's mum and the lodger? Might they find a marriage certificate between Mrs Hennessy and Welsh Harri whose surname was, oh, they don't know because none of the letters mention it. Maybe then check the electoral register for 1965 for the house Mrs Hennessy lived in? That would involve knowing the address, though, and as Ela always writes from London, they don't know that either. What about Auntie Gaynor's cottage by the sea? Asta already knows from her internet searches that the Akter family live there now. Before them, it was Matthew Evans and before him, the Doyles. Would it still be worth taking the three hour train journey to Porthgynffon in the hope of something, anything? Not if the disastrous half-term trip to Eleanor Hennessy's house was anything to go by.

Check the London details maybe? What about Clemmie? How many female Pure Mathematics grad-uates did London universities produce back then and surely only one with a name like that? Perhaps she could investigate the past of their house in London like that good-looking history professor does, find out who lived there and when. Census results? Electoral rolls? So many thoughts, too many to remember. She looks over at Josh's bits of paper, wants to scrawl her own notes on the back of them, decides not to and instead goes into his drawer to get another fresh sheet.

Josh's drawer is like the very opposite of that drawer of trashy junk to be found in every household in the land. At the very front it has a neat narrow tray, like a cutlery organiser, in which pens, pencils, rulers and rubbers sit in organised compartments.

Serial killer precision. Or civil engineer exactitude.

A pile of snowy white A4 nestles behind the tray. She tries very carefully to extract the top sheet without disturbing the tidiness of it all, when something that's been stuffed to the back of the drawer slides forward. She tries to shake it off but as she tugs at the sheet of paper, she catches sight of that familiar handwriting. By now, she knows it almost as well as her own. It's Ela's but what is Ela's letter doing here in Josh's bedroom? How did it get here? Has he been going through her things while she is at school, her parents are working hard downstairs and he is supposed to be applying a second coat of paint in the living room?

But as she reads on, she realises she has never seen this letter before.

8th February 1965

Dear Charlie,

I cannot believe what happened. It is bloody awful
and I am furious.

Is your mum all right? Is George all right? Is the
shop all right?

I'm so sorry about all the damage done. Of course,
I know things have turned rough in there before, there
have been fights in there many a time, but for someone to hit your mum and George. I know you won't
like this but I agree that it was right for Deirdre to
hold you back in the kitchen and not get involved.
Thuggish, drunken customers and their equally brut-
ish beer-soaked mates. If they didn't stint in hitting a
woman and a tiny man in glasses, they would really
have gone to town on your face. As you know, your
face is very precious to me. I'm buying a bottle of
Betty's favourite port and presenting her with it the
very next time I see her.

That's bad enough but for the police to act as they
did. Police in name only! I suppose the one good
thing is that as soon as they arrived, almost everyone
took fright and ran away. But for that policeman to
say what he said about Ada? To blame her for being

the victim of a crime? All she and George try to do is run a good business for people to have hot food of an evening. If the police feel that everyone foreign is up to no good, what hope would any one of them have for reporting a crime?

I can't repeat the things they said to her and about her. It infuriates me even to think about it. I blame that stupid film that came out that makes dimwits think every Chinese woman is that word the policeman used. I long for the day when books and films and all the things people see stop showing us Welsh as simple-minded folk who sing nicely and are covered in coal dust. And for when they show Chinese people like you as you really are. In your case: wonderful, brave, clever and handsome.

And then for them to think none of you would understand what they were saying about you? To talk about you as if you weren't even in the room, to say those disgusting things about you and to treat you like some kind of second-class citizen. I hope they all squirmed good and proper when you spoke to them in English that was probably even better than theirs. I suspect they didn't though, how else does a pig produce such good crackling if it didn't have such a thick skin? Oh no, I'm wrong to say that. Mam's had good help with the police before now and I must try to not let a few bad apples spoil the barrel. Very bad apples. Very, very bad apples.

I'm glad Betty and the other girls were able to help with the clearing up and I know her brother is the best handyman in town so he will have it all fixed up again in no time. It seems good hearts are in no short supply but I wish there were as many of them in the higher-ups as there are in us ordinary folk.

I wish I could do something more from here but for what it's worth, I am sending all my love to all of you.

Ela xxxxx

Asta feels fury as hot and defiant as Ela's was all those years ago and all those miles away. So this is what Grandpa Charlie meant. She thinks of her poor great-grandmother having to put up with that, helpless to do anything other than smile and turn away. George too. She thought he was small and frail because he was so old but it seemed he'd always been this way.

There are two other things dragged out from the back of the drawer when she picks up Ela's letter. The first one is a plain postcard in chunky block letters. She doesn't know this yet but it is the classic style of poison pen letters, an early ancestor of the internet trolling she works so hard to avoid. Her address is on the front while the other document is on rather more lavish paper than the sort Ela uses for her letters. The postmark is too blurry to see the date but judging by the next letter, it must have arrived at about the same time.

POSTCARD Address to be written this side		
CHINESE SHOP 77 JOYCE STREET CAWSMENYN		TELL YOUR SON TO STICK TO HIS OWN KIND. MONGRELS IS FOR DOGS.

Cawsmenyn Town Council
11th June 1965

Dear Mr and Mrs Yau Sum,

I have seen that your son has been stepping out with Billy and Jane Hennessy's daughter.

She is not the first one he has been mixing with, of course. I understand he has been extremely popular with many girls in town. I have no issue with young people enjoying themselves as young people of a certain background always have done, but I was extremely concerned to hear rumours of anything more serious between the two of them.

There is no reasoning with the youth and I was hoping to appeal to you – the responsible adults – as to whether this is a wise course of action.

The Hennessy girl was the apple of her father's eye and it is easy to see how his widow may not have the strength to see what needs to be done. The fact of the matter is

that the mixing of racial char-
acteristics is not to be encour-
aged and the children produced in
this way can look forward only to a
life lived on the periphery of all
right-thinking communities.

It is my hope that this letter
will encourage you to dissuade your
son from pursuing such a selfish
course of action that could prove
detrimental to a young lady making
great strides with her academic
achievement.

Yours sincerely,

Councillor Edwin Bevan

'What's up?' says Josh when he gets back.

Asta has two distinct kinds of anger brewing up inside her. One is for what she's just read and one is for the person who stopped her from reading it all in the first place. Yes, she knows it doesn't make sense and they should cancel each other out but instead she's really fucking furious.

'What are these?'

She waves the letters and the postcard in the air.

Josh goes pale.

'Um yeah, I didn't think they were very nice so I decided to take them out when I handed the letters over to you.'

'*The* letters? *My* letters. Found on our premises and addressed to my Grandpa Charlie, his mum and his stepdad. Mine, not yours. Like I always said.'

Josh gulps and goes back to sit next to Asta. She gets up and takes his place just inside the bedroom door, still holding onto the letters and postcard.

'Sorry, I guess I had no right. I just thought . . .'

'What did you think?'

'I was about to tell you if you didn't interrupt me.'

Josh has raised his voice. Asta doesn't care.

'Well, pardon me for interrupting you trying to tell me you stole my grandad's letters.'

'I didn't steal them and it's not like they were worth any money. Normally we just get told to chuck away anything we find under the carpets and floorboards.

If anything, it belongs to whoever had the house before you . . . '

'My grandfather!'

'Didn't you say the couple Steve lives with had it before your mum and dad?'

'Well, they never found them and they probably didn't want them either.'

'I wasn't to know it was your grandad back then. In any case, you should be pleased we didn't chuck them straight in the bin like nine out of ten contractors would have done.'

'Oh, should I?'

'Yes, and when I'd seen them, I didn't think you needed to see some racist shit from the past, that's why I kept them back.'

'What, you think I haven't seen any racist shit in my life? I've lived it, Josh Palazzo. It's racist shit 2.0, the modern version. Less obvious than what's in these, but you certainly don't need to shield me from it. All this time I've been flailing about, thinking about what happened between Charlie and Ela, when you've had those letters that could have helped.'

'They couldn't. I've already looked. Do you know how many women called Betty there were in Cawsmenyn in 1964? Every other woman in town was called Betty. Not only that, every other one of them was called Betty Jones. It was a complete dead end.'

Josh stops to draw breath.

'As for that council guy, he's lucky he died of a heart attack in 1982 or I would have given him such a slap for that letter. On headed paper too, which is not a constructive use of council money. There was nothing on that postcard either except for psycho penmanship and bad grammar.'

'You still had no right to keep hold of these,' says Asta, 'and you should definitely have said something before now. If I hadn't come across them trying to find a pen and bit of paper, I still wouldn't know about them now, would I?'

'No, you wouldn't,' says Josh. 'And you're just proving my point.'

'How do you figure that out, Head Boy?'

'Because you're taking it so badly now!'

'I'm not angry about what's in the letters!' says Asta. 'They are what they are. I'm furious because you kept them from me.'

It's all too disappointing. She realises that deep down inside she must have known that it was the everyday attrition of a bigoted stick-to-your-own-kind mindset that did for Charlie and Ela in the end. If they really loved each other, they wouldn't have let this kind of thing come between them. She'd rather Ela died in a tragic accident than to think that when it came down to it, Ela just didn't have it in her.

'If that's what you really think, well, that's fine,' says Josh. 'You have all of the letters now. We can still crack on and look at them, see if we can get any further into it.'

'I don't want to do that now,' says Asta. 'I can't trust you any more.'

'Look, I made a mistake. I thought it was for the best. I'm sorry.'

Asta purses her lips, can't think of anything to say. It's shit to argue with someone so reasonable. It's never like this when they have a row at home. Where are the raised voices? The slammed doors? The atmosphere you can cut with a knife?

'I accept your apology,' says Asta, going back over to the desk.

Josh budges up so they can carry on reviewing the letters but instead Asta gathers them all up and shoves them back into her bag.

'I accept your apology,' says Asta, 'but it was a big mistake to think anyone could help me get to the bottom of all of this. Some things you can do as part of a team but there are other things you just have to do on your own. If I'm meant to find out where Ela is, I can do it myself like I usually do.'

'She didn't stay long,' says Vince to Josh after Asta's left, having popped her head into the kitchen to say a polite goodbye.

'Have we got any more butter?' Josh replies, his head in the fridge. 'Eggs? Flour? And did you see where I put the cake tin?'

Chapter Thirty

Asta is in the pet shop, looking at all the different kinds of ball, toy, chew or biscuit available to dogkind. Steve's been out of sorts lately because she's dropped down to three walks a week. She's been spending her time with Sophie, Paige and Callum after school. It's like the ripples you get from chucking a pebble in a pond; the more new people you spend your time with, the more new people you meet. The more new people you meet, the more new people you spend your time with. It is like the opposite of a vicious circle. A social circle!

She ponders a long bit of something dark and chewy-looking with a pretty bit of white fabric running up the edge. She picks it up for a closer look before she realises it's a dried rabbit's ear, a strip of the fur still attached. She winces. It reminds her of the so-called lucky rabbit's foot. For the rabbit, not so much.

No, she prefers her own mascot of lucky leporine origin. She puts a hand into her jeans pocket and feels the cool wooden head of the carved rabbit she found on Felix's floor that must have fallen out of a box of Grandpa Charlie's stuff. She'd put it into her skirt pocket on impulse one day, after reaching for a tissue to take to school and she'd bumped into Sophie at the traffic lights. They'd walked to and from school together every day since. The rabbit had also been with her the very first time she didn't get picked last for the team in games. The day she dropped her mobile onto the hard ceramic floor tiles of the girls' toilets and it had not suffered so much as a crack. The bunny is undoubtedly, and irrationally, lucky and she likes to keep it with her.

Steve is torn.

He wants to play with the squeaky tennis ball the old young owner just gave him. He also wants to eat the carob-coated biscuits she put on the kitchen table and chew the rubbery studs of the orange baton toy she's put into his dog bed. But now she's gone to the porch and has come back with his lead.

Why did she give him all these things before they left for the walk and not after they come back? He eyes Tony Blair as the cat hops up to sit at the kitchen table, a bit too close to those biscuits for Steve's liking. Well, he can have those but he's not having this. He snatches up the squeaky tennis ball.

'We're bringing that with us, are we?' the old young owner asks.

He can't reply, his mouth is full of tennis ball.

When they get close to the meadows, they don't turn towards its kiss gates but instead left at the junction. Steve's disappointed but not too much. He hasn't had a chance to attack that chenille rug in ages.

Scattered all over Elaine's house are photos of her family – her children and grandchildren – but there are more photos of one person than anyone else. These are of her husband, Neil, who died the year before last. Asta has caught Elaine kiss her fingertip and press it to the glass of their photo in the hallway. It's a very nice photo. Neil is looking directly at the camera, dark hair, dark eyes, a lopsided smile of the sort you make when you unexpectedly find yourself being photographed. Younger Elaine is in profile, turned towards him and the way she looks at her husband? Well, if it was posted online, it would definitely attract the hashtag #someonelookatmethewaysheलooksathim.

The radiator is underneath the photo and above it is a small shelf. In a lesser house, this shelf would attract all kinds of household detritus but in the house of an older woman living on her own, it attracts not even dust. Or at least, it didn't until the recent arrival of Max who has been emptying his pockets onto it ever since he moved in. Keys, mints, fluff, tissues. Asta knows Elaine doesn't like it but a mother is reluctant to be too critical of a heartbroken son.

Asta has a solution. She has etched some calligraphy art and put it into a 16 x 9 frame. The two words – Elaine and Neil – are written out in a swooping style of modern lettering but there is no space between their names. Instead the final 'e' of 'Elaine' and the 'N' of 'Neil' are joined by a looping heart shape that binds the names together. Underneath it, she has written the date of their wedding – 2.06.1990 – but instead of dots separating the day, the month, the year, she has drawn in the tiniest of crimson hearts.

'You don't have to put it up in the hallway, if you don't like it,' says Asta, after Elaine has removed the artwork's tissue paper wrapping and scrunched it up into a recycling-ready ball, 'but I did design it with that space in mind.'

'Oh, but I do like it and it will look perfect in there.'

The front door opens. They hear Max pause in the hallway, a series of crunching and clattering sounds, before he appears in the kitchen.

'Look what Asta's made for me,' says Elaine.

Max looks at it carefully before pronouncing it 'very nice' in the tones of the recently dumped who are not interested in this kind of thing.

'You made it?' he asks her. 'You didn't buy it on Etsy or something?'

'No,' says Asta. 'I make the kinds of things that folk sell on Etsy but I've got my own website.'

'Interesting,' says Max, in the conversational-filler tone that people normally reserve for 'right', 'you don't say' and 'mmm hmmm'. He drifts over to the sink to fill the kettle.

'Don't mind him,' Elaine says. 'Let's go put it up.'

She stops to collect the duster and polish from a cupboard before they go into the hall. Elaine sighs to see the empty sweet wrappers and loose change on the radiator shelf. She clears them away and wipes everything down, then rubs the duster on the small greasy mark her finger kisses have left on Neil's face.

'There,' she says, once she's centred the artwork on the shelf beneath the photo. 'Perfect. Thank you, Asta. I love it.' She mutters something under her breath.

'What did you just say?' asks Asta.

'Oh, I just said "my last love". It may seem a little morbid but I won't be looking for another husband at my age, after Neil.' She notices Asta's face. 'Why? What did you think I said?'

It is too good an opportunity to miss. It's only after Asta's told Elaine and Max the full story of Grandpa Charlie and his *lost* love Ela that they notice Steve has been shredding the discarded ball of tissue paper and left it scattered all over the kitchen floor. Under the table, Asta has done something similar to her tights, scratching away at a tiny pinhole until she can fit an entire finger through and dig a nail into her thigh. She's been waiting for Elaine to interrupt, to say she doesn't need anyone to tell her this story because she has lived one half of it already. That moment doesn't come.

'Oh Steve,' says Elaine. 'You are a messy visitor.'

She fetches the broom out of the cupboard.

'Well, there is one person who's closest to the story and still around,' she says between sweeps.

'But I've already asked George . . .' says Asta.

Steve whines and lifts a paw when he hears his old new owner mentioned.

'. . . but he clearly didn't want to talk about it at all,' says Asta.

'Sounds typical of him,' says Max. 'If he refuses to talk about it, it will go away. What about you, Mum, you know almost everybody. There can't be much more than two degrees of separation between you and this Hennessy woman.'

'I was twelve in 1965, I'll have you know, and still living in Swansea with your grandparents.'

'Oh,' says Asta.

'Oh, what?' asks Max.

'I used to think Elaine was Ela,' she says in a small voice.

'Ela's much older than me,' says Elaine.

'Much?' says Max.

Elaine retaliates by shoving the broom against Max's chair, jolting him so his coffee spills out of his mug and down his front.

'What did you do that for?' he says.

He storms out of the room. Footsteps bang upstairs and a bedroom door slams. Asta's jaw drops slightly.

'Don't worry, dear,' says Elaine. 'He'll have stopped sulking when he smells his tea cooking.'

'Now I know what it's like for my mum and dad when I do that,' says Asta.

'There is a big age difference between you and my son,' says Elaine. 'Even bigger than the one between this letter writer and me. I wish I could think of anyone at all called Hennessy who lives, or has lived, in the area, but I've wracked my brains. Nothing.'

'It's a dead end,' says Asta. 'Another one.'

'I don't know about that.' Elaine presses the lever to open the flap on the dustpan and sweeps all the mess inside. 'It sounds like you've seen another side of your grandfather from these letters. You've met him again and known him as a young man. I don't think you ever expected that would happen.'

Asta shakes her head.

'Isn't that something? I don't know if finding the writer of the letters will make much of a difference to that.'

'I suppose not.'

'But you wanted to know why they didn't end up together? Like in a film or a book?'

Asta nods.

Elaine looks up at the ceiling, Max's bedroom on the other side of it.

'Sometimes it's best not to know how it ended. It's just good to know it happened.' Elaine opens the cupboard door and empties all the mess into the bin. 'Like so many things in life.'

Chapter Thirty-One

Steve's on the sofa, one eye on the toasted sandwich George is eating, the other on Susie Dent on *Countdown*. If he had another eye, it would be on the window, awaiting the arrival of Asta for his walk but he's come to realise she doesn't come every day. She has new friends now. Sometimes he can smell them on her – a petrol-type whiff followed by a sugary after-note, those horrible stinks they squirt onto themselves that make him sneeze, good old natural body fragrances as familiar to him as a face or a voice.

He doesn't hold it against her. After all, he has new friends too. Like Tony Blair the cat. The owners like to call what he's doing with Tony Blair now 'spooning'. Whatever it's called, it's cosy. He licks Tony's head, darkening his tabby stripes with saliva. Yum.

Asta *is* meant to be walking Steve today but when she got home on laundry day, instead of the contents of her pockets scattered on top of the duvet, she found both her parents sitting on the bed.

'Where did you get this?' Tim asks.

Asta panics, looks over at her drawer. Mandy spots her glance, goes over to the drawer and flings it open. She has no fear of her daughter's pants or the packets of *Always* Asta deliberately keeps on top of them; they were always designed to deter Felix and Tim. She pulls out the box-fresh vape, the *Talk to Frank* leaflet.

'Out,' says Mandy. 'The shop, the pair of you.'

They troop downstairs, Asta in between her parents, filled with the dread of an imminent interrogation. She hasn't even done anything wrong, she's almost entirely certain about that.

Mandy and Tim slip around to the serving side. It's narrow back there so Asta positions herself on the shop side, that way she has the counter between them and she's closer to the front door for an easy escape.

'What is this?' asks Mandy, throwing the vape onto the counter. 'Are you vaping now?'

'No,' says Asta. 'It's still in the packet.'

'A brand new one doesn't mean you haven't worked your way through dozens of the things. I thought you'd been smelling more fruity than usual.'

'That's Body Shop banana shampoo,' says Asta. 'I've only got the vape because . . .'

'Speak up,' says Tim. 'You've only got it because?'

'. . . I thought it would make me more interesting.'

It all pours out then, how she struggled to settle into the new school, how she missed the old place even though it wasn't that great there. How she worried about what to do, how to behave, how being 'good' was boring while being a vaper, a rule breaker, well everyone prefers Jo March to Meg, Lizzy Bennet to Jane, Marianne Dashwood to Elinor.

Tim shakes his head. 'Who are these girls who are such a bad influence on you? We should speak to the headmaster about them.'

Mandy shushes him.

'Where did you get the money to squander on this kind of crap?'

Asta shrugs.

'It's that online shop you're still running, isn't it? Well, I think it's about time we shut it down. You're supposed to be concentrating on schoolwork. It's why we moved here.'

'No!' says Asta. 'I need that work, it's what I'm going to do when I leave school. I'm going to do the foundation art course and a business course online and really make something of my calligraphy. It's the only thing I'm any good at.'

It looks like Mandy's either going to tell Asta she's good at all sorts of things or she's going to go berserk and insist on her applying for an Oxbridge degree in English. They're both so worried about this, they don't realise that Tim has gone pale and Asta realises they haven't yet broached the subject of why they were in her bedroom in interrogation mode in the first place.

Tim's hands are clenched into fists. Asta knows he would never hit or punch anyone but still it's a bit disconcerting, especially as the knuckles are starting to turn white. Finally, he unfolds one hand.

'What were you doing with this?' he asks.

It's the lucky wooden rabbit. Irrationally, Asta pats her skirt pocket but of course it's not there. She left it in her jeans and in spite of this, today has still been a good day in school with an A* and a conversation with the others about going camping at the weekend.

'I found it on the floor.'

'Which floor?'

'Dunno,' says Asta, implausibly and irrationally.

'I told you it wasn't the one,' says Mandy, turning to Tim. 'It's been years since anyone last saw it. I'm sure it got thrown away and even if it didn't, how could it have got from the Sun House to here? It just looks a bit like the one you had before.'

'No,' says Asta. 'It's not Felix's. It's Grandpa Charlie's, it came from one of the boxes from his bedroom.'

Tim lets out a sigh. 'I don't get it,' he says.

'What don't you get?' asks Asta, instantly worried about the something that's glistening in the corner of his eye and threatening to spill down one cheek. Actual crying now. What else is going to go wrong with her dad?

'This rabbit,' says Tim, 'is the one I gave to your grandfather when I was trying to convince him I should be allowed to go and do my foundation course.'

'You did a foundation course? In art?' asks Asta.

'Yes, both your father and I existed as people in our own right before you and Felix came along, you know,' says Mandy.

'I did,' says Tim. 'Your grandfather didn't want me to, said being an artist was a no-hoper of a job, but then I gave him that rabbit so he could see how good I was. He wasn't that keen even after that but it swayed him. He said I could go and while I was at college, living away from home, having a bit of freedom, I met your mum and you know the rest.'

No, Asta doesn't. Whoever gets to know the intimate details of how their parents got together? Gross! She tries to think of something to say but her silence does a better job at prompting Tim to carry on than anything she could have uttered.

'We knew pretty quickly it was serious between your mum and me. We were young and we would skin you alive right now if you behaved like we behaved. You don't need to know about all that except to say your mum was only seventeen and even though we didn't have to get married, we wanted to.

'Your grandfather was, not furious, but he was disappointed, okay well yes then, he was a bit furious too. Your grandmother was thrilled, though, and as she was having her hernia operation, we moved back here for a bit to help out. Even after she got better, we stayed on. There's not much in the way of kudos, not much chance of using any skills you have in woodcarving or sculpture, but sticking with the family business was the steady job we needed for the new arrival.

'I thought your grandfather would be pleased we'd come back to the family business. It was what he always wanted, wasn't it, and why he didn't ever want me to do the foundation course. I can't even remember now what started it off. Some stupid small bickering over nothing but they're always the ones that escalate, aren't they? The last time I saw this rabbit was when he threw it at me and said he should never have let me go to art college and I would never have met your mother. Sorry, am I boring you in some way?'

Asta isn't yawning but a blank look has spread across her face. She is listening but something Tim said is snagging on her brain.

'How is it that Mum was pregnant when she was a year older than me, but Felix is only nineteen?' she asks. 'He should be twenty-three, shouldn't he?'

'It didn't work out,' says Mandy quickly. 'We don't talk about it with you children but we always remember your brother Leo on his day.'

Asta thinks of a malleable day in the year, sometimes very close to Easter, sometimes a few weeks away from it, when her parents seem to be not quite themselves. *The alien parents have come for their annual visit.* That's what she and Felix used to whisper to each other. They didn't think enough to realise there could be an actual reason for it.

'Where was I?' says Tim.

Asta stares pointedly at the rabbit in his hand. Why didn't she see the resemblance before between this rabbit, cosy in its resting loaf position, and the tense, combative white soap rabbits that occupy most of the bathroom? Because there isn't one. They're all rabbits, yes, but that's the only thing they have in common.

'Ah yes, this guy.' He puts a finger between its tiny ears as if soothing the rabbit and not himself. 'Never knew what happened to him. Thought he must have got thrown away. We made up after the argument, your grandfather and me, he came to realise your mum was a great addition to the family. We took over the business. We looked after everybody for as long as they needed us. I didn't know he still had this, had it all along. Kept it and brought it from the old place to this place.

'I thought I was a disappointment but I was there for him and your grandmother. If we'd finished our degrees, got fancier jobs, made them properly proud of us in the way they wanted, would we have been living far away? Remotely worrying about every cough, sneeze and fall? Instead of seeing them right, all the way to the end?'

Tim splutters and leaves the room.

Like father, like daughter.

Chapter Thirty-Two

'Is it pronounced O-*reg*-uh-no or Oreg-*ah*-no?' asks Asta, lifting up the top sheet of paper and looking at the contact sheet of small grainy images on the second page.

Mr Feather has left the classroom for 'a quiet five minutes for you all to review the text'. Again.

'I'm not really sure,' says Sophie.

'What? Lambert's mum has named her new campsite business after herself and you don't know how to say her name?' says Callum. 'Haven't you met her before?'

'I've met his dad and his step-mum,' says Sophie. 'Loads of times, but his mother's only just come back on the scene and that's why he's trying to support her while she sets herself up.'

'And we can all stay for free this weekend instead of paying the usual price?' asks Paige.

'It's in exchange for testing it out,' says Sophie, 'seeing what little things need fixing, sorting out what could go wrong before it opens to the public.'

'I've never been camping before,' says Asta.

'You won't have done after this either,' says Sophie. 'This is glamping so no putting up a tent or sleeping bags. It's yurts and fire pits and outdoor bathing.'

She takes the handout back from Asta and reads aloud.

'*All in a beautiful off-grid forest setting so you can enjoy the local woodland and wildlife in all of its natural gory.* Oh, that's a typo, must get her to correct that. See? We're earning our free weekend of glamping already!'

'All in the same tent?'

Sophie's voice has gone terribly loud and high. Fortunately, Asta can still push the tragus of her ear in on itself to block out the sound if she needs to. Paige can't do that because of her hooped piercings.

'Yeah,' says Lambert. 'Oh has only managed to get one of the yurts up for this weekend.'

He calls his own mother Oh, Asta notes. Perhaps even he doesn't know how to say her name. She wonders if it was 'Oh' who selected the name Lambert.

'This is the half tipi, half yurt,' says Lambert. 'Room enough for all of us, see?'

He waves his arms around while Asta, Sophie, Callum and Paige, all clustered together by the wood burner that takes up the middle of the tent-like structure, shuffle three hundred and sixty degrees to take in their new surroundings.

In theory, it seems fine, even if it does feel peculiar to be in a completely circular room. The ceiling rises up above them until it reaches the apex of its conical shape, the long thin chimney of the wood burner poking out into the sky. If you sliced the floor plan of this perfectly round room into a pie chart, sixty-five per cent of it would be jewelled throws and mirrored cushions chucked onto extremely firm-looking beds – two doubles and a single – head ends pressed into the walls of the yurt, everyone's toes pointing in towards the wood burner. Another twenty-five per cent looks like a place where cushions and bean bags go to spend their spare time. Piled up into various cairns and hillocks, they look resentful of anyone prepared to make the mistake of sitting on them. Some railway sleepers are piled up in front to make an improvised coffee table. The remaining ten per cent is a tiny kitchen area with a small sink, fridge and cupboard that does not look like it can fulfil the culinary requirements of five hungry teenagers.

'Where do we go to the toilet?' asks Callum.

'Al fresco, of course,' says Paige. 'Do bears shit in the woods, Callum?'

'I don't know,' he says, 'but this bear definitely wants to piss in the woods.'

'No need to do either,' says Lambert. 'There's a toilet out there, just a bit further up on the left. You can't miss it.'

Callum leaves quickly.

'Well, I think it's nice and cosy,' says Asta, dumping her small duffle bag onto the single bed.

'Not so fast there,' says Paige. 'I think we'll keep that one free for Callum, don't you?'

'What?' says Asta. 'I would have thought you could manage to share the bed with each other for a couple of nights.'

'What exactly do you think is the nature of my relationship with Callum?' asks Paige.

'Best of heterosexual friends?'

'No, we're first cousins and I am not sharing a bed with my male first cousin,' says Paige.

Asta removes her bag and dumps it onto the smaller double bed. Sophie and Lambert are already whispering to each other, sat so close they could be conjoined twins, on the biggest bed.

'I don't think Sophie's very happy about how the romantic possibilities of this weekend are panning out,' says Paige, 'I think she was expecting a tent of their own.'

Callum runs back inside.

'Lambert, there's a big note on your toilet saying even we have to pee sitting down, man,' he says.

'Oh yeah,' says Lambert. 'You can't have pee contaminating the main chamber on a composting toilet. It has to go down that chute and the chute only works if you sit down to pee. You get used to it.'

'Nah, I'm not doing that,' says Callum, 'so I just pissed up against a tree instead.'

Sophie and Lambert have gone for a walk and everyone else is too scared to stray far from the yurt in case they inadvertently come across a scene from *Lady Chatterley's Lover*.

It is still a lovely spring day though so Asta, Paige and Callum are sitting in the outside living room which is much nicer than anything inside the yurt. There are reclaimed timber tables and chairs sitting prettily around a shiny satellite dish of a fire pit and although wildlife seems to be creeping into their clearing from the surrounding canopy of trees, it's in the form of a carpet of bluebells. Asta and Paige watch Callum finish his second bag of crisps by upending the packet and emptying the crumbs into his mouth. They've already eaten the sandwiches Mandy insisted Asta take for the journey, even though she knows Asta can easily go a complete forty minutes without having to eat anything. The only other food available is of the sort that needs to be cooked on the fire pit later that evening.

'There's no signal, Paige,' says Callum. 'It's not going to magically materialise just because you want it to.'

'Well, that's where you're wrong,' says Paige, before she stops waving her handset around like she's warming up for the shot putt. 'It does not say there's no service and there is half a bar of signal showing. At least I'll be able to phone for help if we need it. At least it's just a yurt in the woods, not a cabin.'

'Isn't there supposed to be outdoor bathing?' asks Callum. 'I did bring trunks, just in case.'

'I think that's it there,' says Asta, pointing to a roll-top bath sitting on a pedestal of decking to one side of the yurt.

'*That?* I thought there might be a lake or a river or something,' says Callum. 'Isn't that what bathing is?'

'In an Enid Blyton book maybe,' says Paige. 'In the modern world, it means getting in the bath. How does the whole thing even work anyway? It's not like a double room with an en suite for two to share. Yurt for five and one outdoor bathtub where everyone can see you naked?'

'Perhaps you're supposed to wear a swimming costume while you have a bath?' says Asta.

'How are you going to clean your bits efficiently through a swimming costume?' asks Callum.

'They do it on *I'm a Celebrity*,' says Asta.

'They get paid a fortune to have dirty bits for a fortnight,' says Callum. 'Mixed Herbs isn't giving us a penny and it looks like her glamping village can accommodate only one set of people, all of whom have to sit down to take a piss regardless of gender.'

'Don't say gender,' groans Paige.

'Hey,' says Callum, 'what does a man do standing up, a woman do sitting down and a dog do on three legs?'

'Have a pee?' says Paige.

'Wrong! But you see my point? No red-blooded male wants to change the peeing habits of a lifetime.'

Asta wonders what she could be watching on Netflix instead of this, realises it's a rude thing to think, let alone say out loud. 'What is it then? That a man does standing up, a woman does sitting down and a dog does on three legs?'

'Shake hands,' says Callum, 'which you won't be wanting to do with me once I've been to that toilet as there's no facility for washing your hands in there.'

'Good job Asta and I have got wet wipes and hand gel then,' says Paige.

They smile at Callum triumphantly in the manner of well-prepared girls.

Chapter Thirty-Three

Is there anything worse than being wide awake when everyone else around you is fast asleep?

Asta could kick herself for not thinking through this invitation to sleep over with the others properly before accepting, but in her defence, she had been imagining flushing toilets, running water, food cooked all the way through to the middle and a yurt of her own. She looks grimly down at her phone, sticking half out from under her pillow, its screen set never to go dim so she never has to be completely in the dark. This was worse than when Felix couldn't ever sleep over with his primary school friends because of his own little problem. Fortunately, part of being prepared also involved bringing two mini torch/lanterns, which she was going to set up in her individual yurt. She wonders which is the worst thing to have to confess to.

Sorry I can't sleep over, I wet the bed.

Sorry I can't sleep over, I'm scared of the dark.

Asta gets another Philip Larkin moment, one bleaker even than his dead hedgehog and much more famous.

Her head is spinning, she's starting to panic, as she sees the charge on her phone dropping dropping dropping even though it's on low power mode. She knows it will cost her but she has to soothe herself by swiping through photos of Steve. Poor neglected Steve. It's only as she's swiping through that she sees something she's not noticed before.

It's a photo of Vince, smiling cheerily into the camera, pointing at the embroidered logo on the front of his boiler suit – Palazzo & Son and a mobile number. She remembers it now. Max said one of the other teachers needed a builder and could she pass on Josh's number? No, she couldn't, but she could pass Vince's on. She'd taken the photo, sent it quickly on to Max, but hadn't noticed Josh in the background. Josh is looking at the camera, but in a completely different way to how Vince is. Vince is selling his business service, doing a promotional smile but Josh's expression? There isn't one, he's just gazing directly into the camera. Unlike most people, his default isn't to turn away from the lens ostentatiously like the camera-shy but neither does he need to jump around, make a face or play up for the lens. Neither stressed nor stimulated by the thought of a photo, he really isn't doing anything much other than being Josh.

'Hey, it's you,' he seems to be saying. 'You see me and I see you.'

He is a composition of stillness, of composure, of calm.

Has she missed seeing him this last couple of weeks? Of course not. Still, there is something to be said for being more Josh, Asta thinks, as she finally falls asleep.

As soon as it's light, Asta is up and headed over to the single charging point for phones that runs off a solar panel. She carefully removes the handset that's there, Sophie's by the look of the screensaver, unless Lambert is totally into a picture of himself on his phone. She feels a weight lift off her as the little bolt of lightning appears in the top right-hand corner so she pours herself a glass of oat milk and heads outside.

The sky is more red than pink as the sun begins to rise up over the canopy of trees – the ancient woodland of Cawsmenynshire which for so many years was managed, grazed, built up and chopped down by ancestors who long ago abandoned it for life in a town or small city. Asta sits down next to the fire pit, looks at the empty bottles, long blackened edges of burnt pastry, sticks with caramelised bits of marshmallow still clinging on long after the charred puffs of pure sugar have been gobbled down, hot enough to burn your mouth and make you cough. Hang on, where are the raw middles of all the sausages they partly ate? Asta remembers Sophie spitting hers out the moment she thought she'd tasted blood. Callum had speared his onto two sticks and held it like a corn on the cob as he nibbled away on the burnt bits, laying the red raw middle out like it was some sort of flayed trophy that's appeared through the cat flap. In any case, all the meat has disappeared. Asta hopes it was foxes.

The countryside is much noisier than expected and it's mainly birdsong. She can't see any birds, just the sound of lots of rustling in the trees. She can hear the tweets, twitters and trilling sounds though, back and forth, overlapping, threatening to drown each other out until it goes silent just for a moment and then it starts up all over again.

Something moves beyond the edge of her vision and she turns slowly towards it, shivering a little as fresh air breezes over her bare elbows, knees and ankles. She turns to see three rabbits, two of them so young, so brand new, so kittenish, she has to hold her breath in case she scares then away. They hop about, oblivious to Asta's presence, until something itches at the back of her throat, tickles her nose and she has to cough and sneeze at the same time. The explosion of sound sends the rabbit family scurrying back into the undergrowth.

Real wild rabbits, not at all like ones made of soap or wood. She finishes her milk and heads back inside, just as the first fat drops of rain begin to fall.

The rest of the morning is a bit of a washout. Literally. That red sky earlier on means that it rains solidly until well into the afternoon, starting at half past nine which is approximately ninety minutes before anyone else wakes up. There is a peculiar set of morning ablutions during which time Paige swears she has not taken a pee in the rolltop bathtub and Callum returns Asta's bottle of hand gel almost completely empty. Sophie and Lambert go up to the main log cabin/office/guest hub only to find that Oh must have visited very early that morning and absentmindedly locked it all up, leaving the apples, bananas, croissants and quinoa in plain view but completely inaccessible to any of them. Fortunately, Lambert still has some shopping in the boot of his car so they are able to have a fine picnic of hot dog sausages from a jar, cold tins of baked beans, pickled eggs and Monster drinks. It stops raining after that and they decide to go for a walk.

'Oh wants us to check out the area,' says Lambert, 'see if there's enough interesting wildlife to keep the guests engaged. Maybe set up some guided walks?'

'I saw some rabbits this morning,' says Asta.

'That's the spirit,' says Lambert.

It's Sophie who suggests they split up into two parties so they can cover more ground. She'll go with Lambert, of course, and the rest of them should go in the opposite direction.

'What exactly are we looking for anyway?' Callum asks, scuffing his feet on the dirt trail path.

'Weren't you listening?' says Paige. 'Wildlife.'

'Yeah, I know that but does he mean butterflies, weasels, hares, deer, buffalo? What?'

'All of the above,' says Paige. 'Did you see any yet?'

'I can see cows,' says Callum, pointing at a gap between the trees where black and white mis-shapes are dotting a distant green field.

Asta shivers, remembering the cows who bumped up against the fence when she visited Eleanor Hennessy's house.

'What's wrong with you?' asks Paige.

'Just cows,' says Asta lamely. 'Steve and me got chased through a field once by a herd before we moved to Cawsmenyn. We were on the path and they were at the other end and the next thing I knew they were all heading towards us. I picked Steve up and ran but that made them run after us even more. In the end Steve wriggled free and ran zoomies to distract them while I got away.'

'That can't have been very a-moo-sing for you,' says Paige. 'The *steaks* were pretty high there.'

Even Paige begins to wither under the strain of Asta's hard stare.

'I can't believe you have taurophobia,' says Callum, 'what with you being a Taurus too.'

'What?' says Asta.

'Taurophobia?' says Callum. 'Fear of cows.'

'No, how did you know I was a Taurus?'

'You're practical, persistent, chilled out. All classic Taurus.' Callum blows on his fingernails. 'Am I right or am I right?'

'Yes,' says Asta.

'Don't listen to him,' says Paige. 'You told him your birthday is next month that time we were talking about getting provisional driving licenses.'

'Classic Virgo,' says Callum. 'Control freak, judgemental, cynical.'

'Violent,' says Paige, kicking the side of her cousin's trainer with the side of her own.

'But really,' says Asta. 'You know all about astrology and star signs?'

'Do you know, that's such a Taurus kinda question?' says Callum. 'I can read palms as well. If I wasn't so busy doing a Chris Packham right now, I'd have a look for you.'

'Go on,' says Asta. She stops and holds out a hand. 'Do it anyway.'

'Bollocks,' says Paige, stepping between the two of them. 'Knowing about horoscopes, being all mystical, getting to hold your hand. He doesn't believe any of it. He does believe it makes him more interesting to girls, though.'

'They go crazy for a boy who knows all the star signs,' says Callum.

Asta flushes. 'Well, it wouldn't have worked on me.'

They keep walking in silence, the trees so tall on each side it cricks their necks to try to see the tops.

'Look, an eagle,' says Callum. 'It's a wildlife.'

'They don't have eagles around here,' says Paige, who looks up to see a bird flap its enormous wings before gliding and swooping out of sight. 'Shit, maybe they do.'

Asta's squinting upwards too, to try to see what none of them know is a common and not-quite-garden buzzard. That's when they feel the first raindrops.

'Right, that's it. I'm not doing this any more,' says Paige, drops of water like glass beads on her dark curly hair. 'I'm going back to the yurt.'

'Me too,' says Callum from inside of his T-shirt which he's pulled up over his head.

Asta is wearing the full cagoule Mandy made her bring but she doesn't fancy a walk on her own so she agrees to head back too.

They have managed to cover only two hundred metres or so over the course of their walk so in no time at all, they're back in the yurt. They make themselves cups of hot tea, drunk black as the oat milk has now all gone. It's stopped raining again so they head outside, dragging a big golf umbrella with them, just in case. In their normal lives, they would happily sit three in a row, looking at their phones, occasionally giggling or exchanging comments but with limited charge and no signal, they have to do the next best thing. They play charades, then Who Am I? and finally, I-Spy.

'. . . something beginning with Y,' says Paige.

'Yurt!' says Callum.

'Correct!'

'I was going to say that,' says Asta.

'I spy with my little eye something beginning with A,' says Callum, refusing to give up the spoils of his triumphant win.

'Asta,' says Paige.

'Nope.'

'Ant?' says Asta.

Callum shakes his head.

Paige has another go. 'Abyss of despair at a glamping weekend gone wrong?'

'Give up?' says Callum.

'Yes please,' says Asta.

'I really don't care about anything any more,' says Paige. 'Do you think we can persuade Lambert to take us all home?'

'I spy with my little eye . . . it's an argument.'

'What?' says Paige.

Callum gestures they should come and sit next to him so they can see what he can see. Just beyond their clearing, over to one side, only partially hidden by the composting toilet, they can see Sophie and Lambert doing a full-on mime performance of a lovers' tiff, complete with tears, lips moving in impassioned speech, pushing each other away and waving their arms around a lot. At the end, they appear to make up, Sophie sinking her face into Lambert's chest. He holds her close and they sway from side to side. Then they both get into Lambert's car and drive off.

'Hang on,' says Callum, leaping up and running after them like an abandoned dog.

'Don't go, don't leave us!' he howls.

Several hours have passed and Asta's assertion that Lambert and Sophie would be back any minute now is looking less and less likely. It's actually getting dark and Asta's starting to worry about how useful her torches are going to be. She kicked herself earlier on to notice one of them had switched itself on in her bag and its battery is now almost all used up.

'I hope they bring something to eat when they come back,' says Callum, who has already wolfed down most of the packets of mints Paige emptied out of her ruck-sack and is currently working his way through the box of Ferrero Rocher Mandy made Asta bring as a present for Lambert's mum.

'So uncool,' he says, as he stuffs another into his mouth, chucking the wrapper into the fire pit. 'But so good.'

'I'm strongly suspecting they're not coming back today,' says Paige. 'I've pretty much had it up to here with the Beatrice and Benedick of Year Twelve.'

'I thought they were the perfect couple?' says Asta. 'She's always raving about him when we're walking to school and he seems so nice.'

'Yeah, well, you don't know either of them like we know them,' says Callum. 'Remember that shouting match on the tennis court back in Year Nine?'

'How could we forget?' says Paige. 'Four hundred and eighty-one views in the first two hours?'

'And the great break-up of Year Eleven. She had to re-sit her exams after that one,' says Callum. 'Parents went berserk.'

'Yeah, I see that,' says Paige, on seeing Asta's face fall. 'Don't believe the hype. They're not the perfect couple and I'm never, ever going on a camping trip with them *ever* again.'

'They're all right when they're on their own,' says Callum, 'but put them together . . .' He bangs his fists together and makes the same exploding noise small boys do when crashing tiny toy cars into each other.

Asta looks up anxiously at the darkening night sky.

'Do you think I could have a go at charging my phone now?' she asks.

If they get stuck here another night, she's really going to need the torch app.

'Yeah, mine should be done by now,' says Paige. 'Can you bring it when you come back out?'

Asta's relieved to hear Paige mutter something about climbing up onto the roof of the outdoor bath to get a better signal to call Callum's parents to pick them up. By the time she's swapped phones and come back outside, both of the others have jumped up as if on springs. Car headlights are heading towards them from the track, dozens of dotted flying insects dancing about in the dipped beams.

'About fucking time,' says Connor, 'where have you two arseholes been?'

But as the vehicle pulls around, they can see it isn't Lambert's car. It's a van and it has *Palazzo & Son Builders* written on the side.

'It's quite hard to find, this place, isn't it?' says Josh, leaning out of the window. 'Now, Lambert said something about bringing you some grub and breaking into a log cabin?'

Avoiding Josh.

It's becoming something of habit but it's not so hard to do with Callum and Paige there to act as buffers. Even easier after they realise they have yet another problem. None of the lights on the entire glamping site are working. Unfortunately, they only discovered this after they'd put out the fire pit. Josh has put the headlights on the van for now but they can't stay on for long unless they want a flat battery and another unfortunate soul to be stranded here with them.

'You're a practical man, Palazzo,' says Callum. 'Can't you fix it?'

'Solar panels are not my area,' says Josh. 'I'm not even an electrician officially.'

'House breaking?' says Paige. 'You managed to do that, though?'

'That place?' says Josh. 'Lambert is going to have to have a word with his mum about how secure that log cabin is. My dad is not going to believe it when I tell him people still use Yale locks you can open with a credit card.'

'I don't think there is anything much in there worth stealing,' says Paige. 'Now we've eaten all the food.'

When they got inside, the charming shabby chic appearance of the interior had proved to be just shabby. Piles and piles of vintage furniture – the worst of every car boot sale and skip dive within a forty-mile radius and all awaiting refurbishment – exuded a particular smell that hadn't managed to pass through the glass when they'd been pressing their faces against the windows. They'd gathered up the food and run back to the yurt with it. They'd left the quinoa behind.

'So, you're all sure you want to come back to civilisation with me then?' said Josh, after he'd made everyone join in on clearing up the mess five bored teenagers can produce in thirty-six hours. This included a squirt of illicit bleach into the roll-top bath which Paige delivered with more than a pat of butter in her mouth.

There was a chorus of, 'Too right,' 'Yes please,' and, 'Fuck, yes.'

'OK, fetch your stuff while I go double-check the lock on that main cabin then,' says Josh. 'It is rubbish but still better than nothing.'

'What are you doing?' Paige asks Asta as she fusses around on the big double bed.

'Packing up Sophie and Lambert's stuff.'

'Why?' asks Callum. 'They should have to come back for it themselves.'

'Can you lock a yurt?' asks Asta.

'Yes!' Paige and Callum chorus.

'I've nearly done it now anyway.'

Asta shakes the bedding and something falls out. It's a pregnancy test. She holds it gingerly because it's clearly a used pregnancy test and gives one of the very few half-decent possible excuses for Sophie and Lambert's behaviour. She wraps it up in Sophie's nightshirt and stuffs it into her friend's duffle bag. Everything else she folds up as best as she can. She conducts a final scan with the torch on her phone to make sure she's not missed anything before going over to pack up her own stuff and they all go to wait outside on the reclaimed wooden benches for Josh to get back.

'All right, all done,' he says, and opens the back of the van for them to chuck their stuff in.

'No, hang on,' says Paige, after she's dumped her rucksack in. 'We can't leave just yet.'

She goes and sits down on one of the reclaimed timber chairs. She gestures to the others to come and have a seat on the bench next to it. Callum goes over without hesitation, Asta a moment later.

'Switch your headlights off, Josh,' says Paige. 'We need to sit here for five minutes and have a moment of mindfulness, to savour this instance, make sure we never forget this time we had here being at one with nature . . .'

Josh turns the keys in the ignition. The headlights go out and it's properly in-the-countryside dark. No street lights. No neighbouring houses. No torches, candles or iPhones. Asta waves a hand in front of her face, can hardly see it, starts panicking. Josh comes and sits down between her and Callum. She puts her hands on her tummy, tries to slow her breathing.

Josh whispers in Asta's ear.

'Are you all right?'

She realises she seems to be sitting with her side pressed right up against his, entirely invading his personal space, something she would never do if she wasn't so scared.

She nods.

Paige speaks again. 'And if there is one enduring thing we should all take away with us from this special time we've spent here,' she pauses to take a deep breath, bobs her head, unfolds each of the digits of her clenched fist as she exhales, 'it's that we should never, ever go away like this together again if Sophie, Lambert or his mum are involved.'

Asta tries to lean away from Josh. She's sure her trembling must be giving the game away. She's about to shuffle away, just to put a millimetre between them, when she feels him reach over and take her hand. He interlocks his fingers with hers, giving them a small squeeze. She squeezes back. It then feels like the most natural thing in the world to sit there, the four of them in the dark together.

'Is it me or is it getting brighter?' she says.

'It's the night sky. It takes a while for your eyes to get used to it,' says Callum. 'In town, there's too much light pollution, streetlights, office lights, lights off of the rugby pitch. We never think to look up to see the moon, the planets, the stars, 'cos we wouldn't be able to see them properly. But here, we're that far away from civilisation. If it wasn't so cloudy as this, I reckon we'd be able to see all the main constellations, even the Milky Way. Now that's what Lambert's mum should be using to promote this place. Just as soon as she's mastered the basics like accommodation and the plumbing.'

Asta thinks she sees a shooting star but as none of the others mention anything about it, she doesn't either.

'Right, let's go,' says Paige.

As they are about to get into the van, Callum tries to call shotgun.

'Not so fast,' says Josh. 'That's Asta's seat now.'

Chapter Thirty-Four

It's late by the time Asta gets home from the camping trip but still a good twelve hours sooner than Mandy and Tim had expected her.

'Why didn't you text to let us know you were coming back early?' asks Mandy, who's come into the hallway to see which of her children have turned up unexpectedly. 'We would have left you something.'

Asta looks at the debris of a post-work supper spread out over the kitchen table and worktops – scraped out takeaway containers, dirty bowls and dishes, forks, spoon and chopsticks languishing in small pools of sauce, an open bottle of soy, its top carelessly cast aside instead of firmly screwed back on.

'I'm all right. We all had pizza when we got back into town,' she says. 'Is Dad watching *Match of the Day*?'

A whooping sound comes from the living room followed by a shout of, 'Yes! You beauty!'

'He is,' Mandy confirms.

'Look at this mess,' says Asta.

She goes to the fridge and pours herself a shot of Crusha before topping it up with milk. She puts the empty milk bottle back in the fridge. Mandy sighs and takes it back out again, goes to the sink and rinses it out.

'It's a good mess, isn't it?' asks Asta, as she takes her seat at the kitchen table, sweeps her forearm across to clear an empty space for her milkshake and her phone.

'You can go too far the other way,' says Mandy, as she opens the dishwasher, starts loading it up. 'But yes, your dad's let up on the Hinching for a bit.'

'There's a bottle of handwash in the toilet too.'

'He gave most of the soap to the food bank. Pass me those mugs, would you? I expect they got a shock when they opened the box and found a menagerie in there. Still, they do the job, get you clean.'

'Is Dad fixed, do you think?'

Mandy stops wiping the table and sits down next to Asta instead.

'Have you ever heard of *kintsugi*?' she asks.

Asta frowns. It sounds Asian but not Chinese. Is it something she should know about but doesn't? Since when did she become the expert on all things East Asian? No, she'll have to confess to her ignorance rather than try to go along with it.

'It's the Japanese art of mending pottery. The thing is, they don't try to fix it with superglue, pretend it never got smashed in the first place. Instead, they put gold, not actual gold but gold powder into the glue so you can see where it was broken and where it got fixed. You should look them up. They look smashing afterwards.'

Mandy winces at her unintended pun.

Asta thinks of Grandma Lynda's vase. She'd thrown something at Felix because he was annoying her, missed and knocked the vase onto the rug. Instead of smashing into smithereens, it quietly split into three pieces which they hastily stuck back together with some superglue they found in *that* drawer. When Grandma Lynda tried to use it again for a bunch of flowers, water went everywhere. Lips were pursed, eyebrows raised but that was all. The vase ended up in the bottom of a terracotta pot in the garden. If they'd used kintsugi to let the world know what happened to it, perhaps the vase could have carried on fulfilling its purpose of holding flowers instead of getting smashed up into drainage material.

'Your father isn't fixed but he isn't broken any more either. He's different now, like a bowl with a golden scar running through it. Perhaps he won't ever be quite the same as he was before. He got upset the other day because he knows he won't ever be able to eat a Twix ever again.'

'A Twix? Why not?'

'Because it comes as two in the packet and he always used to share it with your Grandpa Charlie, one finger each with their elevenses. It's not logical but he knows he can't do it and that's fine. He has a Penguin instead. He's getting better at coping. We've all been here for him, we helped him to mend himself. You were a big part of that.'

'Me?' says Asta. 'What did I do?'

'You found that wooden rabbit. Your father couldn't believe your Grandpa Charlie kept it, had it with him all that time. It must have meant something to him after all. He feels now your grandfather must have been proud of him.'

'Of course Grandpa Charlie was proud of Dad. He was always telling us to see it from Dad's point of view when we went and complained about him. It was really annoying because I wanted Grandpa Charlie to be on my side, not Dad's.'

'That's what I thought too. I tried to tell your father but it wouldn't sink in for him. I think it took the rabbit to do that. It's like a message your grandfather left behind without meaning to.'

Mandy gets up, goes to put the cleaning tablet in the dishwasher before turning it on. Asta grips her milkshake tightly, starts turning the glass clockwise in her hands.

'Why did you never tell us about our big brother before? What was his name again?'

She turns to look at her mother who is standing facing the window, heels of her hands pressed against the worktop.

'Leonardo William Fung. Leo, for short. We didn't decide one day never to tell you about him. There was never a big plan to keep him secret from the two of you.

When you and Felix were young, we were so astounded and exhausted and happy and miserable all at the same time, it was as much as we could do to manage as we did. You know what you were like when I told you about that kitten I had when I was a little girl, how she ran away when the builders were putting the new boiler in and we never saw her again.'

Asta nods. Poor kitty.

'If a missing cat could upset you that much . . . we decided to leave it until later on. Then "later on" became "it's too late now". And here we are. Perhaps you should tell people things sooner rather than later even if it is awkward and difficult. It never gets less awkward and less difficult, does it?'

Now that her mother has shared a confidence with her, Asta realises she should be more Max to her mother's Elaine. She should tell Mandy everything she knows about Ela's letters and the unsolved mystery of who wrote them. She opens her mouth just as her phone beeps and shuffles across the table. She looks down. It's a message from Josh.

Good night xx

'I have got something to tell you,' Asta says. 'I think it's a nice something.'

'Oh yes?' says Mandy, turning around. 'Bring it on. I could do with hearing a nice something for a change.'

'I think I've got a boyfriend. I think I'm going out with Josh.'

'Josh, the builder's son?'

Asta nods.

'I didn't know he was going on this camping trip with you.'

'He didn't. He only came along when it all went wrong. You should have seen what it was like.'

Mandy opens the fridge, takes out the Crusha and a fresh bottle of milk, gets herself a glass and sits down next to Asta. She serves up another round.

'Why don't you tell me what it was like?'

So Asta does. Not all of it though. She doesn't say anything about Sophie and the pregnancy test. Sometimes you don't have to be told, to know something is a secret.

Chapter Thirty-Five

Nobody likes change, not even dogs.

To begin with, Steve doesn't like the fact that the old young owner has started smelling of someone he's never met. Who is this new human she is spending so much time with? It's like she is wearing him as a scent.

He thinks back to the time he spent with his own mum, his three brothers and five sisters, all living in a tangle in the dogs' home where he was born. How they used to tumble and play fight and shove each other out of the way to get the best feed whether it came direct from his mum or from the big plate of kibble. Then the nine of them became eight, seven and six until it was his turn to leave the litter and go and live with the old young owner.

Happy times. He thought they would never end and then they did. He didn't think he would ever see the old young owner again and then he did.

In short, he's worried about the smell of this new person and what it means for him.

'In you go, Steve. I know it's a bit of a jump,' says Asta. 'Do you need me to lift you up?'

Steve turns around, twists himself into an unhelpful u-shape so Asta can't get a hold of him, before leaping up into the van where he comes face to face with Josh.

He looks at Josh.

Josh looks at him.

Asta looks at them both. It is even more important to her that this goes well than it was for Josh meeting her parents for the first time. They had already met him loads of times before, though.

'Hello Steve,' says Josh.

That's it. He had Steve at hello. Asta can hardly get into the passenger seat for Steve reaching across the gear stick and handbrake and lavishing Josh with wet kisses and a paw on each shoulder.

'Come on, Steve, budge up,' says Asta. 'We're taking you on a trip.'

Steve hops off into the passenger footwell so she can get in, then curls himself obediently at her feet and soon, the movement so close to the engine has lulled him into soft doggy snores.

Not that Asta wants to be mercenary about her relationship with Josh, but having a boyfriend who can drive is fantastic. She's always wanted to visit the reclaimed Coetir Woodland Park at the end of the motorway ever since she heard about it. She imagines it as the kind of place Pemberley or Thornfield Hall might have become after the end of their respective novels if things had gone terribly wrong for the Darcy or Rochester families.

It takes only a short time for a fine estate to become overgrown, neglected, for its buildings to crumble and for people to carve it up and build houses and motorways over and through it. The conversion of the former Cyfoethog Family Manor into a local visitor attraction that is currently #9 on JourneyGuru had taken the work of dozens of committed locals, fed up with the abandoned joyridden cars, the sound of BB guns popping against empty lager cans, drunken raves pulsing and throbbing through the night air. They'd campaigned to lease the land, to clear it up and make it a place for families to visit, runners to squeeze in their trail runs and for dogs to have off-lead romps.

All of the playground, café and meeting points close to the car park are busy with people like Asta and Josh who have decamped here after school and work so Asta waits until they've walked a good distance away from the main thoroughfares before unclipping Steve. He immediately rushes off, snuffling into the grass that edges the wide gravelled path, disappearing into a distant furry dot before hurtling back towards them, tongue lolling and back teeth on display. The path is wide; it used to carry horses and carriages all the way to the big house which is no longer there. As far as they can see, all is lush and green. The estate is edged by a high canopy of sycamore, oak and beech while white ribbons of mayflower are blooming from the hawthorns that fill the spaces in between these ancient trees. The soundscape reminds them how close to civilisation they are, though, as they can still hear the motorway roaring past, invisible yet nearby.

They walk past a steep muddy trail on the right-hand side worn into the grassy bank by local residents coming into the park as a short cut. Steve gambols up it and has to be called back.

'Those are the newest houses,' says Josh, as they peep up into the edge of a children's playground. 'My dad was supposed to be a contractor when they built them but he backed out.'

'Why?' asks Asta.

'All of this bit,' says Josh, 'all the way down to the valley used to be mature woodland. They took some for the motorway and the rest was for new homes which was OK because they still left all of this here. Thing was, there were two ancient redwoods on that side, had tree protection orders and everything. The developer was supposed to build around them but he told the tree surgeon to do a "whoops, there goes my chainsaw". Dad got wind of it, made an anonymous call to the powers that be, but it was too late. Centuries of tree, gone, just like that.

'The developer got fined but it was nothing to him, he probably budgeted for it. Dad got fed up with the big jobs after that, sticks to the small clients. He's retiring next year anyway.'

'He's too young to retire, isn't he?' says Asta.

'Retiring from running the business. He's going to start lecturing in construction management at the Tech. Take it easy as he's going to be a man down after I go away to uni.'

The silence between the two of them moves from the comfortable ones they've shared since the glamping weekend to one that's decidedly not.

'Which isn't for ages anyway,' Josh says, taking Asta's hand. 'Not for months and months. We've got the whole summer ahead of us. What shall we do with it?'

Chapter Thirty-Six

Josh drops Asta off at the end of Steve's street.

She makes sure Steve isn't looking before she leans back into the van to give Josh a kiss and then she floats on air for the last hundred metres. Usually when she takes Steve home, the various members of the Li family who congregate in the bungalow are scattered throughout – Mrs Li and Elaine chatting in the kitchen, George napping in his bedroom, Max and Tony Blair in the front room watching television – but today, she can see everyone is sitting in the conservatory. She waves at them as she walks past to get to the back door and then she notices there's someone else with them who isn't usually there. By the time she gets to the porch and has hung Steve's lead up, that someone else is in the hall. It's Mr and Mrs Li's daughter, the one who suggested she start taking Steve out again. That seems like long, long ago but it's only been a few months.

'Hello,' says Amy. 'Do you want to come and join us? No bubble tea and cakes this time, I'm afraid. Just Glengettie and Welsh cakes but we have got something to tell you.'

'Is it about Steve?' Asta asks, panicked, putting a hand protectively onto the dog's head.

'No,' says Amy. 'There's nothing to worry about. It's all good. Come on.'

In spite of these assurances, Asta's too nervous to take more than a sip of tea and she turns down anything to eat. She asks if she can change seats as the sun is shining directly onto her and she is breaking out into a light sweat. From the sublime to the ridiculous. The best way to get a girl to worry about whether she is going to lose access to her dog is to tell her not to worry and then bribe her with tea and sweetmeats.

Finally, after what seems like aeons of small talk, drained mugs and cake crumbs, these last mainly down the front of George's shirt and tie, Elaine leans forward.

'We've all been working on persuading George here to remember what he can about this Ela Hennessy who was so in love with your grandfather.'

'And then, we've had to persuade him to tell us everything he knows,' says Max.

'That's where I've got involved,' says Amy. 'He listens to me.'

'She's got him wrapped around her little finger,' says Max.

'It's nothing personal to you, Uncle Max,' says Amy to someone who looks more like he should be her baby brother. 'The grandfather–granddaughter bond will always trump the father–son one. Asta knows that, don't you?'

Asta nods.

'He did need some encouragement, though,' says
Amy, 'but there was also the fact that I can translate
what he told us. Now, we could have just got Elaine and
Max to tell you what we found out but I think it seems
only fair for you to hear it direct, or as direct as we can
make it, from the horse's mouth.'

George glares at his granddaughter in that bad-
tempered way you can only get away with towards your
nearest and dearest.

'Especially in the light of how he so expertly dodged
the subject the times you've tried to ask him outright,'
says Elaine.

'Did you find her?' Asta turns towards George. 'Is she
still alive?'

George: (in Cantonese, tetchy) 'I'm not a detective. If
           Charlie couldn't find her all those years ago,
           how do you expect me to? All these years
           later!'

Amy: (in English, calm) 'I'm not a detective. If
           Charlie couldn't find her all those years ago,
           how do you expect me to? All these years
           later!'

Even though it has taken weeks for the joint efforts of
Mrs Li, Elaine, Max and Amy to prise this old story out

of George – he was nowhere near as keen to talk about this part of his old friend's, his one-time stepson's life as he had been to share the good bits, the fun bits – once George starts talking, Amy translating, he is in his element. He loves being the centre of attention.

'When I first saw your grandfather, I knew he was trouble. It was on the platform here at Cawsmenyn Railway Station.

'What had happened was his mother applied for the job for him. I'd put an ad in the Sing Tao paper looking for someone willing to come and work here, in Wales, not in a Chinatown. Bit of a trick that, to be honest. I had been running the shop with my wife but she died so young. I was at a loss. There were good local people here, good friends who helped out but really, what I needed was a qualified chef with years of experience to split the load and maybe partner up with me one day.

'I was going to give it to a man from Sham Shui Po by way of Birmingham when I got this letter from a young widow. Her boy had no father to keep him in place and he hung out with all the wrong kinds. He needed extracting from where he was to somewhere quiet, out of the way of trouble, and teaching a trade to set him up for life. I took pity and that was how I got lumbered.

'You've seen the photos of Charlie. He was well-stocked in the good looks department, wasn't he?'

Asta nods. She doesn't think she's inherited any of it. She has though.

George continues, Amy following on with the translation.

'He was already turning the heads of all the girls even that very first day at the train station. The one good thing was he didn't seem to know it. Yet.

'I was given a job, to get this boy into shape. He was careless and lazy to begin with, insolent too, but I won him around and without having to use the back of my hand like he said his mother used to do. He was a mess underneath it, unsure of himself, lonely too.

'That's where the girls came in. Lots of them. I mentioned it to his mother back in Liverpool and she insisted on coming down to stay, to make sure everything was all right. Which of course it was and I told her as much. She could see it was the case when she got here. The thing is that, after a weekend in the flat above the shop with the two of us, Charlie's mother took a bit of a shine to me. She couldn't help herself, I suppose.'

George smirks with pride all these years later. Amy breaks off the translation to roll her eyes. Elaine joins in. Mrs Li already rolled her eyes a few moments ago because she's following the original Cantonese version of this story.

'The whole Charlie and the local girls situation took a different turn after Charlie's mother and I got married and she moved in with us. Couldn't turn a blind eye to the giggles from his room and high-heeled shoes on the fire escape steps then. She wanted to put a stop to it but, of course, she couldn't. They just went elsewhere but she did start a new rule of, how do you say it . . .?'

George pinches the air in front of him, trying to pluck out the right word to say what he means. When he does, it throws everyone by being in English.

'Grounded.'

Asta leans forward. All of this will be much easier if George has got better, regained his English-speaking voice, but he immediately reverts back to Cantonese. Asta slumps back in her chair. If her grandfather couldn't get better, she was hoping someone else's would. She picks out a familiar word in the midst of what George says next.

'The Ela girl, very intelligent, she was in university in London. Glasses and frizzy hair like a poodle. She was very nice, not like his usual type. I suppose that's why we didn't work out for a long time how serious they were. How could we? We never saw them together and it was about that time his mother decided he should get himself a nice Chinese girl to be his wife.

'Cue a procession of little princesses from Cardiff, Liverpool and Manchester coming to visit. Ada said they were all distant cousins of hers but not to panic, distant enough for Charlie to settle down with if that's what he wanted. He didn't want. He introduced us to this Ela instead who his mother thought was another one of his here-today-gone-tomorrow girls. I knew she wasn't. I knew there was more to it.

'The poor girl, she tried her hardest to get in with Ada. She sent us Chinese groceries you could only get in a big city, brought them with her when she came home, was always kind and attentive, noticed a new hairstyle, admired a new dress, but she didn't stand a chance. You know I divorced Ada, don't you? Your great-grandmother, she had lots of little good points and only one or two very bad points. The bad points got the worst of her in the end. We won't talk about one of them.'

George looks over at Mrs Li.

'The other one was she was entirely unwilling for her son to marry outside. Nobody white, black or brown. Not even anyone from Singapore or Taiwan. She only wanted a good Chinese girl for her Liverpudlian son. Rowing against the tide, of course.

'There were local people as well who didn't think it right for Charlie and Ela to be together. Myself, that was the sort of thing that made me dig my heels in, welcome this Ela girl, but his mother? "Oh no, even the *gweilo* don't agree with this intermingling, we should do something about it." Bollocks.

'Anyway, that summer when Ela graduated from university, she moved back here. We only ever saw Charlie when he was in work with us. The rest of the time, he was with her. Coming back to start work with straw in his hair or sand in his shoes, smelling of ladies' soap and his lips all swollen up. Every morning, he was up and out as soon as the sun came up and gone all day long to be with her. Then there was the time Charlie wanted to talk to me about it because I'd known him as a grown man for longer than his mother ever had. Her parents were moving away, the stepfather was a travelling sales- man and he'd had an offer to go and work in England somewhere. Ela would have to go with them. He didn't want to be apart from her again, like they had before. What should he do?

'Well, he proposed, of course and she said yes. They should have got married straightaway, never mind what anyone thought about very, very short engagements but instead she moved away with her parents. They'd been in love and far apart before so they thought they could do it again, just for one year.

'His mother and her stepfather knew all along what they were doing. It only takes one person at each end to sabotage things – intercept the letters and the phone calls. A travelling salesman and his family can move around a lot and soon the letters came back marked Return to Sender by the Post Office. His mother didn't have to pretend she didn't know where the Hennessy family had gone any more.

'I didn't know about any of this until it had begun and then, what was I to do?'

'You should have told Charlie! That was the right thing to do!' says Asta.

'And go against my wife? "He's my son, not yours!"'
One day when you're with somebody, you'll know what
it's like. Should you side with your wife when she's
doing the wrong thing or do the right thing and have
your wife lose face?

'Charlie went back to his bad ways. Drinking, fighting, smoking. Then his mother did what she'd done
before. She'd extracted him from Liverpool and trans-
planted him out of harm's way down to Cawsmenyn.
She did the same again but from Cawsmenyn to Traeth,
to run the takeaway down there. He didn't want to, of
course, but she shoved him onto the train one morning
after the night before. Didn't even have a pair of under-
pants to his name. He had a hangover, a black eye and a
ten-bob note to start afresh. She carried on arranging for
so-called cousins to visit him down there too. He took
against them all on principle. Eventually, he met your
grandmother, Lynda, while she was on holiday and you
know how that worked out. He lived happily ever after.'

'But did Ela, though?' asks Asta. 'We should still try to
find out what happened to her. Do you remember what
the stepfather's surname was? Harri something or other?
See if we can find out where they moved to and look for
him from there? She can't be far away if we can find him.'

Asta looks over at Elaine, Max, Mrs Li, all of the
others, to get them to back her up. Only Steve gives her
anything resembling a hopeful look and it very much
resembles his hopeful-for-a-snack look.

'No, I can't remember,' comes Amy's English encore of what her grandfather has just said, 'except for it was one of those ordinary ones like Jones or Davies. Too many to look through and find the one that you want.'

'We already tried,' says Max. 'We wanted to solve the whole mystery for you before we told you. At least we know now why it didn't work out for them, even if we can't find out what happened to Ela.'

Asta looks down at where Steve is resting his head on her knee. She ruffles first one ear, then the other.

'Are you all right?' asks Elaine.

'Yes,' says Asta.

Her voice is a bit wobbly. She wants to tell everyone here how much she appreciates all they've done for her, how nice it is they went to all this trouble to try to find Ela. All the time she thought only *she* could get to the bottom of it all, there was an invisible backup team working on her behalf she didn't even know about.

'Yes, I'm fine, thank you,' she says. 'Thanks very much for asking.'

Chapter Thirty-Seven

'Asta, can you stay behind please?' says Mr Feather. 'I need to have a word with you.'

Callum sniggers and Paige throws Asta a sympathetic look as they make their escape to the common room for their regular Thursday afternoon free lesson.

'Callum and Paige? You two too, please,' Max adds. 'Where's Sophie these days?'

The three of them do the teenage shrug that means *dunno*. Her attendance has been pretty intermittent ever since the disastrous glamping break and when she does come in, she gets a lift from Lambert rather than walk in with Asta. Two-thirds of them think Sophie's still embarrassed and is skiving off to spend more time with Lambert. One-third knows there's more to it than this but figures it's for Sophie herself to tell the others. That's if she decides she ever needs to.

Max leads Asta, Callum and Paige into the next classroom and through an enormous glass door into the bookstore. It's a windowless room with shelves so tightly packed with books, it takes patience and a strong index finger to ease a copy of anything out. Boxes of A4 paper are stacked all down one side, the uppermost boxes sporting incriminating evidence of the mugs of coffee and cans of Red Bull that have rested on top. The smell of paper and boiled sweets hovers. In the middle of the room is a small round table and on top of it are two cardboard boxes with letterbox-sized slits in the top, raggedy slips of paper stacked up around them.

'Those are the student votes for the new school motto,' says Max. 'They need collating so we can have the winner in time for the next meeting of the school governors. Mrs Pritchard and I started tallying them but then I figured you . . . '

'. . . don't have a dog and bark yourself,' Asta says at the same time as he does.

'Exactly,' says Max. 'So, as you know, we've been running a poll to select a new school motto.'

'No, we don't know that, Sir,' says Callum.

'I haven't heard anything about it,' says Paige.

'Have we really?' asks Asta.

Max rolls his eyes. 'I'm super-pleased to hear you've been spending so much time studying that none of you have time to notice any of our other school activities.'

He moves slightly to the right to reveal a poster stuck to one of the shelves behind him.

SELECT OUR NEW SCHOOL MOTTO!
Cawsmenyn High School is looking for a
new motto to perfectly reflect it's ethos of
education, inclusivity and aspiration.
With three great suggestions on our shortlist,
we now invite our students to make
the final choice.
Voting slips available from your Head of Year.

'You've split your infinitive and spelt 'its' wrong on there, sir,' says Callum.

'You'll have to speak to His Majesty's office about that,' says Max.

'Who?' says Asta.

'HM? The headmaster,' says Max. 'The only role the English department has is to tally the votes. When I say "English department", I mean the three of you.'

Asta, Callum and Sophie wisely wait until Max has gone off to re-introduce his Year Nines to Adrian Mole before bemoaning the loss of their free lesson. They empty all the slips out of the two voting boxes and, as advised, look through them for obvious multiple votes or faked names.

'Didn't know Daenerys Targaryen was in this school,' says Paige, scrunching up one slip and tossing it into the bin.

'I think I'd have noticed if she was,' says Callum.

'Jessica Jones?' says Paige. 'Come on, who else is in her class? Bruce Wayne? Clark Kent?'

'No, actually, she's in Year Ten,' says Callum. 'I know her.'

'Shall I write out each of the three options on a bit of paper?' asks Asta. 'We can pile the votes on top of each one and then count them up after that.' She starts reading from one of the voting slips.

'No 1 is *Education Diligence Achievement*.'

'That's my address on What3Words,' says Callum.

'The next one is *We support one another to reach our full potential*,' says Asta.

'Do we?' says Paige.

'Paige, don't be so cynical,' says Callum in cynical tones.

Asta carries on reading.

'No 3 is *Strive to achieve more than yesterday, less than tomorrow*.'

She gasps.

I love you more than yesterday, less than tomorrow.

Whoever submitted this for the motto competition must be Ela's granddaughter, maybe even great-granddaughter?

'I like that one,' says Paige.

'Me too,' says Asta.

'Achieve or achieve not,' says Callum in strangulated tones. 'Do not strive.'

Not only has the counting of the votes extended into their free lesson, it's taking up the break that follows it.

'Did you manage to get a result?' Max asks when he comes back to check on them.

'Yes,' says Asta.

Max looks at the three piles of voting slips, each held down by a hardback copy of *Great Expectations*. Callum has written the total for each of the three nominations on a Post-It note stuck to the covers and 'We support one another to reach our full potential' is the winner.

'Not a very good turnout, is it?' says Max, doing a quick mental assessment of votes received and the size of the student population. 'Less than thirty-five per cent. Which is the one you three liked best, did you say?'

'Achieve more than yesterday, less than tomorrow,' Asta, Paige and Callum all recite at the same time.

'No, I don't like the strive bit either,' says Max.

'Did you say there were nominations and this was the shortlist?' asks Asta.

Max nods, inspecting the piles of voting slips closely. 'Where did you get the nominations from?'

Asta wants to know who submitted option three. If a promising lead falls into your lap, it would be a crime to let it get away.

'Can't tell you that, I'm afraid,' says Max. 'I don't even know myself. The headmaster is particularly keen the motto be selected on its own merits and not based on the popularity of the person who put it forward. Apparently, these three individuals were told not to breathe a word as to who they were, nor to engage in any electioneering-type activity, so only he and his PA know who submitted what.'

The bell rings for the end of break.

'Right, the three of you. That will do for now.' Max ushers the three of them out of the room. 'Thanks for counting up the votes we've received so far. Mrs Pritchard and I will do the rest.'

'Are you sure you don't want us to help you and Mrs Pritchard to *reach your full potential*, sir?' asks Callum.

'I'm sure we'll be able to do that without your assistance on this occasion, Callum,' says Max as he steers them into the corridor and on to their next lessons.

Chapter Thirty-Eight

'We need to find out who submitted those mottos,' says Asta.

'Hmmm?' says Paige, looking down at her phone.

'I have no idea what you're talking about,' says Callum.

Asta sighs. It's to be expected. They've just met up in the sixth form common room after having split up for their last two lessons of the day. It's abundantly clear that Paige and Callum have been concentrating on their studies rather than mulling over who submitted *Achieve more than yesterday, less than tomorrow.*

As they meander through the school grounds and out onto the main road, Asta explains to the others about Ela's letters and about getting closer to Grandpa Charlie by reading them. It's only as they reach the pick-up and drop-off area that Asta realises she's told all of this to Josh, Paige and Callum now but has yet to tell either of her parents. She'll tell them soon, just as soon as she's spoken to Ela herself.

'If we can find out who submitted option three,' says Asta. 'I know they will turn out to be Ela's granddaughter or even great-granddaughter? Mustn't they?'

'Huh?' says Callum.

Asta realises that her thirty-second précis of the situation did not mention the incident in the jewellery shop where Ela and Clemmie were shown the necklace with the inscription. She's about to embark on telling them when a familiar van pulls up alongside.

'Finished the job early,' says Josh, leaning out of the window. 'Do you fancy doing something together?'

'Too right, Palazzo, I thought you'd never ask,' says Callum.

'Well, actually, I meant my girlfriend . . .'

Asta wonders if she will ever stop feeling fizzy inside when she hears Josh say that.

'. . . but if you two want to tag along, hop in.'

'Go on, Josh, let me have a bit of your Stella.'

'No way, Callum,' says Josh. 'I nearly wasn't allowed to have this because of you lot.'

They've spent the last half-hour in the beer garden again and only Josh has been able to have an alcoholic drink and even that was made extra difficult by the fact that three of the party are still in school uniform while the fourth one looks as if he should be.

'It'll help me think more clearly,' says Callum. 'So we can find out what we need to do to help Asta find her grandfather's ex.'

'Nice try, buddy,' says Josh, lifting the pint glass up high out of Callum's reach.

He jumps up for it anyway so Josh turns away and downs the rest all in one gulp before banging the glass down on the picnic table. Callum sinks into his seat sulkily. Asta and Paige roll their eyes at each other.

It's just then a man appears from the depths of the pub. In spite of his middle-aged appearance, he still has vast quantities of his own hair. It's a well-maintained feature he makes the most of by growing it long and shaggy while his face looks as if sunscreen was never invented. It's like Mick Jagger's hair on W. H. Auden's head.

'Josh!' he says. 'I thought it was either you or your father when I saw the van over there.'

The man points towards the Palazzo & Son branded vehicle in the car park.

'Well, it couldn't really be anyone else, could it?' says Josh.

Asta, Paige and Callum exchange glances. Josh is never normally like this; he has an extremely high tolerance for all dumbasses and fuckwits.

'A little bird tells me you've got yourself a nice girlfriend,' the man says. 'Aren't you going to introduce me?'

'Asta, Paige, Callum,' says Josh. 'This is my mother's brother.'

'Your Uncle John.'

Josh ignores this while Uncle John turns towards Paige.

'Well, I'm ever so pleased to meet you, Josh's girlfriend.'

'Me?' says Paige. 'Palazzo's girlfriend? No chance!'

'Actually, this is my girlfriend,' says Josh. 'Asta, meet John. John meet Asta.'

If Uncle John is surprised Asta is his nephew's girlfriend, and he is, he covers it up. Well, he almost does.

'Sorry,' he says, 'don't know why I thought she was the girlfriend and not you. Asta, unusual name. Not Chinese though, is it?'

'No, it's not,' says Asta. 'Sorry.'

She isn't sorry. Well, she is a bit. Sorry that Josh's uncle is an old-school idiot.

'Well, good to see you, John,' says Josh. 'But we're just in the middle of something important here so if there's nothing else, um, bye?'

'Don't worry, Josh,' says Paige after Uncle John has disappeared back inside. 'I know all too well the pain of an embarrassing relative.'

She looks pointedly at Callum who is busy throwing peanuts into the air and catching them in his mouth before crunching them down, much to Asta's delight.

'Stop that now,' says Paige. 'What I don't understand is, what makes you so sure that if we find who submitted that motto, it will have anything to do with the Ela person? You said it was from a famous French poem, didn't you? Anyone could know it.'

'I said it was a poem,' says Asta. 'I didn't say it was famous. Not in this country. I've got a good gut feeling about this. I know we'll find her this time.'

'Did you get that gut feeling all those other times too?' asks Paige.

'Yes,' mutters Asta. 'But not as much as I'm getting it this time.'

'Well then,' says Callum. He's a dreamer like Asta, not a hard-headed devotee of the facts like Josh and Paige. 'All we have to do is get into the headmaster's office and find out who submitted *Achieve More Than Yesterday, Less Than Tomorrow.*'

'You make it sound so easy, don't you?' Paige drains her drink and drags her arm from wrist to elbow across her mouth. She leans forward. The others all do the same.

'What you're really saying is, we need to find a time during the school day when there's no one else around, somehow get into the headmaster's office and make sure nobody else comes in or comes back while we work out where the details of this new school motto competition are kept. If they're on paper, we'll have to riffle through all the piles of paperwork, open up all the filing cabinets and desk drawers. If they're being held on the computer system – and we won't know which one it is until we get there – we would have to bypass the security on Mrs

Yates's computer, either by finding out her password or hacking into it and hope that she's named the file something sensible. That way, as soon as we click into the search bar, everything will just pop up for us within nanoseconds so we can make a clean getaway.'

'Yeah,' says Callum. 'That's it.'

'I don't know if you heard me correctly, Callum,' says Paige. 'I did say Mrs Yates.' She pulls a pitbullish face for the purposes of clarification.

Asta does an involuntary shiver, thinking of the harsh stares she's exchanged with the headmaster's PA in her brief tenure at this school. Back in Traeth, none of the admin staff would have been able to pick Asta out of a line-up, but here, she knows her student file is marked with the word 'troublemaker'.

'Geraldine?' says Callum. 'I don't know how she got that reputation. She's always a pussy cat when she's with me.'

'Oh yes,' says Paige. 'I forgot you're on first name terms with *Geraldine*. The thing is, you only get to see the inside of that office if you're very, very good . . .'

'I've never been in there,' says Asta.

'Nor me,' says Paige. 'Or if you're very, very bad.'

'I've been in there loads of times,' says Callum.

'He spent most of Year Six and Seven in there until he got his statement,' Paige explains to Asta. 'Even more proof that you only get sent to the headmaster's office if you've been very, very good or very, very bad.'

'Bagsy very, very good,' says Callum.

'I don't think it's feasible to pretend to be very, very good in order to steal confidential information,' says Paige.

'Very, very bad then?'

'No, Callum, very, very bad would mean suspension or exclusion, so much as we'd like to help you on this one, Asta, we can't.'

Callum pulls an apologetic face.

'Hey you lot,' says Josh. 'Don't be like that. It won't be easy but I don't see why you can't do it. You've got a secret weapon, after all.'

Chapter Thirty-Nine

'You're in a bit of a rush, aren't you?' Mr Feather says as Asta, Paige and Callum scrape their chairs across the floor and Callum's actually falls backwards onto the floor as soon as the lesson ends. 'I wouldn't have any of the three of you down for the athletics meet over at Ysgol Ffuglen. Shouldn't you have asked to leave the lesson early if you were going down there?'

'We're not, Sir,' says Callum, pushing his seat back neatly under the desk. 'We're just excited about the whole thing. Don't you teach PE sometimes, Sir? Why aren't you part of the team?'

'Not us English mortals,' says Mr Feather. 'Just the PE department, the headmaster and Home Economics.'

Paige raises an eyebrow at this last one.

'Don't judge, Paige,' says Mr Feather. 'They're helping out with the sports nutrition aspect of it all.'

'Yeah, Paige, don't judge,' says Callum, before racing out of the room pursued by a bear of a cousin.

Asta gives Max a watery smile and follows them.

*

'What are you doing here?'

Mrs Yates has just emerged from the headmaster's office into her own domain behind the reception at the visitors' entrance to the school. Asta is sitting on the hard leatherette sofa that stretches all along one side of the room. She pushes down on her left knee to stop it trembling.

'I'm waiting for my mum,' she says. 'She's picking me up for a dentist's appointment at two thirty.'

She winces inwardly. Is that too obvious a time for a fictional dental appointment?

Mrs Yates nods before settling down at her desk. She taps briefly at the keyboard and leans into the screen. She's left the door to the headmaster's office open and from here, Asta can see straight inside. It doesn't look that big but it also doesn't look as if it is anything other than a desk, a chair and some bookcases. There is a side table with a sagging display of dried flowers. Mrs Yates's space, on the other hand, looks like it is the beating heart of all headmasterish admin with the appropriate level of organised chaos involved.

While Mrs Yates isn't looking, Asta stretches her neck to look over the counter to see if there is a helpful box file marked 'School Mottos' or even 'Students Mrs Yates Hates' but no such luck. She does spot a bin that's spilling over with empty crisp packets, sweet wrappers and empty bottles of diet Coke. Even though she's seen Max sniff his trainers before putting them on, slam the door after an argument with Elaine and shout at Alexa for playing a slushy bit of Ed Sheeran, it still surprises her to see the human side of teachers and other responsible adults. It almost makes her feel bad for what they're about to do.

Don't weaken. This rule-breaking is for Ela. And Grandpa Charlie.

Asta dares to take a look out of the windows that stretch along the front of the reception on each side of the automated doors. She's often felt the entrance to this school is rather like going into a branch of Sainsbury's Local. Very glassy, the entire visitors' entrance and reception would have a stifling greenhouse effect if it wasn't for the stubby honeysuckle hedge outside. She sees Paige and Callum, their heads stacked one above the other on the leftmost side of the window. They all glance quickly at Mrs Yates who is tapping away at her keyboard, engrossed in her screen. Asta frowns, does a questioning face. The other two respond by raising their eyebrows to show they don't know.

'. . . late!' says Mrs Yates suddenly without looking up.

'Sorry?' asks Asta.

'I said, "Your mother must be running late."'

'Sorry,' Asta says.

Paige and Callum disappear.

If she was anywhere else, with anyone else, Asta would brave a sneaky peek at her phone now to see if it has any updates or words of wisdom for her in this present predicament but she doesn't dare. She sits on her hands with a palm tucked under each thigh, desperately trying to think of a Plan B.

That's when she sees Paige and Callum walk past the window and stop in a spot where Mrs Yates will clearly be able to see them. Luckily, she doesn't seem to notice at first. Asta attempts a cutthroat signal to her friends to get them to move away. They don't notice though because they've stopped walking and are having a loud argument which, of course, eventually attracts attention.

'It was your stupid idea to get involved in this,' says Paige loudly. 'I don't even know why it's any of our business.'

'She's our mate,' says Callum. 'If you can't help a mate out in her hour of need, you might as well not bother.'

'I didn't see you rushing to help me in my hour of need when I broke up with Ryan Matthews last year. I'd been going out with him since Year Nine.'

'That's 'cos I was glad he finished with you.'

'I finished with him!'

'If you say so. In any case, you're better off without him. I've always thought he was as thick as what you flush down the toilet and twice as stinky.'

'You take that back!'

'Make me!'

Paige, who is shorter, rounder and made of more pure muscle than lean, lanky Callum, shoves him in the chest. He shoves her back. She does it again so he repays the favour but this time, she topples over backwards out of sight of both Asta, who's leapt out of her seat, and Mrs Yates, who's rushed out the front door, barking, 'What are you two doing? Why aren't you in lessons?!'

Asta is torn between going to see how her friends are or going over to do what she came to do. She dithers between rushing outside to Paige's side or diving behind reception and starting her searching. Is she really that callous? She looks out of the window again where only Callum can be seen. He is still standing up while Mrs Yates has presumably joined Paige on the ground.

All she can hear is Paige crying, proper angry tears with a touch of self-pity. Unalloyed weeping. Asta's rapidly losing respect for such a public display of emotion when she catches Callum's eye. He gives her a wink.

Those two! This must be Plan B!

She heads over to the PA's desk, hurries to the computer to jiggle the mouse and make sure the screen stays unlocked. She opens up a window, presses Ctrl F and taps in 'school motto'.

Two documents come up but when she opens them, they are just the posters for the competition, one they'd seen before in the book store upstairs asking people to vote from the final three choices. The other is a poster Asta's never seen asking people to nominate potential school mottos with a closing date of a month ago. Seriously, why had none of them noticed this competition was being run? Asta could think of a few choice submissions. None of them quite convey the aspirational, hopeful note the school most likely demands though.

She turns away from the screen and scans the trays of documents, shelves of box files, drawers and surface tops, none of which give any clues as to what she's looking for. She tugs at a filing cabinet drawer. It refuses to budge but then she sees the key is still in the lock. She turns it and sees it's filled with tabs with students' names on each one. She slams it quickly shut. It's one thing to be looking for the nominations for an innocuous school competition, quite another to be caught nosing around in other students' private information. She dashes back to the computer but instead of jiggling the mouse again, she quickly deactivates the lock screen. While she's there, she opens the desk drawers. The top one is a neat tray of all sorts of pens, even one Fudenosuke among all the ballpoints, fibre tips and permanent markers. She's tempted to stop and test some of them but quickly moves onto the next drawer down which is jampacked with whiteboard marker pens. She remembers Max saying something about how he has to bring the old pen that's run out to Mrs Yates as proof he needs a new one.

It's gone suddenly very quiet around here and Asta realises why. Paige has stopped crying. She pokes her head above the parapet of the reception desk and sees Mrs Yates supporting an upright Paige and trying to get her to hop inside so they can take a closer look. Callum stands apart watching them until Mrs Yates says something that sounds quite impatient but can't be made out. Callum comes forward to take Paige's other side and the three of them make slow progress towards the automated doors. They get as far as the sensor that will open them up when Paige spots Asta, a sight so shocking her ankle gives way and she lands on her backside with a bump. Legs inside the school, the rest of her outside, the automated doors repeatedly open and close onto poor Paige's hips. Mrs Yates and Callum dash forward and hoist her inside where they lift her onto the leatherette sofa.

Asta can't tell whether the desperate look Paige is throwing her means 'ouch' or 'get out!' If it's the latter, how is she supposed to do that? There is no way out of this reception now without being spotted.

Paige tries to put a bit of weight on one ankle and cries out in pain before scrunching her mouth up into a tiny sphincter and puffing out her cheeks.

'She's going to be sick,' says Callum. 'Have you got a bucket or something nearby?' He's thinking of the cleaners' cupboard just along the corridor but instead, Mrs Yates rushes behind reception to get her bin.

From where Asta is, crushed into the desk's footwell, the five-point wheeled base of the office chair the only thing between her and Mrs Yates's legs, she sees a sturdy set of ankles pause by the bin stuffed with snack debris, then go into the headmaster's office. She doesn't even have time to think of making a run for it because all too soon, Mrs Yates is back with the headmaster's pristine round bin.

She presents it to Paige who hovers over it for a few seconds making a series of forced retching sounds but is not sick.

Asta dares to poke her head up for a moment to take the scene in, spots the slow shake of Callum's head and dives back down again, bumping her head against the arm of the office chair on the way. She bites down on the back of her fist to deaden the pain.

'What was that?' says Mrs Yates, turning around.

'What was what?' asks Callum.

'Thought I heard something. Never mind. Let's concentrate on you,' she says to Paige. 'I think we're going to have to call your mother to take you to A & E.'

She gets up and heads over to her desk.

'No,' Paige calls out. 'There's no need, I'm okay. I should get back to the common room.'

She reaches out an arm for Callum to take grudgingly, then gets up with a grunt.

'I don't suppose you could help me with my other arm please?' says Paige.

'I think the least he can do is help you after he pushed you over. You're very lucky I'm not taking this further.' Mrs Yates addresses this last bit exclusively to Callum.

Asta bobs up from behind the reception desk, mouths the word 'no' before disappearing again.

'I think I should call my mum after all,' says Paige. 'Is it okay if I use my phone?'

'Just this once.'

Mrs Yates must be coming back to her desk. Asta panics and not for the first time during this last half-hour. There is only one thing for it and that is to do fast baby crawl into the actual headmaster's office and hide behind the open door. She'd much rather close the door behind her but knows it's out of the question. The headmaster won't be coming back after the athletics meet but what if Mrs Yates decides to come inside to do something or even worse, she locks the office door when she finishes up for the day?

Also, it's quite dark in here with all the blinds closed.

'Is she coming to collect you?' Mrs Yates asks.

'Yes,' says Paige weakly. 'Is it okay if Callum waits with me until she comes? It's our free lesson.' Pause while Mrs Yates is presumably communicating silently with one of her many severe facial expressions. 'He's my cousin.'

It can only be a minute or two but feels like an hour or more until Asta realises that Plan B has become Plan A and Plan A is kicking off around about now.

'Hello! It's been ages since I last saw you,' says a familiar voice.

Asta smiles just to hear it and she knows without a doubt it's having the same effect on Mrs Yates. Although, she fervently hopes, not in quite the same way.

'Well, hello there, Josh. What are you doing here? Is there anything I can do for you?'

It's not any old Josh even though it was the third most popular boys name in the year of his birth. It is Joshua Palazzo, holder of five A levels, all A*, and former head boy.

'Well, I was driving past and I couldn't help noticing the tyres on your car are flat. Should we check them and pump them up, do you think?'

'Oh no,' says Mrs Yates. 'Not those Year Nine boys again.'

'Do you want to come with me to make sure it is just letting the tyres down and not an actual puncture? Four actual punctures?'

'I think that would be a good idea, if you wouldn't mind, Josh.'

'No problem at all.'

Josh's voice floats away in continuing amiable small talk with Mrs Yates until the swish of the automated doors open and close behind them.

Asta rushes out to reception just as Paige and Callum join her.

'He took his bloody time,' says Paige, picking up a pile of papers from a pending tray and flicking through them.

'He must have had a good reason,' says Asta. 'Are you all right? Is your ankle OK?'

'It's all right if you know how to fall properly,' says Paige. She hops up and down on each foot to prove her point.

'But the crying?' asks Asta. 'So much of it too.'

'Crying on command is her secret talent,' says Callum.

Paige turns to Asta and demonstrates with a single tear tumbling down the side of her nose. She wipes it away quickly.

'Wow,' says Asta.

With Callum on lookout, Paige goes through the paperwork while Asta works on the computer. She has a bright idea and goes to open up the most recent files. A list of recently opened documents unrolls in front of her, all logically and neatly titled to describe their contents except one called *This is the full list*. She clicks on it and dozens of entries for the school motto competition unfurl themselves under the paragraph Mrs Yates has written to say:

This is the full list of submissions for the new school motto. Only the HM and I are on the judging panel as this . . .

Now that Asta's found the list, she doesn't have eyes for this boring introductory stuff. She scrolls down, marvelling at the fact that efficient, bossy, robotic Mrs Yates failed to name this document something neat and logical but instead, must have just shut her machine down at the end of the day and let the software name the document with its first line. Everybody has an off day, she supposes. Never mind that now, there are way more entries than she ever expected and the competition has clearly been open to everyone who has anything to do with the school. There is even one from Frank the school caretaker.

Aspire to inspire.

It's not half bad and she makes a mental note to add it to her Write4U cache. She's getting distracted but finally she thinks she sees something near the bottom of page four.

Strive to achieve more than yesterday, less than tomorrow. Submitted by –

Callum makes a hissing sound and everyone panics. He dives behind the reception desk and starts helping Paige straighten up everything she's dislodged but they only have time to do a cack-handed job of it before running back to seat themselves on the leatherette sofa. Asta shuts down all the search windows she's opened and goes to join them before remembering Mrs Yates will start asking questions when she realises her computer has stopped locking its screen. She turns back, changes the settings quickly but before she can escape the scene of the crime, someone stops her.

'Asta? What are you doing back there? Where's Mrs Yates?'

Twinset and pearls. Silvery grey hair in an updo. Standing there on the other side of the reception desk, it's Miss Pamela Williams.

'She's had to go and do something with her car?' says Asta. 'All the tyres are flat.'

'And she left you in charge?'

'No. I was waiting here for, well, I was waiting here in reception when the phone rang and I thought I should answer it.' She fiddles with the ends of her hair. 'Yes, that's it. That's what happened. Is there anything I can help you with right now?'

Asta attempts her charming smile.

'Have you got indigestion or something?' Miss Williams asks.

'No, I'm fine,' says Asta, resuming her more usual expression.

'Well, in that case, I was after a copy of the minutes from the last governors' meeting.'

Miss Williams squints towards the back of the room.

'I know where she keeps them,' says Asta, and it's only as she turns away to fetch them that she remembers she's not supposed to know where anything is kept back here. Officially, she has not been rummaging around in a part of the school even more out of bounds than the bin store. If the punishment for that was detention, the punishment for this would be suspension. Exclusion. Very, very bad.

She stops in her tracks and says, 'I must have got it wrong. I don't know where they are.'

'I'll come back there and have a look,' says Miss Williams.

She goes around to join Asta and begins shuffling through the various piles of mess Paige has made, stacking and tidying as she goes. After a few seconds, during which Asta could plausibly just have noticed where the minutes are kept, she points the box file out to Miss Williams who opens it up and takes out a copy.

Callum must have a frog in his throat as he's developed a terrible cough. Asta turns to look at him just in time to see the front doors slide open.

'They've never let all four tyres down before . . .' Mrs Yates is saying.

'It's all sorted now,' says Josh. 'At least you didn't have any punctures.'

'What on earth are you doing back there? That's my office area and students are most certainly not allowed!'

Asta's getting déjà vu from Mrs Yates, a repeat of the bin store incident but unlike that time, she opens her mouth and nothing comes out. Which is an improvement on her previous brattish outburst.

'She's with me, Geraldine,' says Miss Williams, closing the box file and replacing it, a copy of the minutes in her hand.

'Well, you're not supposed to be there either!'

Miss Williams gives Mrs Yates a look. The look that silenced a thousand classrooms.

'I mean,' mutters Mrs Yates, 'you could have waited for me to help you with whatever it is you need.'

'I have waited, Geraldine, for weeks for you to email me these minutes.'

'Sorry, Miss Williams, I didn't mean not to do it. It just, sort of, happened.'

'Well, I have them now, thank you, and that's the important thing. It almost makes me feel you'll be glad when I'm an ex-governor.'

'Oh no, not at all,' says Mrs Yates. 'After you.'

She gestures for the two invaders of her office space to vacate it. Asta lets Miss Williams go first which proves to be a mistake. A handful of papers tucked inside a slippery punch pocket have dropped onto the floor during the illicit and licit searches for documents. If she'd gone first, Asta would have seen them and picked them up or skidded for a moment before regaining her balance. Miss Williams is able to do neither of these things as she does a complete banana skin pratfall but instead of a hip-breaker of a tumble, she falls backwards on top of Asta, who reaches out her arms to catch her underneath the armpits.

Asta's good at this. She had a lot of practice in drama lessons back in her old school. Every session began with trust exercises where one person would close their eyes and fall backwards, confident their partner would catch them. Asta was always an efficient catcher, rubbish at letting herself fall.

Josh dashes around to take both of Miss Williams's hands and help her upright. Her silvery updo is now a little dishevelled because some of it ended up in Asta's mouth.

'Don't move,' he says, and bends down to pick up the Health and Safety-breaching trip hazard on the floor. Asta can see him skimming what the documents say before putting them face down on a nearby table. 'Right, are you all right?'

'Thank you,' says Miss Williams.

'You're welcome, um . . .?'

Miss Williams introduces herself the same way she did to Asta all those weeks ago. Josh insists on shaking her hand politely before she says her goodbyes and disappears off down the corridor into the main school building.

'Your mother's taking her time getting here,' says Mrs Yates as she resumes her seat at her computer.

'I think she told me the wrong day,' says Asta. 'I'm sure now the appointment card said it was next week.'

'And when's *your* mother getting here?'

'She's not,' says Paige. 'I'll have to go back to lessons instead.'

She gets up and extends one arm to Callum, the other to Josh who takes it. Mrs Yates is too frazzled to add anything else. She shakes her head and settles down to catch up on the work she hasn't done during all this disruption.

'That was entertaining at least,' says Paige, as soon as they get outside. She shakes off Callum's and Josh's arms.

'Did you manage to find anything out?' asks Callum.

'No, not me. You?' says Paige, looking over at Asta who shakes her head.

'I nearly saw whose motto it was,' says Asta, 'but then I got interrupted. Does anyone know anyone who can hack into the school system to open a document if I've got the name of it?'

'No need for that,' says Josh. 'I know how to get hold of Ela now.'

That's when the bell rings for the next lesson.

'Come on then, Palazzo. We've got to go. Tell us quickly, what did you see?' says Callum.

'Do you know who she actually is?' asks Paige. 'Has her kid's kid got the same surname? Is it that Hennessy boy in Year Nine with the beard?'

'I can't blurt it all out now, like this, in a rush,' says Josh. 'Tell you what, I'll come back after school, down the pub, tell you there. After I've had a chance to get it straight in my head.'

Paige and Callum usually get the bus home but they walk into town with Asta today. Every time a works van zips past, they turn hopefully like hitchhikers and are disappointed. It's only when they get to the traffic lights that their phones all ping simultaneously.

Didn't have the materials we needed in town, had to drive to Llansamlet to get them. Won't be back in time to pick you up soz

'He's leading us on, he doesn't know who it is any more than the rest of us,' says Paige.

Tell us who it is then, Callum's thumbs ask. Asta can't wait.

'What do you mean I'm the one who can't wait?' says Asta.

'Well you can't, can you?'

'No, but don't bring me into your text, I'll ask him myself.'

'Go on then.'

Almost as soon as Asta presses send, a message bounces back. He must have been about to tell her anyway! Everyone leans in to see.

I'm driving. I'll see your message when I get where I'm going.

Chapter Forty

Josh has no difficulty tracking down where he thinks Ela will be.

The Palazzo family settled in Cawsmenyn in the 1920s. They started out in ice cream which brought delight to many a birthday at either of their two cafés. Not that it did them much good when the war came and locals smashed their windows with bricks even though the family was, by then, more Welsh than Italian. It got more Italian when a great-aunt married an ex-soldier from the prisoner of war camp on the edge of town. In short, they're a local family of long-standing, which means someone will always know someone else who can point him in the right direction.

He thinks about taking his dad with him to follow up on this hunch but he figures he might as well get some practice in for next year when the Vince and Josh team will break up when he goes to university. He definitely doesn't want to take Asta. He isn't certain beyond a reasonable doubt but on the balance of probabilities, he feels confident. It's just too big a coincidence for it not to be Ela but he can't risk getting Asta's hopes up. If he's right, he'll tell her just as soon as he can.

He steps through the gate and up the path to the front door. He recognises the work of Howie, one of the better local gardeners. The lawn is perfectly striped in shades of green, its edges strimmed to perfection. There's that wisteria too, artfully trailing down the front of the house. Leaded panels in the front door, some windows arch-shaped or round instead of square or rectangular; it's the sort of house Vince used to take him to when he was working during the school holidays. That was after Josh's mother left them and the only childcare option was for him to spend the day in a back room with a box of Lego and a bottle of squash. Proper old-school houses.

The Ela family done good.

He has to ring the doorbell twice. It's so loud there can be no doubt about whether it's working or not. Eventually someone small can be seen through the panes of glass in the door. She's leaning into the spy hole and Josh isn't sure what to do with his face when someone is inspecting him like this. Eventually, the door opens.

'Hello,' begins Josh. 'I have a really strange question to ask you. I hope you don't mind.'

'You're not trying to sell me something, are you now?'

'Oh no, nothing like that.'

'Well, in that case, what can I do for you?'

'It's not really for me. It's more for my girlfriend.'

Josh feels the same fizz of excitement when he says this as Asta does when she hears him say it.

'Well, that's not what I was expecting. But I'll help if I can.'

'It's a long story. I don't like to keep you on your doorstep like this. Perhaps if we went inside?'

Uh-oh, Josh can tell from her face he's overstepped the mark. He hopes she doesn't slam the door in his face.

'Perhaps I don't need to tell you everything unless I have to. I might be mistaken so would it be all right if I asked you just one question?'

'Go ahead.'

'Where did you get your necklace from?'

She tucks her fingers up around her neck, plucks at the fine gold chain and lifts it up so that the small gold pendant appears at her throat and tumbles down the front of her blouse. As it falls, the small red stones, arranged into a plus sign, catch the evening sunlight.

'This one? It was a gift from a very dear friend.'

Josh says two words and although they aren't Open Sesame, they have a similar effect.

'You'd best come inside. Would you like a cup of tea?'

What did Josh say to have this magical effect?

Charlie Fung.

Chapter Forty-One

Asta's annoyed.

She has been texting Josh every hour – apart from when she was in school, no need to wind Mrs Yates up any more than she already has – if he will tell her what he knows about Ela and whether he's been able to find her. His replies are soothing, thoughtful and kind but they are no good at all because they firmly decline to give any useful information.

I can't just tell you by message, it's not like I'm firing you from your job. I need to tell you face to face.

It's too much to get into in a message. I'll tell you when I see you.

I'll see you after school!

If Dad and I get this job finished in time #demandingclients

Forgot to say no need to worry. It's all going to be fine. xx

'I suppose it's like my early birthday present to you,' says Josh, as the van's indicator tick-tick-ticks over at the traffic lights.

'I wasn't planning on making a birthday fuss this year,' says Asta.

'You have to,' says Sophie. 'You're only seventeen once.'

If Josh was surprised to see Sophie back at school and sharing the homeward bound walk with Asta again, he didn't show it. He happened to come along at exactly the wrong moment, just as Sophie started to talk about the real reason she's been off school for the last few weeks.

'I know it must have been you who packed up my stuff. If it had been Paige, everyone would know about it. Thanks, Asta, for not saying anything.'

'That's okay,' said Asta. 'Was it a false positive?'

She'd heard about such things and Sophie didn't look, well, she didn't look any more rounded than she did before.

'No, it wasn't. Lambert and me had to decide what we were going to do. Well, it was me who has to decide really. He's good with it, though.'

Asta paused, was waiting for Sophie to tell her what the decision was, when Josh pulled up. The next thing she knew, they were giving Sophie a lift to Lambert's and then going on to something to do with an early birthday present for Asta. It's not Josh's fault. He doesn't know why Asta's decided to hate her birthday, which isn't until next week anyway.

'Where are we going?' she asks.

'You'll find out when we get there,' he says.

'We're here!' says Asta. 'It's this one on the left.'

She turns her head as Josh keeps steering the van along one of the many side roads they've driven along, ever since the sat nav said, 'You have reached your destination.'

It's taken them an hour and twenty minutes to get to Porthgynffon and Asta thinks it would be no problem for a modern-day boyfriend or girlfriend to drive up the M4 to see each other. Back in Grandpa Charlie's day though – the B-roads, cost of petrol, even having a car to drive – it would have been a different matter. Letters back and forth would have had to do.

'That was Seaview Cottages back there,' she says to Josh. 'It's true, you can't see the sea at all from there. Isn't that where we're going?'

'Not quite,' says Josh. 'But nearly.'

Instead, they keep going until they take the sharp bend and there they are, driving along the promenade. On their left, the tide has come in and silvery blue waves are lapping their way up the pebbly beach. Late afternoon and the prom is populated with all sorts of seaside lovers. Day trippers. Dog walkers. Mums with their kids. Teenagers in school uniform. On the other side of the road, the strip of cafés, brasseries and bistros is starting to get busy with early evening trade, the outside tables and benches filling up with groups of women in strappy long dresses, designer shades holding back their sun-kissed hair. There are men there too in their polo tops, pleated shorts, pool slides with snowy white socks tugged up to mid-calf. It's buzzy, it's busy and it reminds Asta of Traeth and home.

She likes it.

Josh reverses expertly into a parking space barely big enough for the van. Asta hops out and waits while he goes to get a Pay and Display. She does a three hundred and sixty degree turn to take in her new surroundings, then closes her eyes and takes a deep breath of salty sea air. No wonder consumptive heroines in novels always get sent to the coast.

'That's a big sigh,' says Josh, as he comes back around to take her hand.

'It's nice to be beside the sea,' she says. 'I've missed it. Shall we get ice creams?'

'No,' says Josh. 'We're not just here to see the sea.'

They cross the road and Asta almost gets flattened by a set of boy and girl twins scootering up the prom while their mother runs to keep up, trying to capture the whole thing on her phone.

'Sorry,' she calls back towards them.

'Are you OK?' asks Asta, as soon as they pass through the iron gates to get onto the pier.

He's started squeezing her hand, rather than just holding it.

'Yup,' says Josh.

'That man over there, he's just sneezed into his chips and now he's eating them anyway.'

'That's nice,' says Josh.

'That seagull over there is being sick.'

'Mmmm hmmm,' says Josh.

He's clearly distracted by the ornate Victorian structure of the pier; he's looking all around at the cast-iron handrails, the wooden walkway edged with memorial plaques forming a brass mosaic edging. Oh well, that's fine, that's a civil engineering wannabe for you. Still . . .

'Shall I take all my clothes off and jump into the sea?' asks Asta.

'Now, that sounds more like it,' says Josh with a smile.

Well, she's got his attention back at least. She leans into him a little and he takes the hint, wrapping an arm around her.

When they get to the end of the pier, Asta breaks off to lean over the edge and looks at the waves hitting the steel supports. She can see the pebbles, as big as duck eggs, turkey eggs, even the occasional ostrich egg, appear and disappear in the sea spray. She wants Josh to come and see it too but now he's looking at something on his phone. She watches him while he doesn't know she's looking; it's become something of a hobby of hers and one she likes very much.

He frowns as he pokes about on the screen, looks up, looks around before coming over.

'Do you think it's stupid to name your café *The End of the Pier* when it's not at the end, it's at the beginning?' he asks her.

'Depends,' says Asta. 'A pier has two ends after all. Perhaps they should have called it *The Near End of the Pier*.'

'Well, they didn't,' says Josh. 'Do you fancy a cappuccino? Or something stronger?'

'Double espresso, extra whipped cream?'

Josh nods.

'Yes please!'

After the dazzling sunny day outside, it's dark coming inside to the inappropriately named End of the Pier café. Asta blinks hard and Josh waves at someone sitting in a booth in the corner, partially hidden by potted palms. As they get nearer, the someone reaches down into her handbag, starts digging around and the top of her head looks as familiar as any little old lady.

Stop doing an ageism, Asta tells herself, she is just a woman in a twinset and pearls, her hair in a silvery grey updo. She tries to ignore the tight feeling in her throat, the fluttering sensation in her tummy and chest. Is this the reason Josh brought her all this way? Finally to meet Ela? Or could it be Auntie Gaynor? Cousin Sali?

She is none of them.

She is Miss Pamela Williams.

'Sorry, we're late,' says Josh. 'We got confused over the two ends of the pier.'

'You're not the only ones to make that mistake,' says Miss Williams. 'Various people have tried to get the leaseholder to clarify the name but it's another case of tradition overcoming common sense, I'm afraid.'

Miss Williams turns her attention to Asta.

'Hello Asta,' she says.

'Hello,' says Asta back.

There is an awkward pause which Asta waits for Miss Williams to fill. She knows the old headmistress is good at that – being a bit bossy, occasionally a bit twinkly, self-assured and confident – but she doesn't seem at all like that today. She angles her left elbow out to nudge Josh, to get him to say something but he's disappeared over to the counter. Eventually, Miss Williams speaks.

'Oh, you don't need to do that here when we're not in school. Please sit down.'

Asta didn't even realise she was waiting for permission. She sits down and squeezes up on the seat ready for when Josh gets back with their order.

Another pause filled with the jangle of spoons, crockery and the steaming sounds of coffee-making.

'Did you have a good journey up?' says Miss Williams. 'I've been visiting some family who live here. They're very lucky. She's the same age as me but her husband is much older, frailer so they live in a granny flat attached to their son's house.'

Asta nods while trying to think of something to say.

'How is your history of the school coming along? Did you finish writing it?'

'Oh that?' says Miss Williams. 'Yes, I have. Thank you for helping me with it. I expect it will just be a dusty old tome for every subsequent headmaster's office but it might be useful to somebody some day in the least expected way. I think the story of the High School is important enough to be recorded. I don't expect it will ever be the new *Wolf Hall*, though.'

'The waitress is going to bring it all over,' says Josh, slipping in to take his seat next to Asta. 'Well, what do you think?'

'What do I think of what?' asks Asta.

'Didn't you tell her already?' asks Miss Williams.

'No, I thought it would be nice if you did it,' says Josh.

'Tell me what?' says Asta.

She's going to fail her A levels.

Mr Feather is so heartbroken, he's joined the French Foreign Legion and Miss Williams is her new English teacher.

Miss Williams is Josh's absent mum's mum.

'That Miss Williams here is Ela,' he says. He smacks himself in the forehead. 'I guess I ended up telling you myself after all.'

Asta folds her arms. 'No, she can't be Ela. Not Grandpa Charlie's Ela anyway. Her name is all wrong for a start.'

The waitress arrives and starts doling out coffees and a pot of tea. The table falls silent until she leaves.

'You do look like him, you know,' says Miss Williams, 'especially when you're a bit put out.'

'She is Ela. I'm as certain as anyone can be,' says Josh. 'Trust me.'

'I understand, Asta,' says Miss Williams, 'but if I can be persuaded by this young gentleman who just turned up on my doorstep, I think, as his girlfriend, you should give us a fair hearing.'

'All right,' mutters Asta.

'Shall we start with my name?'

Miss Williams picks up a biro and reaches for another napkin. Evidence of scrunched-up practice napkins sit on a nearby saucer.

PAM–ELA WILLIAMS

'I never liked the name Pamela. I know most people shorten it to Pam but, as you know, that means 'why?' in Welsh. I didn't want to be everyone's eternal question mark so I went for the unexpected, as usual, and took the back end. I think it suited me well.'

The old woman – Asta isn't quite sure what to call her now – takes a sip of tea.

'I was the first in my family to go to university. It was something my father always wanted for me, ever since he saw me heading for a pile of books over a pile of toys as a baby. He died when I was eight, then it was just Mam and me against the world. Sometimes, Mam sided with the world over me but I did get to go away to London to study even though she didn't like it. She liked the thought of teacher training though; it would be respectable to have a teacher in the family.

'When Josh turned up at my house, told me about the letters, reminded me of what was in them . . . I remembered, of course, but not all of the details I'd written to your grandfather about. It was nice to be reminded of that time. It was a very special time, I was very, very fond of him, you know.'

'Were you in love with him though?' asks Asta, in such a cheeky fashion, Josh turns to look at her. She glares right back at him.

'Yes,' says the old woman. 'Very much.'

'If you did, why did you give him up so easily?'

'I thought he was giving me up. I kept writing letters, every day like we used to but the replies stopped coming. When I phoned, his mother said he was always out and would call me back. He never did.'

'He probably did though, didn't he? But your stepfather. He did what Charlie's mother, my great-granny did at our end and intercepted it all.'

'Is that what happened?' The old woman sighs.

'He looked for you and couldn't find you. All you had to do was come back to find him where you last saw him but you couldn't even be bothered to do that.'

'Do you know what it's like to keep writing letters and receive no reply? To run to the phone every time it rings to find out the call is for someone else?'

Asta nods. In her case, the mobile hardly ever beeped or rang at all and when it did, it was only ASOS or EE or XYZ. Never anyone real.

'The message was loud and clear. We lived so far away too, the thought of coming all the way back only to be told I was too foolish not to take the hint I wasn't wanted any more. Who wants that? It took its toll on me, I won't go into detail except to say it was not a happy time. Still, what doesn't kill you makes you stronger. It must have been difficult for my mam to see me so upset, so inconsolable. She did her best. Harri was very nice about it all.'

The old woman frowns.

'He was a strange one now, looking back.'

She looks across at Asta and Josh.

'So that's what he did and all to no avail. No matter what he did behind the scenes to keep Charlie and me apart, he can't do anything about you two. Nobody can and that's as it should be.

'I always had my doubts about him, but there's no denying he made Mam happy. It was peculiar the way he so wanted me to change my surname by deed poll to his after they got married. I didn't want to, of course. From my father's Hennessy to his plain boring Williams? But he wanted it, and what he wanted, Mam wanted, so there we were. I decided to go the whole hog and go back to Pamela too. It seemed more of a sensible name for a sensible teacher who was working her way up in the world.'

'And you never saw my Grandpa Charlie ever again?' says Asta. 'What about when you moved back to Cawsmenyn to teach at the high school? You could have called into the Yau Sum and seen him there.'

'I did,' says the old woman. 'But there was another young couple running the shop who didn't have very good English . . .'

'That must have been Mr and Mrs Li,' says Asta.

'. . . so I didn't feel I could ask them. I just ordered my meal and went away. Eventually, I realised the children from the takeaway attended my school and were a completely different family. By that time, I hoped your grandfather had moved on, was happy somewhere else. With someone else.'

'He was,' says Asta. 'With my Grandma Lynda.'

'I'm pleased to hear it,' says the old woman. 'And you're the result. You look like him.'

'Didn't you ever find your own Grandma Lynda?' asks Asta.

'No. I suppose you could call it a timing issue. It just never happened for me.'

'You didn't get to live happily ever after,' asks Asta. 'Like I wanted Ela to.'

Asta feels Josh give her foot a gentle dab under the table. She accepts it; she knows she shouldn't have said that. It just came out.

'Oh but I have, Asta,' says the old woman.

She has fielded this sort of comment many times before.

'I have been very happy with my career and my friends and all the children I've taught and seen go on to do magnificent things. I have my family, my second and third cousins. You know about Sali, she still lives here with her husband. They're the ones I came to visit today. Oh yes, everything has turned out as it has and it has turned out well.'

'What do you think, Asta?' Josh asks. 'We did it! We found her! We found Ela in the end.'

'Did we?' says Asta.

'Yeah, of course we did,' says Josh. 'You don't still think it's not her, do you?'

'I do. I just don't know what to call her. I mean, you. Is it Miss Williams? Pamela? Ela?'

'I answer to all of them,' says the old woman.

'Can I call you Ela then, please?' says Asta.

'I'd like that very much. I haven't been called that in years.'

Chapter Forty-Two

Asta thought she'd got away with it.

When she collected Steve for his walk, it all seemed much like any other day but when she dropped him off, the chorus of 'Happy Birthday' began wafting out to her as soon as she opened the back door. There were two cards for her, not one.

'Shall I open them here?' asks Asta after she's thanked everyone.

'You can if you like,' says Elaine.

There is one from Mrs Li and all the family and one from Steve. His handwriting is good, perfect faux calligraphy and extremely accomplished for a dog.

'You did this, didn't you?' she asks George. He shakes his head and points at Steve.

As she walks back home, Asta realises she can't blame the Li family; they don't know but at least her parents and Felix respected her birthday non-wishes. She is seventeen after all, and no longer a baby. It should be just an ordinary day, like any other.

There's nobody in when she gets upstairs to the flat so she goes to her bedroom to get changed. It's only when she comes out again she notices the big red ribbon that's been looped over and around the door to Grandpa Charlie's old room. It's been tied into a big fat knot at the front and looks as if someone is giving her a bedroom door as a present. As she goes towards it, she hears murmurs and shushing and turns around to see her mother's mobile phone propped against a vase on the hall table. The camera has been turned to front-facing so the others inside can see her. She waves at it, braces herself and opens the door.

'Surprise!' says Mandy.

It's not as bad as Asta suspected. It's only Josh, her parents and Ela.

Once the mystery of Ela was solved, Asta showed the letters to Mandy and Tim. Her father was especially pleased and kept reading and re-reading all of them. He said it was like meeting Grandpa Charlie all over again but it was a bloody cheek of him to be so harsh on Tim's own teenage romance with Mandy in the light of 'Rosie, Jeanette, Jennifer, Deborah, Rita, Mary and Angela' and all the other girls he'd stepped out with.

Now Ela and her dad were *as thick as thieves*. That was how Ela put it.

'We know you didn't want a fuss,' says Mandy, 'but Josh and his dad put the finishing touches to the room today and it's not really a birthday do. More a reopening of this room as a study/bedroom.'

Asta looks around at the room that faced out towards the back and never caught the sun. Instead of boring magnolia, it is now painted a lemony shade of yellow. No more net curtains but blinds open wide to let in the light. At one end of the room, an enormous L-shaped desk is surrounded by built-in shelves, alcoves and cubby holes.

'This little one is just for storing calligraphy pens,' says Josh, correctly reading Asta's puzzled face. 'This glass-fronted one is for your dad to display his carvings when he's done with them.'

'Don't worry,' says Tim. 'Your mother and I agreed I should go back to my student days and work with wood, not bars of soap. I've already done one, look.'

It is a dog. He looks rather like Steve, complete with lolling tongue and waggy tail. Next to it sits a familiar wooden rabbit, cosily tucked up into a loaf position.

At the other end of the room is a new sofa-bed, currently in sofa mode. Above it is Grandpa Charlie's old photo of The Beatles. Facing it at ninety degrees on the next wall is a new photo of Grandpa Charlie as a young man, standing next to a bicycle complete with front basket and a bunch of flowers in it. He is looking up at the camera and smiling warmly, his affection for the person holding the camera plain to see.

'That's one of my old photos of him,' says Ela. 'It's amazing what modern technology can do with a crumpled old black-and-white 8 x 5.'

Asta goes over to look at it close up.

'Happy birthday, Grandpa Charlie,' she says. 'My birthday isn't the same without you sharing it too.'

She turns around to see the others all staring at her, heads tilted with concern.

'Do you like it?' asks Mandy. 'Do you like what we've done?'

'Like it?' says Asta. 'I love it.'

Sun House Takeaway
The Ropewalk
Traeth

Darling Ela,

It's been ages since we've written, years and years, and I don't even know if this letter will reach you. Even if you never see it, I know I have to write and get it out there. I figured if I write and send it, maybe one day, you will read it. If I don't, you never will.

Everyone said moving to Cawsmenyn was the making of me, getting me away from my wild and crazy ways in Liverpool, and it was. What they didn't know was I still felt wild, crazy and restless down here. That explains all the girls, the drinks, the fighting, getting friendly with another outsider like Miguel. I was starting to get fed up with it all, wanting someone who looked past my face and my 'exotic' accent, but I realised too late. I was just a bit of fun to the girls around here so they could say they'd been with a Chinese guy.

Meeting you when I did was one of the best things that ever happened to me. Everything that's happened to me since — running the shop in Traeth, meeting my fiancée Lynda, standing up to my Mum when she's

wrong — none of that woulda happened without you.
So I guess this is me saying thank you for that.

Wherever you are now, I hope you're as happy in
your life as I am now in mine. I guess we were each
other's stepping stones to where we're supposed to be.

I loved every single minute of it. I wouldn't change
a thing. Well, maybe one thing.

I wish you a wonderful life and a Happy Ever After
as good as mine. The kids who get to have you as their
teacher are gonna be the luckiest kids in the world.

All my love

Charlie x

Acknowledgements

Hello there and thanks for reading the acknowledgements. I'll bet you never let the streaming service rush you over to the next episode without clicking to find out who all the behind-the-scenes heroes are!

Patient and kindly Editor.............................Jennifer Edgecombe
Patient and kindly Editor............................Rachel Hart
Stylish copy Editor.......................................Caroline Kirkpatrick
Eagle-eyed Proofreader...............................Sam Matthews
Cover Designer and Lettering Artist ....Emily Courdelle
Publicist and English Literature Expert ... Felicity Hu

This book wouldn't be in your hands if it hadn't been for all the wonderful support from my Welbeck family – Jon Elek, Mark Smith, Marcus Leaver, James Horobin, Rosa Schierenberg, Rob Cox, Móz Rahman, Nick Brink, Maddie Dunne-Kirby, Margarida Mendes-Ribeiro, Nico Poilblanc and Alexandra Allden. Families can drift apart and drift back together again; I hope that happens to us.

And to my new team at Mountain Leopard Press –
Beth Wickington, Jennifer Doyle, Jennifer Edgecombe
(so good she appears in the acknowledgements twice!) and
everyone else in my leap of Mountain Leopards. Yes, like
a fluffle of rabbits, it *is* a leap of leopards.

Gerald, Ian, Carol, Justin, Jonny, Ming and Huanxin –
paid colleagues in my main job, unpaid ideas generators
for this other little job I have here.

For support during the ups and downs, acceptances and
rejections of a writer's life and for swapping dog pics – Lou
Morrish. I really hope you're not a chatbot in disguise.

In my unpublished writer days, I attended an event
where Steve Coogan described being told by Stephen
Frears to write the script better. 'So are you asking me
to make the implicit, explicit?' Coogan asked. To which
Frears replied, 'Oooh, get you!'

Well, that's how I feel about adding my own family to these acknowledgements, but in the interests of
making the implicit, explicit: I couldn't have done this
without Soong, Simon, my Mum and my Dad. All the
aunts, uncles and cousins too.

As Asta discovers, even when you are trying as hard
as you can, there is always an unseen team working hard
on your behalf without you even knowing it. To my
unseen team, thanks ever so much.

Last and definitely not least, there is you, dear reader,
who has reached all the way to the end. As Ela wrote,
flowers crave to be sniffed, bicycles would like someone
to ride them and this book wanted to be read.

About the Author

Julie Ma won the Richard and Judy Search for a Bestseller in 2020 with her debut novel *Happy Families*.

Born in Wales, with Chinese heritage and a career that includes postwoman, fraud investigator and customer service manager, she believes in finding the extraordinary in the ordinary to write into her novels.

When not reading, researching and writing, she continues to work hard in a Chinese takeaway so her dog can have a better life